# Thirteen Tales for Halloween

### Andrew Noles

Copyright © 2021 Andrew Noles

All rights reserved.

ISBN-13: 979-8458976183

No part of this book may be reproduced, distributed or transmitted in any form or by any means without the express written permission of the author.

This is a work of fiction. Names, characters, places, and incidents are either the product of the author's imagination or are used fictitiously, except as noted below. Any similarity to real persons, living or deceased, is entirely coincidental.

*They Called Me Lucy* based on the 1897 novel *Dracula* by Bram Stoker, available in the public domain

### Cover Design by Andrew Noles
All Free Stock Media via Canva.com
Silver Stone Rough, Beth Ellen, Badhorse, and Beauty Salon Sans Fonts via Canva.com
Double Feature and Nemo Regular Fonts via 1001fonts.com and free for commercial use

For
Devin,
Kristina,
Daniel, Zachary,
My Mom and Dad,
My Godmother,
Nic, Katie, Kratz,
Emily, Miranda,
Flo, Håkan,
Alana, Erin,
and Sam.

# THE TALES

|   | Our Own Brand of Magic | i |
|---|---|---|
| 1 | The Trick-or-Treaters of Shaded Oak Lane | 1 |
| 2 | When Witchy Comes to Town | 10 |
| 3 | The Porcelain Ladies | 15 |
| 4 | Truth or Scare | 25 |
| 5 | The Halloween Candle | 41 |
| 6 | Murder! At Castle Bloodstone | 62 |
| 7 | The Haunted House | 85 |
| 8 | They Called Me Lucy | 91 |
| 9 | Who Was That Guy? | 110 |
| 10 | Marceline Starlington | 117 |
| 11 | Madness! At Castle Bloodstone | 129 |
| 12 | A Trick-or-Treating They Will Go | 145 |
| 13 | The Thirteenth Story | 158 |
| + | It Happened on Halloween Night | 207 |

# OUR OWN BRAND OF MAGIC
## Miranda Enzor

October 31st just feels different. It's in the chill in the air as the sun finally sets and darkness descends. It's in the golden glow of jack-o-lantern faces lighting the paths of delighted trick-or-treaters, anxious to fill their pumpkin pails to the brim. It's in the quiet moonlit night as the frivolity dies down, the witching hour approaches, and the veil grows thin.

It's magical.

For those of us who have never outgrown our love of Halloween, adulthood means trying to recapture that magic we felt as young trick-or-treaters on a night of endless possibility.

Luckily, it's never far from reach. Some keep the magic alive by practicing and passing traditions on to their children. Others host a huge Halloween bash, aspiring to pull off a party that would make the adults of Salem in *Hocus Pocus* jealous.

And then some weave their own brand of magic through creative expression.

That creativity is how Andrew and I first met. When he was setting out to start *Your Best Halloween Ever* in 2018, he did a Google search and found *Spooky Little Halloween*. He was kind enough to sign up for my emails and immediately replied to my question about what he loved most about October 31st: that even as an adult, it held on to its sense of magic like no other holiday.

It was no surprise to me when Andrew added original short stories to his blog lineup in its second year that each tale spun a web of wonder more magical than the last. His writing style is intoxicating, and he captured what we both loved about the holiday so perfectly with his words. That season, I found myself looking forward to Saturday mornings in bed with coffee and a new story to read – partly because I couldn't wait for more and partly because it triggered a fond memory deep inside of me.

When I was a girl, my family had a story-a-day book for The Holiday We Do Not Speak of Before October 31st. (You know the one…) It was one of my favorite traditions to sit down with my mom or dad each evening and read that day's story. We only read that book during the holidays, which made it feel even more special. I loved visiting those fictional friends year after year.

Reading Andrew's writing felt like that tradition, improved. Now I had Halloween stories to read once a year! But, of course, I found myself wishing I could once again have a book to take off the shelf on October 1st, read throughout the month, and quietly tuck away again on November 1st until next Halloween.

Sometimes spooky wishes come true because that is exactly what you hold in your hands right now. I couldn't be more excited for you to enjoy all the Halloween feels these words will bring you this October. You will meet the trick-or-treaters of Shaded Oak Lane who are after more than candy. You may be emboldened enough to light a spooky candle alongside cousins Jack and Brandon that will make all your wishes come true…or will it? And if you're lucky, you'll even meet Witchy as she travels into town, a sure sign October 31st is on the way.

But above all else, you will once again experience, through the written word, that thing we all love so much about Halloween: its magic.

Happy reading,
Miranda Enzor
spookylittlehalloween.com

# THE TRICK-OR-TREATERS
# OF SHADED OAK LANE

The Halloween that I dressed up as an astronaut was the first year that they came. I was glad that it was a warm night for late October so my parents didn't make me cover my costume with a coat which, at seven years old, would have been absolutely devastating.

My mother had taken me trick-or-treating earlier in the evening just as the sun was starting to set. My little brother was too small to go out, so he stayed at home with our father, who was passing out candy. I can still remember running from house to house, my vision distorted by the plastic space helmet I'd been wearing every night since it came home with us from the costume shop a few weeks earlier. Mobs of other kids and their parents crowded the sidewalks and driveways, all in costume and cheerfully wishing us "Happy Halloween!" as they passed. Finally, once the plastic jack-o-lantern pail I was using to collect my hard-earned candy was almost too heavy to carry, my mother suggested we head for home.

In every way, it was the perfect Halloween.

Later in the night, I was still in my costume (though I'd finally agreed to take the helmet off) and sprawled out on the floor of our living room surrounded by candy and pages of note paper with math problems scribbled all over them. Just as I was about to finish my homework, my father called from the kitchen, asking me to turn off the porch light and blow out the jack-o-lantern if it hadn't burnt out yet.

"Okay," I said, jumping up and heading for the porch. I stepped outside and immediately noticed that the wind had picked up since my mother and I had returned from trick-or-treating. It was now blowing through the trees, the air much cooler than it was just a few hours prior.

I bent down and lifted the top off of our jack-o-lantern, the flame inside flickering low on the candle wick, and before I could blow it out, I heard something I couldn't quite place. I looked up and into the darkness, glancing down the street but no one was out anymore. In fact, our house seemed to be the last one with porch lights on and a lit pumpkin. We had just moved to Shaded Oak Lane over the last summer, and I was still getting used to calling the neighborhood home. Shaking my head, I bent down to blow out the candle when I heard it again, more distinct this time.

Whispers. I was hearing whispers, almost as if they were carried on the wind itself. I turned to look inside to see if my parents were playing some kind of joke on me, but there was no one in the doorway. I could see my father's shadow in the kitchen through one of the windows and I knew my mother was upstairs putting my brother to bed. I shuddered and turned to blow out the candle as quickly as I could and gasped when I saw the silhouettes of ten trick-or-treaters standing at the end of our driveway.

"H-hello?" I called to them. They didn't answer. I tried to make out their costumes in the dark as best as I could. One looked to be dressed as an old clown with a pointed hat and an umbrella, another had a mask with horns and a tail. One girl in a witch hat was holding a broom and I could just make out another girl's pigtails; I think she was supposed to be a cowgirl.

"Happy Halloween!" I yelled. Again, they said nothing. A boy in a top hat glanced toward a girl dressed as a ballerina before looking back to me.

"W-we still have some c-candy, if you'd like some?" I said, trying to keep my voice from quivering. I carefully backed toward the front door and turned around to reach inside and grab our candy bowl.

When I turned to face them again, they were at the base of our porch, silently holding out what looked like old pillowcases to collect their candy. How had they moved to the porch so quickly? I tried not to think about it as I started passing out the little candy bars. I could finally see their faces now that they were up close - those that weren't hidden behind masks, I mean. They were all pale with dark circles under their blank eyes and sad expressions. There was a strange sense of melancholy among them all.

I smiled when I dropped candy into each of their bags. One by one, they nodded toward me and walked away. Once I'd given candy to the last trick-or-treater, a boy in worn out overalls and a burlap scarecrow mask that covered his whole head, I watched him walk toward the end of our driveway and rejoin the others. They stood there, staring at me.

"Happy Halloween!" I called again, still very uneasy about the whole encounter. I bent down and blew out the jack-o-lantern and when I stood up, they were gone. I ran to the edge of our porch, looking up and down the block, but I couldn't see them anywhere; it was like they just vanished. I shuddered and jumped inside, slamming the front door behind me and quickly turning off the porch light. I quietly set the candy bowl down onto its post.

"Everything okay, Sport?"

I screamed, unaware that my father had walked into the foyer.

"Y-yeah, I'm fine, Dad," I said, looking down at my feet, "just a little spooked because it's so dark outside, I guess."

My father smiled at me and laughed.

"That's alright. Go on and get your backpack ready for school tomorrow. It's almost bedtime."

Later that night while I was lying in bed, I couldn't get the image of those strange kids out of my mind. Who were they? Where had they come from? I hadn't seen them while I was out trick-or-treating earlier. Maybe they were from another school in the area? I figured they were older than me because most of them were taller than I was.

I rolled over to my side and tried to put them out of my mind, but even the shadows my night light cast around the room started to remind me of those trick-or-treaters. I burrowed deep beneath my blankets and eventually fell into a restless sleep.

\* \* \*

They came back the next Halloween.

It was the first year that my parents let my little brother go trick-or-treating and we both dressed up as pirates. A few of my friends from school came over, and we went out in a group with our parents keeping pace just behind us. Afterward, we went back to my house and played outside in our costumes until well after the street lights came on and all of the other kids had gone in for the night.

I had spent a week or so after last Halloween nervous about those weird kids coming back to my house. I asked around at school the next day, but no one in my class had seen or heard of anyone in costumes like they were. Since I was still the new kid in class, I didn't want to make a big deal about it and draw too much attention to myself, so I decided to try and forget about the whole thing. They were probably just a group of kids from a neighborhood or two over, or maybe the other side of town. After a few weeks and no sign of those ten kids, I was more excited for the approaching holidays and by the time spring arrived, I had all but forgotten about them.

Halloween fell on a Friday that year, so my parents let me stay up and watch an old horror movie with them after my friends had gone home and my brother went to bed. I had made it about half way through when I started to fall asleep, so my father gently suggested that it might be bedtime. I had had a long, fun night so didn't protest too much. I sleepily wished them good night and left them in the den to finish the movie.

On my way through the foyer, I noticed a flickering light reflecting from the porch and realized my father must have left the jack-o-lantern lit. I decided to let it go, figuring it would burn itself out before long. But then something else caught my eye outside of the front window just as I started up the stairs. I whipped my head around and my eyes went wide; I threw my hands to my mouth to keep from screaming.

Those trick-or-treaters were back, all ten of them, and they were standing at the end of our driveway just like the year before. Even from inside the house, I could feel their eyes staring through the window and right at me. I stood for a moment, paralyzed by fear, my hands trembling. Before I could stop myself, I ran upstairs to my room, two steps at a time, and jumped in bed, yanking the blankets over my head.

I curled into a ball under the covers, trying to decide what to do while catching my breath.

*Maybe they'll go away?* I thought to myself.

After a few minutes, I had to know if they were still there, so I worked up every bit of courage I could muster and slowly got out of bed. I walked over to the window and peeked out through my window blinds.

Sure enough, they were still standing at the end of our driveway staring at the porch. They looked as though they hadn't aged a day. The witch with the broom, the burlap-faced scarecrow, the boy in the top hat, and even the clown with the umbrella - it was so strange to see them all standing outside of my house again, like watching a memory. I tried not to make any noise or sudden movements, but as I studied them, they suddenly jerked their faces toward my window in unison, staring right back at me.

I jumped back from my window, and covered my face with my shaking hands.

"W-what do they want?" I asked myself out loud, my voice trembling. And suddenly, I knew. I knew what they wanted, what *all* trick-or-treaters wanted. I walked back to my window and peeked through the blinds again.

They were standing closer to the house now, beneath my window, arms outstretched with the same tattered pillowcases I'd put their candy in the year before.

"They're trick-or-treating," I whispered to myself, "and they're here for their candy."

There was no way I'd be able to go outside like last year without rousing my parents' suspicion, but I had an idea. I lifted my blinds and nodded toward them, holding up a finger to let them know I'd be right back.

As quickly and quietly as I could, I snuck down to the foyer where our bowl of Halloween candy was still on the stand by the coat rack. I grabbed a handful and ran back to my room, taking care to avoid the stairs that creaked.

When I was back in my room, I opened my window and leaned out toward them. A rush of chilly nighttime air blew into my room, and I could hear their whispers on the wind, just like the year before.

"Happy Halloween," I whispered into the night as I tossed the candy down to them. They carefully picked up what pieces hadn't landed in their bags, and dutifully walked back to the end of the driveway, just as they'd done before. They stared up at me for a minute or two until a huge gust of wind roared through the trees. I glanced down the street for a moment and when I looked back at the driveway, they were gone.

I closed my window and crawled into bed, though I didn't fall asleep until long after I heard my parents turn in for the night.

\* \* \*

A few weeks later, on a bright Saturday afternoon, I was playing outside with my little brother when our mother announced it was time for him to go in for a nap. I asked if it would be alright if I stayed outside for a little bit longer.

"Sure," my mother said, "just come in if you get cold."

In the time since those trick-or-treaters had made a second visit to our house, I hadn't thought of much else. I had asked around at school again to see if anyone knew of any kids that fit their description, but no one did. I didn't tell my parents or anyone else about them, because I was sure no one would believe my story. I wasn't even sure that I believed it myself.

I was putting my bicycle away in the garage when I noticed the tub of sidewalk chalk our parents had gotten my brother and me the previous summer. I hadn't used it in a while, and seeing the chalk gave me an idea. I grabbed the tub and ran to the end of the driveway, my intentions set.

I started with the clown, drawing him with his pointed hat and umbrella in a blue chalk, before moving on to the boy in the cape and the ballerina. I lost track of time, working diligently on drawing each of the trick-or-treaters as I remembered them from their two visits to my house.

When it was late in the afternoon and the sun was starting to get low in the sky, I heard the sound of approaching footsteps and looked up to see one of our neighbors, Mr. Owensby, out for a walk. He was a nice old man that lived a little way down the street and would go for walks almost daily when the weather allowed for it.

"Hey buddy," he called to me.

"Good afternoon, Mr. Owensby," I said politely. He stopped quickly when he saw my drawing of the trick-or-treaters. He inhaled sharply through his nose, his eyes darting from one of my drawings to the next. Finally, he looked at me.

"Do you know these kids?" he asked slowly. I looked over my handiwork then back to him.

"No," I said, "not really. They're just... they're some kids I saw trick-or-treating on Halloween." He looked at my chalk drawings again.

"I wondered where they'd gone off to," he said to himself quietly before looking at me directly. "If you've seen these kids, then you know that they're not kids like you or your friends."

I stared at him, confused.

"Now, I don't want to go and spook you," he said, "but they're spirits."

"Ghosts?" I blurted out.

"You could call them that, yes," he said. "I don't know anything about how they came to be that way or who they were, I just know that every year on Halloween for a good number of years, they came to my house late in the night after all the other lights had gone out looking for treats like any other kid on Halloween. Nearest I can figure, it's the last lit jack-o-lantern they look for."

I stared at him quietly.

"Two Halloweens ago was the first year they didn't come in all the time I've lived on Shaded Oak Lane," he said. "I stayed awake for as long as I could, but it got to be a little too late for me, and when I went to blow out my jack-o-lantern, I saw that the candle was already out. I guess the wind got it. I've been wondering ever since what happened to them.

"It's all good and well, you see, I'm planning to move sometime in the next year once the weather warms up in the spring, so I'm glad to know they've found a place to... I don't know... keep being kids for a little while longer. Or as long as they need to, I guess."

"Were you ever afraid of them?" I asked.

"Oh no," he said gently, "not at all anymore. Of course, it gave me quite the surprise the first time I saw them standing outside of my house, but it makes me happy to know I was able to bring them a little bit of peace in my own way."

He took one last look at my drawings before tipping his hat toward me and continuing on his walk. I sat on the ground after he'd gone, thinking about everything he'd said. Before too long, I was starting to get cold, so I cleaned up my things and went inside.

\* \* \*

All of that happened a long time ago.

Every Halloween since, I've taken care to make sure our jack-o-lantern is the last one lit on the block and that I have candy ready for the ten ghostly trick-or-treaters who find their way into its candlelit glow. Even when I went away to school, I made sure to come home each year on Halloween to ensure that those ten kids had a treat waiting for them.

And now it's Halloween again. I've spent the evening in costume and handing out candy to the neighborhood kids with my whole family. They're all inside now, but I'm sitting on the porch, waiting for our last trick-or-treaters of the night.

I glance at my watch. It's getting late. I stand and look down the street just as the last house on the block goes dark; there's no more shining porch lights, no more glowing jack-o-lanterns. The wind picks up and I hear a familiar whispering. I turn my focus to the driveway and there they are, the trick-or-treaters of Shaded Oak Lane, standing in a line just like they did so many years ago when I was a kid.

"Hello, old friends," I say with a smile, shaking the candy bowl. "Happy Halloween!"

# WHEN WITCHY COMES TO TOWN

We always know Halloween is on its way when Witchy comes to town.

Of course, it's widely accepted that most small towns and villages have a witch or two, but don't believe the rumors you may hear about them. I'm sure there's been a few bad ones over time, but Witchy is cheerful and kind. She's an old woman with graying hair that falls around her shoulders who lives at the edge of the woods in a stone cottage, and mostly keeps to herself. Our town grocer even makes a weekly trip to deliver her food, bringing back her trinkets to sell in his shop. For most of the year, we hear very little from our local witch.

But when Witchy comes to town, it's nothing short of magical.

It starts when the first leaf changes colors. Some trees turn a bright yellow, others a deep red. The days are still warm, but the nights start to cool and if you listen very carefully, you can hear her singing in the wind as she tends to her garden of pumpkins.

"Dance with me, let's spin and sing!
'Tis nigh on the hour of Halloween!

When the leaves doth change, and the days condense,
Magic builds in the air, and my power hence!

So I say with glee to those most dear:
Happy Halloween to all - the time grows near!"

She makes her first trip into town on the first of October when the sun is at its highest point, the squeaking wheels of her horse-drawn cart announcing her arrival. The children playing in the streets gather to welcome her as she rounds the corner into the square, a toothy grin on her weathered face.

"Hello again, my darlings!" she calls, lifting the wide brim of her black pointed hat to greet the children. They rush to her, knowing she's brought them gifts to take home.

"For you a paper bat, my dear," Witchy says, handing out a handmade decoration, "and for you a pumpkin pail! A hanging ghost for you, young one, and for you all, a spooky tale!"

After the last of the decorations has been handed out, the children gather round and she tells them stories of Halloween. She shares chronicles from the woods and tales of the spirits, bringing them to life with her magic, until the shadows grow long and she must begin her journey home. She packs her cart and departs the square, waving goodbye as she goes.

"I'll be back in two weeks' time, when the leaves all start to fall," she calls. "And I'll have with me in my cart, dress up costumes for you all!"

\* \* \*

True to her word, Witchy returns in two weeks. The days are shorter, and the air more brisk. It's a windy, gray day when the squeak of her cart can again be heard. The children of the town throw on their jackets and run to the square to await her arrival, and as she turns the corner, they welcome her with a cheer.

"Hello again, my little ones!" she calls to the excited children. "It's lovely to see you all! I hope my last gifts brought you joy, as the days give way to fall!"

She jumps down from her cart, her bangles clanging as she lands; her black dress is covered in crescents and stars that shimmer, even on this dreary day. She reaches up and pulls down an old trunk that hits the ground with a bang.

The children look over one another, eager to see what Witchy has for them today. She flings open the trunk and starts passing around carefully wrapped packages.

"For you a sweeping cape, my darling," she says excitedly. "Oh! You look divine! For you a black cat mask, young one, and for you a hat like mine!"

Witchy continues handing out costumes and as she does, the children happily put them on. Before too long, the last of the parcels has been handed out and she is surrounded by a group of little goblins and ghouls, all excitedly playing in the costumes she's given them.

"Now take these home, and do take care," she says. "I know they bring delight! But carefully these costumes wear so they last 'til Halloween night!"

With that, she gives each child a hug and sends them on their way home. She carefully puts the trunk back in her cart and as quickly as she'd come to town, Witchy is on her way back to her cottage.

* * *

The next week Witchy comes to town again, though this time overnight and with only a few days until Halloween. As the sun goes down, she loads her cart full with the pumpkins from her garden, and once the town has gone to sleep, she sets out on her next errand.

Witchy quietly rides through the town, wrapped in her orange cloak stitched with owls, bats, and cats. She hums to herself cheerily as she goes, leaving a pumpkin at each door with a note that reads:

"Here's a pumpkin, orange and stout,
and all your very own.

But now a task to you I hand,
imperative you don't postpone.

For soon the moon glows in the darkest of night,
and walks a spirit horde.

And only the light of this jack-o-lantern,
off the monsters will ward.

So carve a face and light a candle,
to carefully place inside.

And leave it lit the whole night through,
'til the sun outside doth rise!"

Witchy continues on her midnight mission until the last of her pumpkins have been delivered to the homes in the town. When she's finished, she quietly heads back to her cottage, singing to herself along with the gentle *clip clop* of her horse's hooves as she goes.

\* \* \*

Witchy makes her final trip to town for the year on the morning of Halloween, loading up her cart with treats for all. And by the time the children of the town wake up, she has completely transformed the square into a Halloween wonderland with decorations and games for everyone to enjoy.

In the late afternoon, once they have finished their schooling for the day, the children dress up in their costumes and head to the square with their parents and carved jack-o-lanterns in tow. They spend hours playing games and sharing the treats Witchy has brought.

"For you a candied apple, dear," she grins, "and you a little pie. And for you a bag of chocolate treats, better than money can buy!"

The sun starts to set and the townsfolk light the candles in their jack-o-lanterns, bathing the square in an orange glow. They light a bonfire in the middle, and a few of the adults play music from fiddles and pipes. Witchy joyfully leads them in a dance, her pointed shoes clacking on the stones in the square.

One by one, the children start to grow tired, and their parents take them home. Before long, there are only a few of the adults from the town helping Witchy carefully pack everything away in her cart.

And as the town settles down to sleep, with jack-o-lanterns still lighting their windows, Witchy drives her cart back to her cottage, singing to herself in the moonlight.

"Dance with me, let's spin and sing!
'Tis still the hour of Halloween!

Lo, as belov'd October wanes,
The magic of this night yet reigns!

So I say once more, to those most dear:
Happy Halloween to all, and I'll see you next year!"

# THE PORCELAIN LADIES

When I was little, I spent every Halloween with my nan. She owned an old antique store a few towns over and lived in the apartment above. Nan's store was filled with all kinds of treasures, from old toys and books to dishes and lamps. There was even a corner full of clothes - large brimmed hats, oversized coats, and those sorts of things - that I would spend hours playing dress up with.

But the most interesting thing in Nan's shop was her collection of porcelain lady figurines. She had maybe fifteen of them, all of which were just over half-a-foot tall, and each was as elegant as the next. She kept them scattered around the store, tucked into the cases and shelves that were brimming with fascinating things just waiting to be discovered. No one ever asked about them, and if they did, Nan would politely let them know that her porcelain ladies were not for sale.

And from an early age, I knew that they were alive.

It happened on Halloween night when I was six. Nan had taken me trick-or-treating around the block, and when I couldn't fit another piece of candy in my witch bucket, we returned to her cozy apartment for some cider and an old movie. I was curled up on the couch under my favorite blanket that Nan had crocheted, when I decided I wanted a glass of water. I looked over toward Nan, and she was asleep in her chair.

*I'll get it myself*, I thought, quietly getting up and tiptoeing into the kitchen. I stood on the stool Nan kept in the corner to get a glass from the cabinet, when I heard a strange noise. It sounded like laughter - a low, cruel cackle - and it was coming from the door that lead to the shop downstairs!

I stood on the stool, afraid to turn on the faucet; I was terrified to make a sound. After what felt like an hour, and just as I was convinced I was imagining what I'd heard, there was a crash from downstairs and a very bright light flashed under the door to the stairs.

"NAN!" I screamed, running to the living room.

"Sophie!" she yelped as I lunged into her lap. "What happened, my darling?"

"I got up to get a drink from the kitchen and I heard a weird noise from downstairs and there was a crash and a light under the door and I don't know what any of - "

"Shhh, there, there," she said gently. "You must have had a nightmare, dear one."

"But - "

"Now come on," she said, "I think you've had enough Halloween fun for one night. Let's get to bed!" Without another word of protest, we walked to my room and she tucked me in.

"No monsters here, Sophie dear," she said before giving me a kiss on the forehead. "And if there were, they'd have another thing coming!"

She sat on the edge of my bed for a minute, carefully rubbing my forehead.

"Now off to sleep with you!" She turned off the lamp next to my bed and closed the door on her way out, leaving my moon and stars night light to cast a soothing glow in the room.

I was exhausted, but I couldn't fall asleep. I laid awake in my bed for a long time, my mind racing. I knew that what had happened in the kitchen wasn't a dream! I had heard that awful laugh, I had seen that bright light.

I had to know what happened down in the shop.

Carefully, I slid out of bed and crept to the door. The clock on the dresser read 1:28 a.m. Just as I was about to sneak out into the hall, I heard a noise from the corner of my room. I spun around. There was nothing in the corner but a rocking chair with a teddy bear on it. Confused, I walked over and jumped when my foot stepped on something cold.

It was the vent! The noise I was hearing was coming from the vent!

Carefully, I got down to the floor and put my ear to the metal. I couldn't make out much, but there was definitely something moving down in the shop. There were creaks and groans and what sounded like small footsteps, lots and lots of small footsteps, with something else, something I couldn't quite make out.

Suddenly, I realized what I was listening to. The noise was soft, but unmistakable: the quiet *clink* of porcelain as it hit the surfaces downstairs, from the glass countertops to the metal racks, and even the wooden floors. It was the ladies! The porcelain ladies in the shop downstairs were moving around; they were alive!

I laid on the floor in my room, listening to the sounds downstairs intently. Without realizing it, I must have fallen asleep, because the next thing I knew, I jolted awake. I was still on the floor, though I'd rolled away from the vent. The reddish light of daybreak was just starting to stream through the window.

I put my ear back to the vent. Silence. Whatever the ladies had been doing down in the shop, they probably finished hours ago. Exhausted, I climbed into bed and fell into a deep sleep.

When I woke up a few hours later, there was a stack of pancakes on the kitchen table and Nan was downstairs. I was surprised to find that the shop was just as we'd left it the night before; nothing was out of place. I spent the rest of that visit trying to convince her that the porcelain ladies in her shop were alive, but she insisted I had imagined the whole thing.

\* \* \*

Over the next six years, I spent every Halloween visit with Nan trying to catch the porcelain ladies moving around the shop with no success.

"I know you're alive," I whispered to the one Nan named Rowena. She didn't move, her painted features staring right through me; I stared back.

"Sophie, can you come help me?" Nan called from the back room. I looked toward the door and back to Rowena's face.

"You're not fooling me," I said, before running off to help Nan. She was sorting through a box of donations in the back, and knew how much I loved helping her with those. I got to find the best things that way!

"Are you talking to the ladies again?" she asked, laughing.

"They're alive, Nan," I said. "I know it, and I'm gonna prove it."

"Is that so?" she asked with a smile. "Well, keep me updated on your progress, dear."

We sorted through the boxes for the next half hour or so, until the bell at the door jingled.

"I'll be right back!" she said, going to greet the customer. I continued digging in the box. At the bottom there was something delicately wrapped in an old green cloth. I picked it up and carefully unwrapped it to find the most exquisite antique mirror I'd ever seen.

"Wow," I said aloud. It was stunning, with a handle and decorations around the looking glass made of silver. I stared into the mirror, looking past my reflection at the masterful antique. It almost pulsed with life in my hands.

"Hello."

The voice broke me from the trance. I looked toward the door to see a girl about my age. She was tall and pale with dark hair.

"H-hi," I said. "Can I help you?"

"Oh, no. I'm just out shopping... with my dad," she added quickly, nodding toward the room where I heard Nan talking with someone. "I'm Mia. What's your name?"

"Sophie."

"I haven't seen you around," she said. "Are you new here?"

"I don't live here," I said. "I come stay with my nan every year for Halloween. It's our tradition."

"Oh, fun!" she said, looking around the room. "This is… one of my favorite stores in the neighborhood."

"I love it, too," I agreed. "There's so much to see and play with! Wanna come look at some of the fancy dresses?"

"Sure!" she said. We lost track of time combing through the collection of old clothes. Suddenly, Mia looked at the clock on the back wall.

"Oh my gosh! It's getting late!" she said. "I've gotta get going. My dad will wonder where I'm at!" She put the big, fancy hat she'd been wearing back on the rack.

"Are you doing anything on Halloween? We could go trick-or-treating? Or you could come watch a scary movie with me and Nan? She won't mind if I have a friend over."

"Sure," Mia said, smiling. "That'll be fun."

"Cool!" I said. "Nan lives upstairs, so you'll just come back here and we'll come down and let you in."

"I'll see you around, Sophie," she said before turning to run out of the shop. I looked around and saw that Nan was back in the storage room, going through another box.

"Who was that, dear?"

"Her name's Mia," I said. "She lives in the neighborhood."

"Oh, how nice," Nan said. "I saw you two having fun and didn't want to pull you away."

"Is it alright if she comes back on Halloween?"

"Of course!" said Nan. "The more the merrier. Let's finish going through this box and we'll close up for some dinner, alright?"

* * *

On Halloween morning, Mia stopped by Nan's shop to say that she wouldn't be able to go trick-or-treating, but that she would still like to come back and watch a movie later in the evening if that was alright.

And so I found myself running downstairs to let Mia in after returning from another wonderful year of trick-or-treating with Nan.

"The shop looks a lot different at night," she said, as we ran up the stairs. I stopped on the landing and looked back at her.

"Yeah," I said. "It kinda creeps me out."

"Really?" she asked. "Why?"

"Well," I said, wondering if I should tell her about the ladies. I mean, we were friends and what's the worst that could happen? She'd think I was making it up like Nan? She looked at me intently. "You know all of those porcelain lady figures down in the shop?"

"Yes."

"They're... well, they're alive."

"What? Really?" she said, giving me a weird look.

"Yeah," I said, looking at my feet. "I, uhh, I heard them moving around down there from my room when I was little."

She was quiet.

"It's okay if you don't believe me," I said quickly.

"Oh no," she said. "It's not that, not that at all. I just... how scary for you!"

"Kind of," I said. "I don't know, I'm not really afraid of them? If that makes sense."

"I guess," she said. "Let's go watch that movie!"

We ran the rest of the way upstairs where Nan was waiting with a few buckets of freshly popped popcorn. All through the movie, I kept wondering if Mia thought I was making up the whole thing. She was acting normal enough, and she didn't mention it to Nan, so maybe she believed me?

When the movie ended, Nan was asleep in her chair and I went to the kitchen to get Mia and myself a drink. I didn't see her follow me into the kitchen, and I jumped when Mia's hand clasped down hard on my shoulder. I spun around to face her.

"I believe you, Sophie," she said. "What you said earlier, about those ladies downstairs being alive? I believe you. I was thinking about it during the movie. Figures like that shouldn't be alive, but if they are, then they must be evil..."

I stared at her.

"...and if they're evil, they must be destroyed."

* * *

Before I could stop her, Mia had me back down in the shop. We'd snuck quietly down the stairs, even though we didn't really have to worry about waking Nan up.

"Where are they?" she whispered. I stood in the middle of the store, my eyes adjusting to the darkness. I looked from shelf to shelf, but with a growing panic, realized that none of the porcelain ladies were where Nan usually kept them.

"I don't see them," I said as quietly as I could, my voice shaking. "I don't know where they went! Mia, I think they're gone!"

"I don't think they're gone, Sophie," she said impatiently. "I think they know we're coming for them." She had an edge to her voice that I hadn't heard before.

We continued searching the store, but couldn't find a single porcelain lady. As I walked by the register, something on a lower shelf caught my eye. I bent down for a closer look and gasped when I realized it was the mirror from the box I had gone through the other day - and its glass was glowing!

"What is it, Sophie? What did you find?"

I couldn't look away from the mirror, its glass was shining brighter and now it looked like there were green clouds swirling underneath. I was so transfixed by whatever was happening with the mirror that I didn't realize I was slowly holding my hand out to touch the handle.

"Nothing," I said lethargically. I barely heard myself; had I even answered Mia's question out loud? The mirror still held my complete attention. I was vaguely aware of Mia standing behind me. She was breathing heavily.

"What's going on?" I said aloud, each word hanging in the air.

"Sophie! Look out!" Mia shouted. Her sharp yell broke the mirror's mesmerizing hold on me. I spun around just in time to see two of the porcelain ladies pop up on the counter. "Behind you!"

"Ahh!" I screamed, as more and more of the porcelain ladies stepped out of the shadows. "Mia!"

She didn't say anything.

"Mia?"

She was standing there, a wild look of fear on her face.

"Get them, Sophie," she whispered. "Smash them all."

I spun around and realized none of the porcelain ladies were looking at me. Every one of them was facing Mia. I turned back to her and gasped in terror. Mia's face contorted in rage and her eyes began to glow a pale green, just like the mirror.

"I said get them, Sophie!" she commanded, her voice much deeper than it had been just moments ago. "Get them NOW!"

As Mia yelled, her bones cracked and her face shifted into a grotesque monstrosity as though she were a wild animal. Her ears pointed and fangs dropped from her gums; she batted clothing racks out of her way as she moved toward me. I fell to the ground and backed away as quickly as I could, hiding under the counter as she advanced. She had almost doubled in height. I tried to yell for Nan, but my voice stuck in my chest.

"No one can help you now, stupid girl," the monster Mia had become said, its voice a raspy growl. It was getting closer to where I was hiding. "You or your pathetic nan."

"I wouldn't be so sure," a commanding voice said. I looked up to see Rowena on one of the shelves on the far side of the store.

"You're no match for me," said the monster, looking up from me toward her. Hot tears ran down my cheeks.

"Ladies," Rowena said.

The monster turned and snarled; I couldn't believe what I was seeing. The porcelain ladies that had been scattered around the store rose into the air and floated toward the beast.

"What is this?" it snarled. The porcelain ladies began to glow and spin in a circle around it. They spun faster and faster, up and down around the monster.

The mirror began to rise from the shelf and floated toward

the white light that was growing in the center of the store. With a gasp, I realized I'd seen this light before! Six years ago, from under the kitchen door upstairs. As I looked back toward the light, I could barely see the monster or the mirror anymore; the shop was so bright.

"NO!" the monster cried out, as it was encased in the white light from the porcelain ladies. "I was so close! After so long!"

It howled in agony and without warning, the room went dark. The monster was gone and the white light had disappeared. I hid under the counter, trembling, for what felt like hours.

"It's alright, Sophie. The monster's gone," a voice said to me. I looked up and could hardly believe what I was seeing. The entire collection of Nan's porcelain ladies was standing on the counter, all of them looking at me warmly.

"W-what?"

Rowena stepped out from the rest.

"The beast that came into the shop through that mirror is gone. And the mirror has been destroyed, so it won't be bothering you again," she said. "I'm sure you have a lot of questions."

"You're alive? You're alive! I knew you were alive!" I shouted, wiping my eyes. "A-and there was a monster in that mirror?!"

"Yes, yes, and yes," she said. A murmur went through the other ladies.

"But what are you all doing here? What are you?"

"We're guardians, Sophie," she said. "And we've been tasked with protecting your nan and this shop whenever things that are... less than favorable, like that beast, find their way here. Which, more often than not, happens around Halloween."

"Those creatures get so worked up around Halloween, don't they?" the porcelain lady Nan called Ingrid said quietly to another, both shaking their heads in disapproval.

"But... I stay with Nan every Halloween?"

"To renew your protection charm," Rowena said. "It's strongest when cast on the eve of All Hallows, you know."

"What?!"

"You have a long and storied family history, dear girl," she began. "And I can see you don't know any bit of what I'm talking about."

"They've kept things from me? My parents? And Nan?"

"And for the best until now, I'm sure," she said. "But you're almost thirteen, and there's no sense in keeping secrets any longer."

"But... wait. What happens when I turn thirteen?" I asked. She looked to one of the other ladies in response.

"Bernadette, go wake Nan," Rowena said, turning around. "I suspect that beast put her under some sort of sleeping hex." One of the ladies in the back of the group rose into the air and floated toward the stairs to the apartment.

"We'll brew some tea, Sophie dear," Ingrid said. "It's going to be a long night." She and another of the porcelain ladies hopped down and scurried toward the back room of the shop, a familiar *clink* sounding with each of their foot.

I looked from Rowena to the other ladies, all of them smiling at me. For so many years, I'd known they were alive, that I hadn't made up what I'd heard that night. It was like a dream to finally face them after so long. The adrenaline from the monster's attack was subsiding, and now my mind was racing... was Nan okay? Did my parents know about all of this? Who was that monster? What did it want with me? And most important of all, what were these porcelain ladies about to tell me? My whole world was about to change.

I could hear Nan coming down the stairs and smelled our favorite tea brewing. I took a deep breath and smiled.

"Tell me everything."

# TRUTH OR SCARE

"You know what it means when that cemetery gate is open, right?" Gabi yelled back to the four of us. As she usually did on our walks home from school, she'd run ahead from our group to get to the crosswalk first. Gabi, Peter, Eliza, and I were all in the same fifth grade class; my little brother, Joey, was in first.

"What?" asked Peter as we caught up to her. It was a chilly day in late October; the sky was gray and most of the trees were bare with just a few orange and brown leaves hanging on.

"You know, when the gate's open," she said, pointing to the old cemetery entrance gate that was just barely open. "It means there's a ghost out of the graveyard!"

"Nuh uh," said Joey. "That can't be true! Ghosts aren't real."

"Oh yes they are," Gabi fired back. "Mrs. Bloom was reading us a story about them today and in it, the ghosts could come and go from the graveyard so long as the gates were open. And if any ghost is out of the graveyard, the gates can't close!"

"Is that true, Johnny?" Joey asked, looking up at me.

"No," I said. "It's just from a story our teacher read us today."

The light changed and we continued our walk home. We passed that cemetery every afternoon, but only since our teacher had started reading us scary stories in between our lessons had

Gabi taken an interest in it.

The graveyard was old, dating back at least two hundred years, with crumbling headstones and shadowy statues keeping watch throughout. And though I had never known there to be a fence surrounding the property, an old entrance gate still stood on one corner near the road. It was more of a decoration than anything, really, since you could just as easily walk around it to get onto the grounds.

"I like how Mrs. Bloom has been reading us those stories all month," Eliza said.

"Yeah," agreed Peter. "It's fun! Like the one with the - "

"I'm telling you guys," Gabi cut in. "When the gate's left open like that, there's a ghost out of its grave... probably sneaking around out here with us!"

"I don't know if I believe that," Eliza said quietly.

"Me neither," Peter said.

He tried not to, but I saw Joey look back toward the graveyard and shiver. We were safely across and had reached the entrance to our street.

"Well if you're all so sure that ghosts aren't real, why don't we go back tomorrow night?"

"What?" I asked.

"After everyone's done trick-or-treating," Gabi said. "Let's meet here and see if we meet any ghosts out in the graveyard on Halloween. If none of you think there's such a thing as ghosts, there shouldn't be anything for you to be afraid of!"

"I don't know," Eliza said, her voice trailing off. We all stood there awkwardly for a moment until Gabi said those four fighting words.

"Unless you're all chicken."

That did it.

In a rush to prove our bravery, Peter, Eliza, and I all agreed to Gabi's plan; Joey stood anxiously behind us, kicking a pile of leaves.

"It's settled," Gabi said. "We'll meet back here tomorrow night, unless any of you scaredy cats decide not to show!"

"C'mon, Johnny, let's go home," Joey said as he grabbed my

hand and started pulling me toward our house.

"Fine," I said to my friends. "See you guys at school tomorrow."

Later that night, just as I was about to fall asleep, I heard a soft knock at my bedroom door.

"Johnny?" Joey whispered.

"Yes?"

He walked in and stood at the foot of my bed.

"I can't sleep," he said. "I had a nightmare."

"Is it because of what Gabi was saying on the way home from school today?"

"Yes."

"Sit up here a second," I said, patting the space next to me. "Gabi is a bossy know-it-all who was just trying to put on a show for Peter and Eliza. She knows that story from school was just a story, but she's gotta feel like she's braver than the rest of us."

"I guess," he said.

"Look," I continued, "if you don't want to go tomorrow night, you don't have to."

"No," he said firmly. "I want Eliza, err, your friends to see I can be brave, too."

"Okay," I said with a grin. I had figured Joey's not-so-secret crush on Eliza was part of this. "But remember, if you change your mind, you don't owe them anything."

"Ghosts aren't real, right?"

"Right."

"Then Gabi was right, I guess," he said. "We don't have anything to be afraid of."

\* \* \*

The next day was Halloween, and despite trying to enjoy our classroom party at school and trick-or-treating with Joey and Peter, I couldn't help but feel anxious about our plans for that night. It was like a dark cloud that had hung over the entire day… Gabi had even passed me a note during math class to make sure I didn't forget.

I knew there was no such thing as ghosts, so why couldn't I shake that uneasy feeling?

"We're going to meet up with Eliza and Gabi," I explained to my mom when we returned from the last house on our block.

"That's fine, boys," she said. "Don't be out late - and Johnny, look after your brother!"

And so the three of us found ourselves walking toward the graveyard that we passed by every day on the way home from school. My vampire cape rustled the leaves behind us as we walked; I could hardly deny the dread building in the pit of my stomach. We were going to show Gabi there was no such thing as ghosts, and get back home as quickly as we could.

"Well, well, well," Gabi said as we walked toward her and Eliza. "Look who decided to show up."

"As if you'd let us forget it if we didn't," Peter said, his voice muffled behind his green monster mask.

"Guess you guys weren't the scaredy cats I thought," she said with a laugh, adjusting her cat-eared headband.

"Looks like you're the only cat here tonight," I said. Gabi rolled her eyes while Joey tried not to laugh.

"Hey guys," Eliza said. She was dressed as a witch with an orange and black pointed hat and held a broom at her side. "Nice cowboy costume, Joey."

"Thanks," he said, squeezing my hand tightly.

"Let's get on with it," Peter said, lifting his mask. "I wanna get home and dig into this candy!"

"Sounds good to me," Gabi said. She turned to lead us into the graveyard, but stopped short. "Look at that, the old gate's still open. There must be ghosts out tonight."

\* \* \*

We were all a little jumpy as we walked down the main path into the cemetery, the gravel crunching under our feet. There were lampposts with flickering gas lights along the path, but it was a dark night, so I was glad that Joey had had the idea to bring our flashlights; Eliza and Peter had brought theirs, too.

Maybe it was my imagination working extra hard, but I couldn't shake the feeling that we were being watched. Every statue we passed, every shadow beneath a tree... I felt like there was something observing us as we walked by. I could feel through his hand clutched in mine that Joey felt uneasy, too.

The cemetery was quiet except for the occasional car in the distance and the breeze kicking leaves up before dying down just as quickly.

"There's nothing here but gravestones and grass," Peter said impatiently.

"Shh," said Gabi. "Did you hear that?"

"Hear what?" asked Eliza.

"That," Gabi said, looking toward a dirt path between two tall evergreen trees that led deeper into the graveyard. "Come on."

I didn't want to admit it, but I had heard it, too. I couldn't tell if it was a howling or what, but we definitely weren't alone. We followed her quietly, all of us huddled close as we walked along. The headstones just off the path were looking more weathered the further we went. I shivered, realizing we must be walking toward the oldest part of the cemetery.

"Look!" I whispered to the others. There was a light ahead of us through the trees, and I could hear a high-pitched sound that almost sounded like...

"Music," said Peter. "Someone's playing music!"

Joey's grip on my hand tightened.

"Well let's see who it is!" Gabi said defiantly. We walked on, closer and closer to the clearing, and as we did my heart started racing in my chest, each step feeling heavier than the last. Just as we were about to reach the light, the music stopped and a voice cut through the silence.

"Who's there?"

Peter inhaled sharply and Eliza gasped. I looked at Gabi with my eyes wide, jerking my head toward the light.

"Go on," I whispered. She rolled her eyes.

"Hello!" she yelled back, walking toward the light. For what felt like an hour, the four of us stood on the path until we heard her yell back to us.

"Get out here, you chickens!"

We walked toward the clearing and I was surprised to find Gabi standing with another group of kids who must have come to the cemetery after trick-or-treating like we did, since they were also in costumes.

"These are my friends: Eliza, Peter, Johnny," Gabi said. "And that's Johnny's little brother, Joey."

The clearing, which had seemed so bright from far away, was only dimly lit by one of the cemetery's gas lampposts in the center, and I had a hard time making out the other kids' faces.

"This is Wallace and Minnie," she said, introducing the first two before turning to the others. "And this is Grace and this is Elmer." I wasn't sure what both of the girls were supposed to be in their frilly dresses, but the boys were both dressed as hobos with hats and oversized jackets, almost identical except that Elmer was wearing glasses.

"And who are you three?" I asked the kids standing in the shadows toward the back. There was a girl dressed as an angel, with big wings that almost looked like stone, and two boys: one was dressed as a soldier, the other wore a baseball uniform. The baseball player must have been the one playing the music, because he held a small fiddle.

"High schoolers," Grace said quickly.

"They won't tell us their names," Elmer added. "They don't want their friends to know they dressed up for Halloween."

"We were just getting ready to start another round of Truth or Scare, if you guys wanted to play with us?" Wallace asked.

"What's Truth or Scare?" Peter asked in reply.

"Oh, it's great fun!" Minnie spoke up. "We take turns asking each other 'truth' or 'scare'. If someone picks 'truth', you can ask them a question - any question you want! - and they have to answer truthfully. And if someone picks scare - "

" - they have to do something scary?" Gabi interrupted.

"Exactly," the boy dressed as the soldier said slowly from the shadows. "And once you've finished either your truth or your scare, you get to choose who to ask next."

I pulled Joey closer to me as I looked toward Peter and Eliza. They shrugged their shoulders.

"Sounds like fun," Gabi said. "We'll play."

"Excellent," Minnie said with a grin.

"How long do we have to be here?" Joey asked me quietly.

"We'll just play a round or two," I answered. "Then we'll be on our way home."

"It was your turn," Elmer said to the angel. She stepped toward the rest of us and in the glow from the lamp post, it almost looked like her dress was made of stone just like her wings were painted to be. She turned to Peter.

"Peter, right?" she asked. She spoke in a hushed tone, barely above a whisper.

"Yeah," he said.

"Truth or scare?"

"Uhm... truth," Peter said quickly. The angel smiled.

"Do you believe in the Governess?" she asked.

"The who?" Joey asked with a squeak.

"The Governess," repeated the angel.

"Who's the Governess?" Peter asked.

"She's a cloaked statue with no face that watches over a mass burial plot of kids that died a long time ago in a fire," said the boy in the soldier costume. He spoke quietly, just like the angel. "Legend has it that she walks the cemetery at night, looking for trespassers."

"They say you can hear her coming by the echoing of her hollow, metal footsteps, ringing like a bell," said the baseball player, "and sometimes, you'll hear her whisper through the trees. But you won't know she's near until it's too late."

I could feel Joey shudder next to me.

"Well," asked the angel, "do you believe in the legend, Peter?"

"A statue that walks at night?" he asked. "No, of course not! That's silly - it's like something out of our teacher's storybook."

"Interesting," the angel said with a giggle. "Better not let her catch you, then."

"W-what happens if she catches you?" Eliza asked suddenly.

"She'll take your face and wear it as her own!" Grace shouted, her hands raised. "So beware!"

Joey whimpered quietly.

"Ooh, spooky!" said Gabi, laughing. "Alright, Peter - you're up! Who's next?"

Peter shifted uncomfortably, then turned toward Wallace.

"Truth or scare?" he asked.

"Truth," Wallace answered.

"Uhm, I dunno," Peter said, kicking his feet in the grass. "D- do *you* believe in the Governess?"

Before Wallace could answer, a noise stopped us cold. It came from far off in the graveyard, but something about it sent a chill down my spine.

"Did you hear that?" the soldier asked the angel.

"What was that?" Minnie asked, her voice shaking.

"Johnny, I'm scared," Joey whispered to me.

"Shh," I said, patting his shoulder. "It's fine."

We stood around the lamp post, waiting to see if we'd hear it again. And just as I was starting to wonder if we'd all imagined it, the noise rang out again. This time it was closer, echoing through the graveyard and unmistakably metallic… like a bell.

"Wait," Peter said, turning to me and Eliza. "You guys don't think…"

"Whooo'sss out of theeeir graaaaavvvess…" a metallic-sounding voice called out through the trees.

"It's the Governess!" shouted Elmer.

"Don't let her take my face!" Joey screamed before darting into the woods.

"Joey, get back here!" I shouted, running to catch him.

\* \* \*

I ran as fast as I could to catch my little brother. Over tree roots and under branches, I followed the sound of his footfall for what felt like at least a mile, my lungs burning in my chest. I finally caught up to him in another clearing; he was huddled in the shadows of a low, marble bench.

"Joey?" I called.

"Y-yes," he said, with a sniffle.

"Hey, it's me," I said. He cautiously stuck his head up. As soon as he saw me, he jumped on the bench, leapt through the darkness and wrapped his arms around me in one quick motion, sobbing into my shoulders.

"Can we go home?" he asked, still sniffling.

"Oh yeah," I said, "we're out of here. We just have to find the others."

We heard the crack of a twig and Eliza emerged from the trees, followed by the angel and the soldier.

"That kid can run," the soldier said with admiration.

"You guys okay?" Eliza asked. Joey jumped down and stood next to me, wiping his eyes.

"Yeah," I said. "We're alright. Where are the others?"

"We lost them in all of that back there," Eliza said.

"We know our way around," the angel said softly. "We can help you find your friends."

"Thanks," I said.

"I know you guys have already had quite the scare," said the soldier, "but what do you say we play another round or two while we look for them?"

I looked at Eliza, who raised her eyebrows at me. I didn't know if we could trust these two high schoolers, but for the moment we were going to have to believe they would help us find Peter and Gabi.

"Sure, I'll go," I said, turning to the soldier. "Truth or scare?"

\* \* \*

Halfway across the graveyard, Peter and Gabi realized they had lost us and finally stopped running. They were on a dark, dirt path deep in the cemetery. Not long after, Elmer, Grace, and Wallace caught up to them.

"What happened back there?!" Peter demanded.

"It was the Governess," Grace said. "She almost caught us!"

"No way," Gabi said, defiantly. "She can't be real!"

"Says the girl who swears there's ghosts out tonight," Peter shot back, aiming his flashlight at her.

"Okay, fine," Gabi said. "I know ghosts aren't real! I was just trying to scare you guys."

Peter sighed.

"Where are we, anyway?" Gabi asked the other three kids.

"We have to be in one of the oldest parts of the graveyard," Elmer said. "There's not even any of those lights back here."

"Great," said Gabi.

"How are we going to find our friends?" Peter asked.

"We'll look for them with you," Grace said. "Minnie's gone, too. She's probably with them."

"Okay, then," Gabi said. "Let's start looking."

They walked a short distance down the path when Wallace turned to Peter.

"I guess that answers that truth then," he said.

"What?" asked Peter.

"About the Governess," Wallace said. "The answer is yes, I do believe in the legend."

"Yeah," said Peter. "I guess it does."

They continued on for a few minutes, whispering our names, when Wallace let out a chuckle.

"Hey Elmer," he said. "Truth or scare?"

"What?" Elmer answered.

"Truth or scare?"

Elmer thought for a moment.

"Scare," he said.

"I was hoping you'd say that," said Wallace. "Look."

Peter held his flashlight up. Both he and Gabi gasped when they saw that they were standing in front of a plot with a marker memorializing the kids who'd died in an orphanage fire over a hundred and fifty years ago, the one from the angel's story.

It was filled with weathered headstones, most with unreadable carvings that had been beaten away by the elements over time. And in the back of the plot was an empty bench, low to the ground.

"Wallace, no…" Elmer said, his voice trailing off.

"Oh yes," he said with a grin. "I dare you to sit on the Governess's bench!"

\* \* \*

"Truth," the soldier answered. He and the angel were walking ahead of Eliza, Joey, and me. We were so turned around, I couldn't tell if we were going deeper into the cemetery or not.

"Do you really know how to help us find Peter and Gabi?" I asked without thinking.

"Oh yes," he answered, looking over to the angel. "We certainly do."

"We're almost to the central convergence of the cemetery's paths," the angel said. "We'll be able to find them from there."

"And with that," the soldier said, "we have now had three truths in a row!"

"And?" asked Eliza.

"And the rules say that after three truths - or scares - in a row, the next has to be the opposite," he explained. "So whoever I choose has to do a scare."

I inhaled sharply as Joey's nails dug into my palm.

"And I pick little Joey."

\* \* \*

"Aaaand time!" Wallace called to Elmer from the path. Elmer jumped up from where he'd been sitting on the Governess's bench and raced out of the plot to rejoin Peter, Gabi, and the others on the path.

"Easy as can be," he said, catching his breath.

"Great, you did it," Gabi said sarcastically. "Can we go find our friends now? It's getting late."

"What's the matter, Gabi," Grace asked. "Not getting frightened, are you?"

"N-no," she said. "That's not it at all, it's just… it's getting late and we need to go. Don't you guys have to get home, too?"

Grace looked at Wallace then back to Gabi and Peter.

"Yes," she said. "I guess we should be going soon."

"Hey, not fair!" Elmer said. "I did my scare; I still get to go!"

"Alright, fine. Are you guys up for one last round?" Wallace asked Peter and Gabi.

"Sure," said Peter. "Then we need to find the others."

"Of course," Elmer said before looking at Gabi. "Truth or scare?"

"Scare," Gabi said, folding her arms.

Elmer grinned what Peter described to me later as a wicked grin.

"Excellent," he said. He pointed to one of the few headstones that was still legible in the plot. "I dare you to lie on that grave and count to a hundred."

"Easy," she said. "Peter, come count with me."

"Alright," he said and the two walked off, leaving the three other kids on the path. They stepped carefully into the grass, which was starting to dampen with late night dew.

"That's the one," Elmer called when they stood in front of the one he'd pointed to.

"'Minerva Eastauffe'," Peter read aloud. "I wonder who she was?"

"Who cares," Gabi said, lying down on the ground and shifting to a comfortable position. "Peter, start counting."

"One, two, three…" he counted.

"This is nothing," Gabi said from the ground. Peter counted on.

"Seventy two, seventy three, seventy four - "

Without warning, a piercing scream tore through the night air. Peter stopped counting and snapped his head to look at the three kids behind him on the path, but they were gone.

"Did you hear that?" he asked. He turned back to Gabi and gasped, horrified to see that a thick, swirling mist was rising from the grave around her as she lie on the ground.

"Gabi!" he yelled, her eyes jolting open as he grabbed her hand to pull her up. "Let's get out of here!"

\* \* \*

"You don't have to do this," I told Joey, glaring at the soldier for picking him.

"What do I have to do?" he asked quietly.

"Tell you what," the soldier said, "how about I give you something that's not *too* too scary?"

"That'll be alright," Joey said. I could tell he was scared, but I also knew he was trying to put on a brave front for Eliza.

We continued our walk to the center of the cemetery, calling for Peter and Gabi while the soldier thought over what scare to give Joey. Suddenly, he and the angel stopped.

"I know just the thing!" he said.

"W-what?" Joey asked.

"It's simple really," the soldier said. "See that statue over there? For your scare, I want you to dress it up for Halloween."

Joey looked at him, confused.

"Just your cowboy hat, your neckerchief, and your holster," the soldier continued. "Told you it'd be easy."

"That's not so bad," I told Joey. "Right? And I'll come with you."

"We'll all come with you," Eliza said.

"Yeah," Joey said slowly. "That's not so bad."

We all walked toward the statue the soldier had pointed toward. It was carved in the likeness of a tall boy standing next to the entrance of a small mausoleum. The closer we got, I couldn't shake a feeling of familiarity with it.

*Maybe we passed by it earlier,* I thought.

"Well, might as well get on with it," I said. We set about tying Joey's bandana around the statue's neck and fastening the holster around its waist from behind.

"Only the hat left!" the soldier said, looking around. It almost seemed like he was nervous about something.

I took Joey's cowboy hat and just as I was about to place it on the statue's head, I stopped and looked into its face. I dropped the hat and clapped my hand to my mouth when I realized where I'd seen the statue before: it was the high school boy who was dressed as the baseball player!

"Guys!" I shouted. "Look at this!"

And just as they reached the statue's front, a scream erupted from behind us. We spun around to see the soldier and the angel frozen in terror. I followed their gaze and found myself looking directly at the faceless, shrouded statue known as the Governess.

* * *

"Ghosts out of their graves, statues running amok," the Governess lamented from beneath the hood of her metal cloak, "and children in the cemetery well past their bedtime!"

I held Joey and Eliza close to me, the three of us very still.

"Tsk, tsk... Halloween night is more troublesome year after year," the Governess said with an echoing sigh. "Come with me, children. I'll see to it that you're escorted safely from this place."

Joey, Eliza, and I were frozen in fear next to the statue.

"Please don't take my face!" Joey whimpered.

"Take your face? Why would I want to do that, little one?"

"But, but..." Joey started. "But they said..."

"Ahh," the Governess said, turning toward the angel and the soldier. "Probably a tale to keep you away from me. I've no interest in your face, dear - only in keeping the cemetery in order.

"And speaking of which, you'll want to be picking that up," she said, gesturing toward Joey's cowboy hat on the ground. "Don't want any statues to be slipping out of the graveyard tonight."

"W-what?" I asked.

"Oh yes," she said. "All it takes are three articles of clothing and one object well-loved for a statue such as this to pass among the living, and none would be the wiser."

"The fiddle!" Eliza said suddenly.

"He's held onto that fiddle for years," the angel said bitterly. "Do you know how hard it is to come by objects like that in this graveyard?! He dug it up himself!"

"That will be quite enough out of you two," the Governess said, turning toward the angel and the soldier and raising her arms. "Back to your posts."

The soldier and the angel stood, as though being

puppeteered by an unseen force. Their limbs contorted at odd angles and they backed away with jerking movements into the shadows of the graveyard until we couldn't see them anymore.

"What is going on?" I asked. "Who were those kids?!"

"Couldn't you tell?" the Governess asked, her tinny voice echoing. "You've been in the company of statues all night. And probably a few spirits, too, I'd wager."

"Ghosts!" Joey screamed.

"Oh yes," said the Governess. "Quite common, especially at this time of night - and on Halloween, no less! Everyone's out and about, visiting and playing games... Now come along. I believe we have two more of your party to find before I see you safely out of the cemetery."

\* \* \*

It didn't take us long to find Peter and Gabi. They had heard the angel's scream when she saw the Governess, and started heading in that direction. We told the Governess about the other kids that we had been playing Truth or Scare with as she was leading us back to the entrance.

"Those weren't kids," she said. "Elmer, Grace, Wallace, and little Minnie... they were four of my own charges."

"Charges?" Peter asked.

"Yes," she said. "Four of the little spirits I was brought to this cemetery to watch over. They're always trying to sneak out while they think I'm not looking. Ghosts are free to come and go, you know, and the entrance gate will always stay open for them to return. But I prefer my little ones stay put where I can keep an eye on them."

We walked in silence after that, following the Governess toward the cemetery gate. Even Gabi seemed frightened by the whole ordeal, walking quietly with her head down.

"Best be getting home now, children," she said once we reached the gate. We filed past her without a word, through the entrance and toward the crosswalk. When we reached the street, I turned around but the Governess was gone. In fact, the whole cemetery looked still as the entrance gate slowly swung open, its hinges squeaking.

I didn't want to think about how late it was, or how I would even start to explain to our parents that Joey and I had gotten lost in the graveyard while playing a game with a group of kids who turned out to be ghosts and statues that had come to life.

While we walked, Peter told us what had happened to him and Gabi after our group had split up. I carried Joey on my hip, his head resting on my shoulder. I was sure he'd be asleep by the time we got home.

"And the three of them just disappeared!" Peter said, finishing his story.

"Wait," said Eliza. "You were only with three of the kids, err, ghosts?"

"Yeah, we were with Grace and the boys," said Peter. "Wasn't Minnie with you?"

"No," she said, "we were just with the statues."

"You're awfully quiet back there," I said to Gabi, who was walking behind the group. "I thought you'd be pretty pleased with yourself since you were right about ghosts being real."

"And then some," Peter added.

Gabi started to laugh.

"We won," she said. I stopped and looked at her; she didn't sound like herself.

"Who won what?" I asked.

Just then, the moon overhead came out from behind the clouds, and as it did, Gabi's eyes began to glow brightly. Joey screamed and we all stared at her, our mouths hanging open.

"Minnie," I said as I realized what was going on.

"Correct," she said with a grin. "That mean, old Governess never lets us have any fun! So my friends and I made a wager with those statues to see who could sneak out of the cemetery first tonight. And we won! It helps that we don't need anything from the living to leave the graveyard like the statues do, just someone to lie on our graves so we can hide in them.

"So I guess that gate won't be closing tonight," she said with a shrug. "Anyone up for another round of Truth or Scare?"

# THE HALLOWEEN CANDLE

We found it just before Halloween, the last year that we went trick-or-treating. Brandon was staying the weekend while Aunt Winnie was out of town for one of the craft fairs that she had a booth at every year. We were digging through the attic on a rainy, gray afternoon looking for anything that we might be able to use as costumes. Luckily, my mom was a fan of estate sales and antique shops, so we had quite a bit to choose from.

"Think we could use this for anything?" I asked, pulling a fur coat off of a rack and sending dust everywhere.

"Oh, Jack! What big ears you have," he said, laughing. I laughed and hung the coat back up. No one could crack me up like Brandon did.

"Good point," I said, adjusting my glasses. "I don't know that I want 'Big Bad Wolf' to be my last Halloween costume."

Brandon and I were cousins, our moms were sisters, and we were both in our sophomore year of high school. When we were little kids, our moms took us out on Halloween together; the last few years, we'd gone out on our own. I was older by a few months, but between the two of us, he was the one that called the shots. He was athletic and good at video games, while I was always picked last for teams in gym and right at home in the library. He was more outgoing, and I kept mostly to myself.

Sometimes I wondered if we would even be friends if we weren't related, but then he'd ask if I wanted to run off on some adventure or another and I'd know that he didn't just tolerate me out of some sort of familial obligation. We were always more like brothers than cousins, anyway.

"Who says anything about there being a *last* Halloween costume?" he asked, pulling a box down from a shelf. He knelt down to open it. "Just because we won't be going trick-or-treating doesn't mean we can't dress up."

"True, true," I said. "Anything good in there?"

"Not really," he answered, closing the box. "Hey wait, what's this?"

He crawled over to the shelf and dragged out an old wooden chest. It had worn, leather straps and metal hinges. Brandon spun it around so we could open it up, and when he did, we were surprised to see a word spelled out in brass letters nailed above the rusted lock.

"S-P-L-E-N-D-I-N-I," he spelled aloud. "Splen-dee-nee? Is that right?"

"Doesn't ring a bell," I said.

"Hey wait," he said, sitting back on his knees. "I think I remember my mom telling me some story about a great uncle or something, someone on grandma's side that ran off and joined a traveling carnival back in like the '30s."

"Stop it," I said, rolling my eyes. "That's probably some trunk of random junk my mom picked up at an old house."

"No, seriously!" Brandon said. "I'm remembering this now - my mom said he'd gotten into a fight with his parents and left home that night. I guess he would have been our great-grandma's brother? Maybe great-great? From the Splenden family... Anyway, he became like a famous magician or something before completely disappearing."

"What?" I said, not believing a word of his story.

"Yeah, he was like famous all over the country, and then one day he just vanished - no one heard from him ever again. The carnival people sent his trunk back to the family, and they held onto it hoping he'd eventually come home. I guess it's been handed down over the years, and your mom stored it up here. Or maybe Grandma put it up here without her knowing?"

"Dude, he probably enlisted to go fight in a war or something."

"I don't know man," Brandon said, looking over to the trunk. "That thing looks pretty old-world-carnival-magician to me. I guess there's one way to find out…"

"What, open it up?"

"I'm game if you are," he said, his eyes lighting up. "We could find some cool costume stuff in there?"

I sighed.

"I'll go get the tool kit to get that lock open," I said. "But you're dealing with any spiders we find in that thing!"

Twenty minutes later, Brandon had jammed the smallest screwdriver I could find and an unfolded paperclip into the keyhole on the lock and was tinkering around. Thunder rumbled in the distance.

"How did you learn how to do that?"

"I didn't," he admitted, twisting the screwdriver. "I mean, I guess I saw it on TV, but really I'm just hoping for the - "

*Click.*

"…best," he said with a grin. "Nothing to it!"

"Let's see what's in there," I said, kneeling down. He slid the lock out of the latch, and together we lifted the lid, which made a long, echoing creak. The air in the trunk was stale, musty. There wasn't much inside but a tattered tailcoat and a top hat. Various trinkets were scattered throughout and in the back corner, there was a stack of black and white pictures tied together with fraying twine. Thankfully, there weren't any spiders to be found.

"This is neat," Brandon said, carefully lifting things from the trunk. "I bet no one has looked in here in almost a hundred years!"

"Seriously though," I said. I had untied the twine holding the pictures together and was looking through them. They told the story of life in an old carnival: from the crowds of people packed in a striped tent to a rickety carousel lined with chipped wooden horses, a group of sideshow performers posed together on a stage and even a shot of the empty midway at night, lit only by the strands of lights from above which, for some reason, made me feel a little sad.

And as I flipped through the pictures, I started to notice the same man again and again: a magician, just like the one in Brandon's story. One photo showed him standing between two clowns with frilly collars. In another, he was leaning over a water tank and smiling cheek to cheek with a mermaid, who I figured was just a woman wearing a costume. There was one of him on stage in front of a crowd, his arms open in triumph, and in the last, he was sitting alone, leaned back and reading a book with his feet resting on the very trunk we were looking through.

If Brandon's story was true, then this man had to be Splendini!

"Hey now," Brandon said suddenly. "What's this?"

He had found a trick compartment under the lid of the trunk and a small parcel rolled out.

"I don't know if I'd open that," I said, leery of what an old magician might have hidden in his trunk.

"It'll be fine," he said. He untied the string holding the paper together and an old candle rolled out of his hands, falling onto the floor. He picked it up quickly.

"It's just a candle," he said, inspecting it closely.

The candle looked very old, with yellowed wax drippings melted all down its sides. It had the same musty smell as the trunk, and bizarre symbols were carved all over it. As Brandon rolled the candle in his hands, I noticed a slip of paper that had fallen from the candle's wrappings.

"Look at this," I said, picking it up. "There was a note with it… oh weird! Listen:

> 'Behold you now afore your eyes,
> a fabled ware to handle,
> for in your hands, you do hold
> the ancient Halloween candle.

Imbued with magick and charm alike
as a gift from the Hollow King,
its wick will light but once a year –
on the night of All Hallows' Eve.

So light it once and you will find
a wish you do receive,
but light it twice and pay the price
before he takes his leave.'

"What do you think that's about?" I asked him. I didn't like the sound of that last line.

"I don't know," he said, examining the candle in his hands more closely before looking at me with a grin. "Let's light it and find out!"

"You can't be serious," I said, folding the paper in my hands.

"Oh c'mon, Jack," he said. "What do we have to lose? It's just a candle."

"Alright, alright," I said. "I'm sure we've got matches somewhere."

We went downstairs with the Halloween candle in tow, finally finding a small matchbook tucked away in a cabinet in the garage behind some old glass mugs. Brandon gave me the candle and pulled out a match.

"Here goes nothing," he said, striking the match against the side of the box. The flame ignited with a burst of light before falling back toward the stick. I held the candle steady in my hands as he went to light it with the match. But just as the flame grazed the wick, a crack of thunder exploded outside and the side door flew open. A gust of wind howled through the garage, extinguishing the match. I screamed and ran back in the house, knocking my glasses off in the process.

Brandon caught up to me at the bottom of the stairs to the attic.

"You okay, Jack? Here, you dropped these," he said, handing me my glasses.

"I'm alright," I said, embarrassed. I wiped my glasses off and put them back on. "Thanks."

"Talk about a weird coincidence," he said. The thunder cracked again outside and soon after, it started pouring down rain.

"Yeah," I said. "Weird"

I didn't want to mess with that old candle anymore.

"Well hey, let's take that back upstairs and finish picking our stuff for Halloween," he said. "The hat and jacket in that trunk would make a great magician costume!"

"You sure you don't want it?"

"Nah," he said. "I think I'm kinda leaning toward that 'Big, Bad Wolf' coat."

\* \* \*

Halloween was five days later, and we had the time of our lives trick-or-treating that night; I had used the top hat and tailcoat from the trunk with some other clothes I already had for a magician costume while Brandon dressed up as a mad scientist, repurposing an old apron and some goggles we'd found. We ran from house to house, collecting handfuls of candy until our pillowcases were totally stuffed and almost too heavy to carry.

When we got back to my house, our parents were still over at the Stein's bonfire down the street, so we dropped our bags on the kitchen table and went to the living room to watch a scary movie. We were about fifteen minutes in when Brandon suddenly perked up.

"Hey, what happened to that candle?" he asked.

"Huh?"

"That creepy old candle," he said. "The one in the trunk. Did you put it back upstairs after you grabbed your costume stuff?"

"Yeah," I said. "Why?"

"Let's light it!"

I sat up on the couch.

"Why do you want to do that? You saw what happened last time, it wouldn't light."

"True," he said, "but it's 'The Halloween Candle' and now

it's Halloween! Didn't that paper say something about how it would only light on Halloween, and if you lit it, you would get a wish?"

"Yeah, something like that," I said slowly.

"Well come on," he said, getting up and walking toward the stairs. "Let's go see if it's true!"

We stopped in the kitchen to grab a lighter and Brandon's bag of candy, each of us snacking on a mini chocolate bar on the way upstairs. I had an uneasy feeling in my stomach that wouldn't go away and wasn't helped by the sweetness of the candy. Once we were in the attic, Brandon dropped his bag by the door to the stairs and went over to where we'd left the trunk. Again, it creaked as he opened it.

"Here it is," he said, pulling the candle. I handed him the lighter and he clicked it three times before the flame took. Carefully bringing it to the candle, he held the lighter to the wick.

With a spark and three pops, the wick ignited and the Halloween candle was lit. The flame immediately shot up tall, causing Brandon to drop the lighter, before settling down to a low, flickering glow. A warm, spicy smell filled the air.

"Now what?" I asked. Brandon grinned.

"Well, I guess I need to make a wish," he said, staring into the candle's flame. "I... I wish... hmm... oh! I know! I wish for more candy!"

He was obviously joking around and I started to laugh, but was cut short by a tearing sound from the other end of the attic by the door. I jumped as there was a sudden gust of air that extinguished the flame.

"What was that?!" Brandon yelled, dropping the candle as we ran toward the door to the stairs. And there, right where he'd left it, was the tattered remains of Brandon's pillowcase underneath a mound of candy that was easily double, maybe even triple, the amount of candy he'd carried up here.

"Whoa," he said, his eyes opening wide. "It worked!"

I was speechless, staring at the massive pile of Halloween candy on the floor.

"Come on, man," he said, grabbing me by the arm. "You get

a wish, too!"

Before I had even fully processed what had happened, I found myself holding the Halloween candle in one hand and Brandon putting the lighter in the other. I clicked the lighter just as he had done and lit the candle. It sparked like it did for Brandon, before settling down to a low flame and again filling the attic with that warm smell of fall spice.

"What are you gonna wish for?" he asked, excitedly. Shadows cast by the candle's flickering light danced around the walls of the room.

"I-I don't know," I said, transfixed. "I guess I wish for a new computer?"

Again, a gust of air blew through the attic and the candle went out. We were heading downstairs to see if I had a new computer on my desk when I caught something out of the corner of my eye. I stopped and spun around to see a brand new computer on top of a stack of boxes, just like I'd wished for!

"This is incredible!" Brandon yelled, catching up to me. "Here, let me see that."

"What are you gonna do with it?" I asked, handing him the candle.

"We should wish for a million dollars or something," he said.

"But we've each lit it," I said. "And that note said we should only light it once."

"Okay, but *you* just lit it," Brandon said. "So if *I* light it now, I won't be lighting it a second time right away since you just lit it... see what I mean?"

"I don't know, man," I said. I remembered the last line of that poem sounding like a warning against lighting it twice.

"It'll be fine," he said, reassuringly. I nodded, thinking of all the things our families could do with that kind of money, though I still had a bad feeling.

Brandon picked up the lighter and again lit the Halloween candle. Just as before the wick sparked and the flame shot up. He was grinning a big, goofy grin and I couldn't help smiling myself; there was just an air of magic in the room - and we were about to be rich!

But as the flame lowered to the wick, it turned a sickly shade of acid green. And where before the candle had filled the attic with the best smells of fall, we were now surrounded by a smell so rotten, so horribly putrid that I had to stop myself from dry heaving.

"Something's wrong," I managed to choke out. Brandon had a panicked look in his face. "Blow it out!"

"I can't!" he yelled, looking at the candle with terror on his face. The candle was now glowing green, just like the flame, and the glow was spreading from Brandon's hand to his arm.

Suddenly I heard a crash from downstairs, the shattering of glass followed by the quick patter of several little feet. They were racing up the stairs, getting closer to the attic; they were coming for us.

"Brandon - " I started to yell, but was cut off as the door from the stairs was kicked open. I turned and screamed as three short, red monsters raced in the room. They had pointed ears and fangs, with tails swinging back and forth behind them. They giggled and snarled, their faces pulled into twisted grins.

"*Light it twice and pay the price!*" the lead creature chanted over and over again. The others joined in and Brandon, now fully enveloped in a green glow, looked at me with panic in his eyes. I was frozen where I stood, unable to even lift my feet. I watched, helpless, as the three of them surrounded my cousin and lifted him in the air.

"Off to the Hollow King with you!" one of the red monsters said. Again, the three of them hollered and laughed, running toward the wide window. I was sure they would run through the glass, but just as they reached it, there was a flash of light and I was alone.

As soon as they had gone, I was able to move again. I ran to the window and looked out to see them carrying Brandon off toward the woods behind our house, the green glow of the Halloween candle lighting their way.

"NO!" I screamed, beating my fists against the window. "Bring him back!"

But I was powerless to do anything to stop what had already

happened. They darted in between the trees, and for a second I could still see the candle's light, but when I looked again, they were gone.

\* \* \*

I grabbed my top hat and ran as fast as I could, down the stairs and out the back door toward the line of trees behind the house.

"Brandon!" I shouted as loud as I could. "Brandon! Bring him back!"

I stopped just short of the trees. I had seen these woods every day for as long as I could remember, but there was something about that night that made them different. They were darker, menacing. And I could still hear the faint giggles of those monsters who'd carried Brandon off. My hands were trembling and my legs felt like they were going to buckle, but I knew I had to go in after him. I took a deep breath and ran straight between two trees.

"Brandon! Where are you?!" I yelled. I ran a little further down the path, screaming his name along the way, but had no luck finding him… or anyone for that matter. The woods that night were different, quieter than they usually were when we'd go exploring. I felt lost in an endless sea of trees and leaves.

"Brand - unnf!" I tried again to call his name, but suddenly a hand clasped over my mouth from behind, the stranger's other hand firmly grabbing my shoulder to hold me in place.

"Quiet, kid," I heard a man whisper. "You trying to call those imps back here?"

I was panicked, my heart racing! I tried to yell, struggling against his hold, but couldn't break free. My eyes welled with hot tears under my glasses; I was trapped.

"I'll let you go, but you have to promise me you'll be quiet," he said. I nodded as quickly as I could.

"Okay," he said. I jumped back the second he let go and spun around to face him. He wasn't much taller than I was, and was very thin. He was in a dirtied, button-down shirt and pants that had been mended a time or two. His wavy hair was messy and long, and when he pulled it from his face, my mouth fell open. It was dark among those trees, but I knew it was him: the magician from the photos in the trunk!

"S-Splendini," I said. His eyebrows raised and he broke into a beaming smile. He looked as though he hadn't aged much at all from when those pictures at the carnival were taken.

"So they're still talking about 'The Amazing Splendini', huh?" he asked. He pulled out a deck of playing cards and shuffled them in his hands, pulled one to look at and then looked back at me.

"What's your name, kid?"

"Jack," I said.

"Well, Jack, how did you find your way into the Hollow King's woods?"

"The what?"

"The Hollow King's woods," he repeated, gesturing all around us. "Our current whereabouts? The forest we're in."

"But these are just the woods behind my house!"

"Not anymore they're not," Splendini said. "Tonight they're the Hollow King's woods. I'm guessing a certain candle had something to do with it?"

I didn't say anything.

"So it's Halloween again," he mumbled to himself, looking down. "Finally."

"How did you know?" I asked.

"Because that's how I found myself here, too," he said. "Where did you find the candle?"

Before I could stop myself, I spilled the entire story. I told him how Brandon had come to stay last weekend, how we'd found the trunk in the attic. How we had discovered the candle, but it wouldn't light. How we'd decided to try again since it was Halloween, and how we thought it would be okay for Brandon to light it again since I had lit the candle after he did. Splendini turned around and was quiet for a few minutes afterward. Finally, he looked over his shoulder toward me.

"You're lying," he said quietly.

"W-what?!" I said. "No I'm not!"

"You're lying," he said again. "That trunk should still be with the rest of my things at The Columbo Brothers' Traveling Carnival of Mystery and Intrigue, not in some stranger's attic."

"The what?"

"The carnival," he said. "My new home."

"No, they sent your trunk back to your... old home," I said, remembering the story Brandon had told me. "After you disappeared."

"But... but," he said, "I've only been gone a year!"

"I don't know how to tell you this," I said slowly, "but all of that happened almost a hundred years ago."

"Impossible!" he said. "It can't be!"

"Look," I said, taking off the top hat. "I got this from the trunk, too!"

He grabbed it from my hands and flipped it upside down, plunging his hand into the hat before pulling out a dingy playing card a few seconds later.

"My Ace of Spades," he said to himself quietly. He handed the hat back to me and pulled the deck of cards from his satchel, shuffling the card into it. I fidgeted quietly, anxious to keep looking for Brandon.

"So if I've been in here for almost a century," he said slowly, "then most likely everyone I know... is gone..."

He was quiet for a minute.

"Well, come on, kid," he said. "We've gotta get out of these woods."

"No," I shot back. "I'm not leaving without my cousin!"

"Kid, listen," he said. "If the imps ran off with him, the Hollow King's probably got him in his circle already. It's a lost cause! And if you were able to enter the woods, you'll be able to leave the woods - and if I'm with you, I can get out, too! We're going!"

"Not without Brandon," I demanded with a surge of bravery. "And if you can't leave without me, and I'm not leaving without him, then it sounds like we'd all better get comfortable."

Splendini scowled at me, pulling the deck of cards out from

his satchel again. He shuffled quickly, and held them toward me.

"Pick a card, any card," he said. I hesitated, but reached out and pulled one from the deck. He looked at me carefully and then snatched the card from my hand.

"The King of Hearts," he said to himself. He smiled and then put the deck away. "Alright, kid, we're gonna do this your way. But listen to me very carefully: I know these woods and I know the Hollow King. If we're going to save your cousin, we need to move quickly. And once we've got him, I'm coming with you both. Deal?"

"Deal."

\* \* \*

Not long after, I found myself racing to keep up with Splendini. He jumped over logs and ducked under branches, moving with surprising agility as he sped through the woods while I was just trying to keep my glasses from fogging up between my eyes.

"How do you know this is where we need to go?" I asked, trying not to shout after him.

"All the paths lead to the Hollow King's circle," he said, stopping so I could catch up to him. "Sorry, kid - I'm used to running these woods by myself. I didn't realize you were so far behind."

"It's alright," I said, catching my breath. "So what about you? How did you end up in these woods?"

"Well, like you, I found the candle," he said. "Or rather, it was gifted to me... in a manner of speaking. C'mon, let's keep going."

I followed him quietly through the dark woods. He was quiet for a few minutes.

"You meet all sorts of interesting characters in the carnival circuit," he finally said. "Sideshow performers, animal trainers... the best that humanity has to offer. And sometimes... well, the opposite.

"But Madame Celestina... she was something else entirely.

One of a kind. She joined the Columbo Brothers when we were set up on a three-week arrangement in Florida. I can still hear the racket that vardo - you know, one of those traveling carts - kicked up as she came driving down the gravel road the first time. For an old cart, she had it done up like the belle of the ball.

"She was peculiar - superstitious about the strangest things... wouldn't even let me take a photograph with her when Mr. Columbo picked up a new camera out west.

"And she knew things, too. Things about people... things no one had told her, things she couldn't have known. She knew about..."

His voice trailed off.

"About what?" I asked.

"...about the fight I had with my folks. How I'd left home in the night with nothing but a small pack and a few bucks to my name. How it... it was eating me up inside that I'd left my brothers and sister. It was all over a misunderstanding, I see that now, but back then... and really for so long afterward, my pride kept me from going back. Making things right."

I followed him silently as the path wound to the left and then to the right; we were descending into a valley.

"But then she came to me one night. Celestina, I mean. It was the night before Halloween. 'You're different from the rest of them,' she said to me. 'You could have so much more.' I followed her back to her cart - actually, I think I was the first person she'd let inside of it. It was all done up, bright colors, crystals, gems, fabrics... exactly what you'd imagine, but *so* much more beautiful.

"And then suddenly she was handing me this little candle. It didn't look like much, but she promised me it could provide everything I'd ever need in my life and then some. All I had to do was light it on Halloween... which is what I did.

"I lit that candle, and it did much the same as it did for you, I'm sure. That flame kicked up and the smell, oh that sweet smell... I'll never forget it. Then I made my wish. I wished to be the most famous magician in the carnival circuit.

"From that day on, things changed. I felt an energy on those stages, when I was doing those illusions. Those tricks. And the audiences, they were different. They didn't shout 'Boo', they didn't throw things anymore. They were... amazed. I was no longer Seamus Splenden, nobody runaway with a goofy hat and a deck of cards. I was 'The Amazing Splendini', and it was everything I'd ever hoped for in my life. At first.

"It was almost two years after that, Madame Celestina parted ways with all of us at the Columbo Brothers. She said she was heading north. I went to say goodbye, but I had something else on my mind, too. Halloween was coming again, and I wanted another crack at that candle.

"See, I was no longer content to be the greatest magician in the circuit... I'd seen how well some of the others in my line of work were doing, and I wanted more. I wanted to be the greatest magician in the world.

"So when I was there, I swiped that candle as soon as her back was turned. I knew where she'd hidden it away, and it was an easy grab for me, being so good with sleight of hand tricks. And off she went into the night, leaving me with what I had hoped would be my own ticket to the big times.

"I knew I was doing something I shouldn't... I'd read the inscription. *'Light it twice and pay the price'*. But I figured I had nothing to lose with everything to gain, no matter what that price may be. And it had been a couple years since I lit that candle, anyway, so maybe it wouldn't know if I lit it again."

"But it did," I said quietly. "No matter if it's years or minutes, it knows... just like with Brandon."

"Yes," he said. "It sure did. And it turns out that the price I paid was in time... time I won't get back."

We walked in silence, the path before us leveling out.

"Can I ask, why did you have me pick a card back there?"

"That?" he asked. "Oh, kid, the cards can tell you a lot about someone. And not just the tarot cards, like the ones Madame Celestina had... everyday playing cards. Things speak to you if you only know to listen.

"And truth be told, sometimes that deck of cards is the only thing that's kept me sane the last year, or... well, I guess it's been longer than that that I've been in these woods. I've had 'em since... since before I left home. They were an old birthday present from my sister, you see. And they were the only thing I could grab before those imps carried me off into these woods that night."

Without warning, he held his arm out, putting his hand to my chest to stop me from walking on. We had reached the bottom of the hill and were near a clearing with drums beating ahead. There was a flickering light in the distance and I could again hear the laughter of those little monsters that had carried Brandon off, although now there had to be hundreds of them.

"We're here."

* * *

My breath caught in my chest as I followed Splendini toward the opening in the trees. The music grew louder the closer we got, and I could see there was a huge bonfire in the middle, with hordes of those imps dancing around merrily. We held our position, keeping watch on the clearing.

"You said your real name is Seamus Splenden?" I asked him.

"Yeah," he said. "I wasn't born 'The Amazing Splendini', you know."

"Well, sure," I said. "It's just that Brandon had heard of you. And not from old newspapers or anything... he'd heard of you through stories from our great-grandma's side. Or great-great, we're not sure... anyway, they kept your trunk all those years, hoping you'd come back."

"Really?" he asked, slowly turning his face toward me before looking back to the clearing. "So all these years... they kept it... which makes you..."

"Family," I said. "Splenden's an old family name in mine and Brandon's family. I'm surprised you couldn't tell right away."

"Wow," he said. He was quiet for a few minutes until the drumming in the circle stopped. The laughter of the imps died down, and they quietly knelt to the ground. There was a distant rumble that shook the ground under my feet.

"What's that?" I asked.

"That means the Hollow King's coming."

I watched in horror as a large figure approached the far side of the clearing. At first, I could only just make out the shadow but as it approached, I could see him more clearly.

He had to be at least twenty feet tall, maybe thirty, with the body of a man, but a jack-o-lantern was perched on his shoulders where a head should have been. Straw stuck out from the cuffs of his clothing around his wrists and feet, and he had twisted, thorny vines sticking every which way out of his shoulders. As he approached, the bushes and trees at the far side of the clearing bent and grew, forming a throne on which he could sit to look over the entire clearing.

He took his seat, and I gasped, my eyes going wide as Brandon emerged from the shadows, trailing behind the Hollow King and still suspended in the green light. The Hollow King raised a hand and in a rapid-fire motion, the imps rose and the drumming began again; the bonfire in the middle of the clearing blazing brighter than it had yet.

"N-now what?" I asked Splendini.

"Follow my lead," Splendini said. He nodded toward me, and took off toward the clearing. I followed as closely as I could, hoping he knew what he was doing. When he reached the treeline, he paused and then jumped into the open.

At once, the festivities ground to a halt.

"What's this," the Hollow King said, his voice deep and echoing through the trees.

"The magician! The magician!" I could hear the imps hollering from where I crouched just beyond the treeline.

"We've found him!" they cheered.

"Bring him to me," the Hollow King said slowly, sending a hush over the clearing.

"No," Splendini said firmly. "We can talk just fine right here."

The flames in the Hollow King's jack-o-lantern face flared.

"How long have I evaded you, Hollow King?" Splendini shouted. "All the power you can muster in these woods, these little imps everywhere… and yet, I was always just a step beyond your grasp."

A low rumble escaped the Hollow King's carved mouth.

"Before tonight, I thought it had only been a year," he continued. "But it seems to have been much, much longer… Enough is enough, Hollow King. I'm tired of running. And I'd like to present a trade."

"A trade?"

"Me for the boy," he said, pointing toward Brandon. I gasped and several imps looked toward my hiding spot.

"Come out, Jack," Splendini called. "You've only lit the candle once. He can't hold you prisoner."

Cautiously, I stood up and walked toward Splendini.

"You see," he yelled to the Hollow King, "I've recently come to realize that blood truly is thicker than water. Even when you don't realize it. Jack here came running into your woods to rescue his cousin, unaware of the dangers this place holds.

"And a long time ago, there were those I would have done the same for," he said. "All these years, I thought they'd abandoned me… but I learned tonight, that they held onto my things, they never gave up hope. Because that's what family does… I think my two great-nephews can attest to that. Or is it great-great?"

"What are you doing?" I whispered to him.

"It's fine," he shot back, clasping his hand on my shoulder.

"So what do you say?" he asked. "Me for the boy. And they're allowed safe passage out of your woods."

The fire crackled and popped and the woodland bugs chirped; the Hollow King was silent.

"Your terms are acceptable, Splendini," he finally said.

The green light surrounding Brandon disappeared and he fell to the ground, dropping the Halloween candle. He got to his feet and ran toward us as a pair of imps rushed to pick it up.

"Brandon!" I shouted.

"Jack!" he said. "You didn't have to - "

"Yes I did," I said. "We're cousins… brothers. You'd do the same for me."

"This is nice, but you two need to go," Splendini said.

"Who's this guy?" Brandon asked.

"I'll explain along the way, c'mon!" I said.

"I'll be right behind you," Splendini whispered. We turned and ran from the clearing as a deep cackle boomed through the woods.

At the treeline, I stopped and turned to see the imps again hollering and jumping around as Splendini stood facing the Hollow King. But he was different, his stance powerful and his arms opened wide, a white light surging between his hands. He turned toward us, his eyes filled with the same brightness, and as he jerked his head toward the woods, I felt a force pushing us away from the clearing.

*Go*, I heard his voice say in my mind. *I can handle them. I've picked up a few tricks of my own during my time in these woods; I'll be right behind you. Now go!*

Brandon and I ran through the dark woods.

"Where are we going? It's so dark in here!" he said, keeping pace behind me.

"All paths lead to the Hollow King's circle," I said. "So if we run away, it should take us back to my house."

Behind us, a white light exploded and the laughter of the imps turned to shrieks. We heard the low rumble of the Hollow King's shouts, but we kept running.

We ran as fast as we could and without looking back, up the hill and away from the bonfire, the imps, and the Hollow King himself. The path wound every which way, and just as it seemed we'd never get there, we reached the edge of the woods and could see my backyard. I hoped Splendini was okay.

"He's going to catch up with us," I said, looking back. "I don't want to leave until he's here. He can't leave the woods unless he leaves with us."

"Okay," Brandon said quietly. "Hey, thanks again, man... for coming to get me. I don't know what would have happened if I'd been stuck with that pumpkin guy."

"Don't mention it," I said. "Like I said, you'd do the same for me."

"Yeah I would," he said. "Sorry I lit that candle twice."
I had to laugh.

"We had no idea what would happen," I said. "As far as we knew... it was just an old candle and a meaningless poem."

"But still," he said. "You were right, and I'm sorry."

"We're good, man," I said, giving him a big hug.

From far away, we heard a clock tower ring out with the stroke of midnight, and as it did, the wind blew up around us with a sudden force, the likes of which I'd never felt. And I can't explain how, but the dark woods seemed to lighten, even though it was nighttime, like the shadows were being drawn back to the deepest part of the Hollow King's woods.

"He's not coming, is he?" Brandon shouted over the wind, grabbing a tree to steady himself. The clock tower rang out for a fourth time.

"No," I yelled back, trying to stand my ground and focus down the path behind us. I grabbed my top hat as it blew off of my head. The clock rang an eighth time, and there was no sign of anyone. "He's not."

"We gotta go," Brandon said, pulling me toward the treeline. The clock rang a tenth time.

"Thank you!" I shouted into the woods as Brandon and I fell onto the grass just beyond them. A few blocks away, the clock rang a twelfth time and all was quiet.

We stayed on the ground for a few minutes, catching our breath. Finally, Brandon sat up.

"Dude, it's late," he said. "Let's go inside."

"Alright," I said, standing up and brushing myself off.

"So that was *the* Splendini, huh?" Brandon asked as we walked back to my house.

"Yeah," I said. "It was. I guess he was our great... or maybe great-great uncle."

"Let's ask your mom about him tomorrow," Brandon said.

The night was getting chilly, so I folded my arms, and that's when I felt something in my tailcoat, something that was definitely not there earlier. I stopped walking to reach inside, and gasped when I pulled out Splendini's tattered deck of cards.

"Playing cards?" Brandon asked.

I explained to him that they were more than that, that these were the cards that Splendini had used to keep his sanity all of the time he was in the Hollow King's woods. That they were the only thing he could grab before the imps carried him off the night he lit the candle for the second time, and they were one of the last things he had that tied him to his family. Our family.

"He knew he couldn't escape the Hollow King," I said aloud as the realization hit me. "Even with his power, he knew he wasn't going to make it out of those woods. He told me he was a master of sleight of hand tricks... and this was his coat, he knew this pocket was inside... I'm sure he put the cards in it when I was standing by him in the clearing... because he knew."

Brandon looked at me sadly; we glanced back to the woods but there was no longer anything out of the ordinary about them. The night was still. We set off again for the house, and I started shuffling the cards in my hands as we walked.

"You gonna take up magic now? Continue the family legacy?" he asked. He was joking, of course, but he was also being a little serious; Brandon just had that way about him.

I grinned and fanned the cards out in my hand, holding them toward him.

"Pick a card," I said. "Any card."

# MURDER! AT CASTLE BLOODSTONE

Part 1: The Guest List

"Ms. Steele!" the voice shouted from the third-floor laboratory over the crackling intercom. "Ms. Steele! Come to my lab immediately!"

Throughout the castle, ornate candelabras flickered against stone walls as the mechanical woman known as Ms. Steele walked past on her way toward the laboratory. The cogs and wheels throughout her body whirred as they worked to make her movements appear as naturally effortless as possible. Her metallic footfall echoed and her eyes glowed blue in the dimly lit hallways as she climbed the stairs in the eastern turret. Finally reaching the door to the lab, she pushed it open and greeted her creator as she entered.

"Good evening, Dr. Bloodstone."

"What took you?" he asked, not bothering to look up from the papers he was shuffling through. He was a tall, thin man; his dark hair wild and streaked with gray. His desk was a mess of beakers and tubes, and equipment was scattered about his lab.

"I came from the kitchen, sir," Ms. Steele said, her synthesized voice even and devoid of emotion. He looked at her, lifting his goggles to his forehead.

"No matter," he said quickly. "It seems I've misplaced this weekend's guest list, and I want to make sure everything's in order for their arrival on Friday evening. Run through the list for me."

"Yes, sir," she said. She stood for a moment, processing his request. "Ready, sir."

"Proceed."

"The delegates from the Coven of the New Moon are due in no later than 9:00 p.m. They will be arriving via broomstick to the south tower."

"And who's coming?"

"Miss Snow. Miss Pumpkin. Mr. Mist."

"Ahh, they're sending a wizard."

"Affirmative."

"Make sure one of the bots is at the tower to greet them. Next?"

"Priestess Amaranth will be arriving by means of chariot. She will need space in the stables for two griffins."

"Easily taken care of," he said. "Amazing how light those mummies travel, isn't it?"

"Count Darknoire and his companion, Mr. Gold, will be arriving in bat form once the sun sets. Their coffins will be arriving tomorrow morning and they have requested exclusive use of the crypt."

"Vampires," Dr. Bloodstone said, shaking his head. "Always have to make an entrance… and so particular about their moldy coffins!"

"Obsidian Leatherwing of the Northern Gargoyle Clan will be delivered tomorrow afternoon in stone form. He's requested a private space in which to awake. He indicated that the process can be hazardous for bystanders."

"Very well," said Dr. Bloodstone. "Have one of the bots take him to the north turret when he arrives, and instruct them to keep their distance. I don't have time to rewire anyone who gets impaled by a gargoyle shard this weekend."

Ms. Steele nodded.

"The werewolves Sir Tawnywood and Madame Crimson will

be arriving in their coach and have also requested space in the stables."

"Ahh, the joys of hosting werewolf nobility," said Dr. Bloodstone. "Have they indicated what will be pulling their coach?"

"Negative, sir."

"Well, let's hope the Priestess' griffins don't decide they want a midnight snack," he said with a sneer. "Who else is coming?"

"Captain Shamrock's ship is due into the harbor between 10 and 10:30 p.m. depending upon the Aegean current, sir."

"Excellent," Dr. Bloodstone said. "Make sure we give him a room in the lower levels of the castle. I'd rather not spend the weekend mopping up after a sea creature."

"Understood," said Ms. Steele. "The Sapphire Lady has sent word that she will be in attendance, but did not indicate when or how she would be arriving."

"Lovely," Dr. Bloodstone said, rolling his eyes. "Have someone keep an eye on the paintings, Ms. Steele. Make sure that old ghost isn't hiding in one to spy on us ahead of time."

"Yes, sir," said Ms. Steele. "Finally, Princess Thistlebush of the Grecian Dryads has confirmed her arrival on the east wind."

"Fantastic," said Dr. Bloodstone. "And preparations for the welcome feast at midnight?"

"Ongoing," Ms. Steele replied. "The kitchens are on schedule, though could fall behind if tomorrow's delivery of provisions is later than planned. If that will be all, sir, I will return to my post assisting them."

Dr. Bloodstone nodded and she turned toward the door.

"Oh, Ms. Steele?" Dr. Bloodstone called. She spun around to face him. "Set a place for a thirteenth guest at the welcome feast."

"Sir?"

"For yourself," said Dr. Bloodstone. "I want you to count yourself among the guests this weekend."

"Yes, sir," she said. "Thank you, sir."

"That will be all, Ms. Steele."

\*\*\*

Part 2: The Midnight Feast

All of the guests arrived to Castle Bloodstone as expected and were shown to their chambers by the various bots and automatons that Dr. Bloodstone had created. In their rooms, they each found a note inviting them to a welcome reception in the castle's library, where Ms. Steele was on hand to greet them. Finally, just before 11:45 p.m., the sound of a theremin over the intercoms called them to dinner. Ms. Steele led the group to the Great Hall, which had been set with a long feasting table.

"Tell us, Ms. Steele, where is Dr. Bloodstone?" asked Priestess Amaranth as she took her seat next to Obsidian Leatherwing. Several of the guests murmured similar sentiments.

"Dr. Bloodstone will be joining us momentarily," replied Ms. Steele. "He had work to complete in his laboratory prior to the feast."

"Work, work, work," Count Darknoire said as he draped his arm around Mr. Gold.

"We're all very intrigued about this announcement of his, you know," said Miss Snow. "Any hints as to what he's got in store?"

Captain Shamrock and the Sapphire Lady paused their conversation and turned toward the mechanical woman. Princess Thistlebush and the werewolves, Sir Tawnywood and Madame Crimson, followed suit.

"No, ma'am," Ms. Steele said. "I have not been privy to any of Dr. Bloodstone's plans for the weekend after this meal."

Mr. Mist and Miss Pumpkin glanced at each other and looked down at the table.

"Come now, Ms. Steele," the Sapphire Lady said in a singsong voice. "You can clue us in a little, couldn't you?"

Just then, the clock struck midnight and the doors to the hall opened. A line of bots entered the room to the sounds of gizmos and hums, serving the first course, with each meal catered to the nutritional needs of each guest. As quickly as they came, the bots exited the hall and the guests sat in silence.

"Should we wait for Dr. Bloodstone?" asked the vampire Mr. Gold, looking from the ornate goblet filled with blood in front of him to the other guests at the table.

"We should eat while it's fresh," said Captain Shamrock, the writhing tentacles on the plate in front of him squishing over one another with wet plops.

"It would be rude to eat without our host," Madame Crimson stated, replacing the cloche over her plate of raw steak.

"Ms. Steele, would you be able to fetch Dr. Bloodstone?" Priestess Amaranth asked.

"Right away," Ms. Steele replied. She stood and walked quickly out of the room, the echo of her footsteps growing quieter as she went.

The guests sat around the table with only the pops of the fireplace and cracks of thunder in the distance until Count Darknoire broke the silence.

"Alright, now that his robot's gone, what do we really think is going on here?" he asked.

"We haven't the faintest," said Sir Tawnywood, nodding toward Madame Crimson.

"It can't be coincidence that he summoned us all out here for the weekend, arriving tonight of all nights," said Miss Pumpkin.

"What do you mean?" asked Obsidian Leatherwing, his deep voice booming through the hall.

"Friday the Thirteenth? And the Harvest Moon as well?" asked Miss Snow.

"He's a scientist," replied Priestess Amaranth. "He doesn't pay as much mind to the mystical arts as some of us, dear."

"Nevertheless, the fact remains," intoned the Sapphire Lady. "Here we all are."

"The invitations said he had news of something that would be revolutionary for supernatural kind everywhere," Mr. Mist reminded the others. "Looking around this room, I can think of precious little that would affect all of us so greatly."

"You don't trust him," Princess Thistlebush said to the wizard.

"Science has had a complex history with witchcraft and wizardry," replied Mr. Mist. "Not all of us can spend our days dancing around the woods, Thistlebush."

The leaves in the dryad's hair rustled as she inhaled sharply; the gargoyle uttered a low growl, coming to her defense.

"Now, now," Miss Pumpkin said quickly, raising her hands to quell the tensions rising around the table. "Our brother spoke with no sinister intent."

The werewolves smirked toward each other and Priestess Amaranth looked at the clock in the hall.

"Where has Ms. Steele gone to?" she wondered aloud. "It seems to have been an awfully long time she's been gone."

After a few minutes of idle chatter, they heard the sound of the mechanical woman's footsteps as she approached the Great Hall. She was walking quickly, and the guests looked at each other curiously as she approached.

"Ladies and gentlemen," Ms. Steele said as she burst through the doors, "I regret to inform you that Dr. Bloodstone has been murdered."

Shouts erupted around the Great Hall and each of the guests jumped up from the table in shock. Ms. Steele calmly raised her hands to get everyone's attention.

"Additionally, his death has activated a heretofore hidden subroutine in my programming that alerted the Bureau of Supernatural Affairs of his demise. Two inspectors have been dispatched to the castle, and I must insist that no one leave until they arrive."

\* \* \*

Part 3: The Dastardly Deed

While his guests were arriving for the weekend, Dr. Bloodstone was perched on a stool in his laboratory, furiously scribbling notes on sheet after sheet of paper. He glanced nervously at the clock on the wall.

"All of them should be here by now," he muttered to himself. He got up and walked to the window, looking out into the dark sky. This high in the eastern turret, he could see lightning sparking from a distant storm.

"That's tracking this way," he said aloud.

The door to his lab slowly opened as he looked out into the night. The person who entered stepped softly, their silent footfall masking their entrance. They closed the door without a sound. Suddenly, Dr. Bloodstone spun around.

"You! I thought…"

"You thought wrong."

For just a moment, the intruder and Dr. Bloodstone stood staring at one another, each daring the other to make the first move. Without warning, the intruder dove toward the pile of notes Dr. Bloodstone had been working on, knocking over a series of beakers and tubes with a crash, sending shattered glass in every direction. The scientist tried to intercept, but he was too late; the intruder had the pages.

"What are you doing with those?!" shouted Dr. Bloodstone.

"Finishing this," said the intruder.

"I'll finish you first!" Dr. Bloodstone bellowed, lunging toward the intruder with his fists raised. The intruder threw everything to the ground and grabbed the doctor by the throat.

Without warning, the intruder pulled a sharp, heavy object from their cloak and raised it high into the air.

"Think again."

\* \* \*

Part 4: The Aftermath

"You can't keep us here, madam," Sir Tawnywood shouted defensively over the roar of heated conversations in the Great Hall to Ms. Steele. The mechanical woman stared at the werewolf with no reply.

"I've tangled with a few inspectors from the B.S.A. in my

time, Tawnywood," said Count Darknoire, his calm voice bringing a silence over the room. "When they arrive, they're going to want answers and they're going to do whatever they need to ensure they get them."

"So what do you suggest?" Obsidian Leatherwing shot back.

"Well," the Count said slowly, "it would be most helpful if we could ascertain whether or not there is anyone else in the castle this evening."

The group turned toward Ms. Steele.

"I can confirm that all guests in the castle are present and accounted for in this room, sir," Ms. Steele said.

"What about the little robots that served our meal?" the Sapphire Lady asked.

"The worker bots that Dr. Bloodstone created to aid in the day-to-day operations of the castle are designed with one or two functions at most," Ms. Steele said, her modulated voice steady. "I can assure you that none of them would have been able to carry out the task of murdering Dr. Bloodstone."

"Even if they were compromised?" asked Miss Pumpkin.

"Even if they were compromised."

The guests sat quietly for a moment, the fire crackling in the fireplace behind them.

"Where is the doctor now?" asked Mr. Gold.

"Dr. Bloodstone's body is still in eastern turret laboratory," Ms. Steele replied. "The same subroutine that sent the notice of his death to the Bureau of Supernatural Affairs prohibits me from moving the body."

"But could we go up there ourselves?" asked Priestess Amaranth. Ms. Steele looked around the room.

"Provided the body is not disturbed, you may all access the eastern turret laboratory."

"Then take us up there, my girl!" said Captain Shamrock, jumping up from his soggy chair. "We haven't any time to waste!"

\* \* \*

"As you can see, there are obvious signs of a struggle," Ms. Steele said to the others as they filed into the messy laboratory. Papers littered the ground with shards of glass from broken equipment. The mad scientist lay face down in the center of the room, a small puddle of blood drying around his head.

"Any indications that his spirit is still with us?" Priestess Amaranth asked the Sapphire Lady. The ghost shook her head in reply.

"What about the body? Any bite marks on the neck? Signs of a mauling?" asked Mr. Mist. The vampires gave the wizard a dirty look and the werewolves snarled.

"No, sir," Ms. Steele said quickly. "It would appear that Dr. Bloodstone sustained blunt force injuries to the head. Nothing that would implicate any particular suspect."

"Suspects? What do you mean by that?" asked Madame Crimson, offended at the notion she might be associated with the guilty party.

"She's right," said Count Darknoire. "When those inspectors get here, we're all going to be considered suspects. And until we get to the bottom of this, no one is above suspicion."

All of the guests murmured in agreement, looking from one to another.

"Ms. Steele, how much time do we have until the inspectors arrive?" asked Princess Thistlebush.

The mechanical woman looked toward the window and paused, her circuits communicating with those at the Bureau of Supernatural Affairs.

"The inspectors have been delayed by an approaching storm. They will arrive in approximately two hours' time."

"Then we have two hours or less to solve this murder," said Miss Pumpkin.

* * *

Part 5: The Investigations and What They Found

Obsidian Leatherwing and Princess Thistlebush walked quickly down the corridor, the shadows on the stone walls dancing in the flickering lights. They stopped at a juncture where two additional halls split off from the one they were in.

"The footprints go that way," the gargoyle said, pointing down the corridor to the left. "Come on."

They continued walking, hand in hand, down one twisting hall after another. Obsidian had first noticed the footprints in the laboratory, and they followed the trail through the castle until it led them to a door deep in the castle.

"What's this?" asked Princess Thistlebush.

"The crypt," Obsidian answered.

"Isn't this where the vampires are staying?"

"It is," he answered. "Normally, I would insist it's rude to invade their space, but..."

"In light of recent developments, I'd say it's imperative," said Princess Thistlebush. "And if they raise any trouble, I'll claim diplomatic immunity, being royalty and all."

The gargoyle smiled.

"You know, that's one of the things I like best about you."

"That I'm a royal dryad?" she asked playfully.

"No," he said. "Your resourcefulness."

The gargoyle put his arms around the dryad and pulled her close. She smiled. And just as they were about to kiss, the Sapphire Lady burst forth from the stone wall behind them.

"Oh, for all the spirits, you two!" she yelled. "There's a murderer about! And we haven't any time to waste in getting to the bottom of it! And you're busy doing... whatever this is?!"

"Are you following us?" Princess Thistlebush said, jumping back. Obsidian growled, and the ghost looked from one to the other.

"Yes," she said, matter-of-factly. "I saw how quickly you two rushed out of that lab and thought you might be on to something. What did you find?"

"Nothing yet," the gargoyle said. "Just some footprints."

"Footprints?" she asked.

"Yes," he replied. "I saw them in the lab around the body, but it appears no one else can see them. I would assume it's to do with gargoyles' ability to see outside of what's considered to be the standard vision spectrum."

"And they led us here," said Princess Thistlebush.

"Well let's get on with it then," said the ghost. The gargoyle pushed the door open and the three of them entered the crypt. It was a dimly lit, eerily quiet room, with only a faint dripping sound in the distance; the whole space was musty and damp.

They explored the crypt for a few minutes, but found nothing significant. Even the footprints that had led them here seemed to have vanished.

"It's a dead end," Princess Thistlebush said. The gargoyle let out a deep sigh, agreeing.

"Not so fast," said the ghost. She had her gaze fixed on a far wall in the crypt. "There's nothing behind that wall."

"What do you mean?" Obsidian asked, following the Sapphire Lady as she floated toward the wall.

"What I mean is that there are likely all sorts of things in this castle that aren't as they appear," she said. She pointed toward a perfectly square stone in the wall, her wispy finger generating a ghostly mist. "Push that stone, please."

Obsidian pushed the stone and as he did, a part of the wall slid into itself, revealing a door.

"What's this!" shouted the dryad.

"A secret door," said the ghost. Obsidian walked toward the threshold and flared his wings.

"The footprints!" he said. "They continue away into this passage!"

"Then let's see where they lead," said the Sapphire Lady. Obsidian lead the group into the hall followed by the ghost, and no sooner had Princess Thistlebush stepped over the threshold then the door slid shut, plunging them into darkness.

"This should help," said the Sapphire Lady, who willed herself to glow brighter, illuminating the passage enough that they could see.

"Nowhere to go but forward," said Obsidian. They walked on quietly, the gargoyle following the footprints around twists and turns in the dark corridor. Before long, they found themselves surrounded by damp earth instead of the stone passageway. They continued on until they came to a wooden door, which opened easily and led into what appeared to be a small cabin.

"We're down in the harbor!" Princess Thistlebush shouted. They walked out onto the dock, where they saw Captain Shamrock's ship gently bobbing with the waves.

"That makes sense," Obsidian said slowly.

"What?" asked the Sapphire Lady.

"The footprints," he said. "I can't believe I didn't think of it sooner - they must have been left by someone with a form of bioluminescence in the part of the color spectrum that only gargoyles can see!"

"Which would mean…"

"Captain Shamrock."

The ghost and the dryad looked at each other, excited at the breakthrough.

"He could have docked here, and snuck into the castle through the crypt!" suggested Princess Thistlebush.

"But weren't the vampires some of the first to arrive?" asked Obsidian.

"Maybe they were in on it," the Sapphire Lady suggested.

The three of them looked toward the sea monster's ship then back to the castle. It was starting to rain and the thunder was getting louder.

"We'd better get back up there," said the ghost.

\* \* \*

Not long after the gargoyle and the dryad excused themselves from Dr. Bloodstone's laboratory, Mr. Gold smelled something unusual. He followed the smell around the room, from the corner by the door directly to the body. Confused, he looked at Count Darknoire and gestured for him to come over.

"Do you smell that?" Mr. Gold asked.

The Count subtly sniffed the air, and his eyes went wide.

"That's what I think it is, isn't it," said Mr. Gold.

"Indeed," said the Count. "And I think I know where it's coming from."

"What's going on over here, gentlemen?" asked Mr. Mist, walking toward them. The vampires exchanged a look, annoyed that the wizard who'd just accused them of murdering Dr. Bloodstone was now trying to strike up a conversation.

"Relax," said the wizard. "I want to get to the bottom of this as much as you two do. The witches and I are definitely not trying to tango with any B.S.A. inspectors anytime soon."

"Very well," said the Count. "Come with us."

*"Are you alright over there?"* Miss Snow said telepathically to Mr. Mist from across the lab. She was standing in a group with Miss Pumpkin, Priestess Amaranth, and Ms. Steele.

*"I can hold my own against these two,"* Mr. Mist replied, not looking at her so the others wouldn't know they were talking. *"They seem to have found something of interest… I'm going to tag along."*

*"Excellent. Let Pumpkin and me know what you find."*

"After you, gentlemen," Mr. Mist said, holding the door to the laboratory open. He followed the vampires out into the hall and down the stairs of the eastern turret. The trio walked in silence until they reached the main floor, where the vampires stopped and sniffed the air.

"What are you two tracking?" asked Mr. Mist.

"Griffins," said the Count.

"What?"

"We both smelled them up in the lab," said Mr. Gold. "They carry a distinct odor that's very subtle, but hard to mask from those with enhanced smell."

"And they're only found in certain parts of the world," added Count Darknoire.

"…like Egypt," Mr. Mist concluded.

"Precisely," said the Count.

"So you think…"

"That's correct," said Mr. Gold. "Who in the castle would be the most likely to track the smell of a griffin all the way up to the scene of Dr. Bloodstone's murder?"

"Priestess Amaranth."

The vampires nodded.

"And if I'm not mistaken, I saw a group of bots loading her chariot into the stables when we flew in," said the Count. "So that's where we're heading."

Mr. Mist followed the vampires out of the castle's entrance and over the grounds. As rain started to fall, he cast a simple charm over the three of them to keep them dry. A crack of thunder sounded as they reached the stables.

"And there they are," said the Count, latching the door behind him. Even though the stable was dimly lit, they could see two griffins roosted near an ornate chariot with hieroglyphics carved on the trim.

"Let's take a closer look," said Mr. Gold. As they moved toward Priestess Amaranth's chariot, the griffins grunted ominously, causing them to stop.

"*Creatures great and fierce as thunder; Fall thee now to deepest slumber*," whispered Mr. Mist, his hands raised. Immediately, the griffins settled down into a heavy sleep.

"They won't be bothering us for a while," he said cooly. "Shall we?" The vampires and the wizard moved toward the mummy's chariot, carefully looking over the exterior. They found nothing out of the ordinary, but were unable to gain entry.

"What's that?" Mr. Gold asked aloud. Count Darknoire and Mr. Mist looked where he was pointing. In the shadows, they could just make out the outline of another coach, this one larger than Priestess Amaranth's chariot.

"Someone else must have arrived via coach," said Mr. Mist. They walked toward it curiously, the vampires sniffing the air. Two horses stood in stalls near the other carriage.

"You smell that?" Mr. Gold asked Count Darknoire.

"Yes," he said. "Werewolves."

"So Madame Crimson and Sir Tawnywood have also been in here," said Mr. Mist.

"And the scent of the griffins is strong enough to mask the scent of werewolves," said Count Darknoire. "It could have been them we were smelling in the lab."

Outside, the storm was beginning to unleash its fury.

"Let's get back to the castle," the Count said. "I have some questions for a few of our friends there."

\* \* \*

"*Is he alright?*" Miss Pumpkin asked Miss Snow telepathically.

"*He'll be fine,*" the other witch answered. "*Let's see what we find up here.*" They continued to explore the laboratory as the rest of the guests filtered out. Before long, they were alone in the lab with Priestess Amaranth, Ms. Steele, and the corpse.

Suddenly, Miss Pumpkin had an idea.

"Ms. Steele?" she asked. The mechanical woman turned to face her. "How advanced are the security systems that Dr. Bloodstone installed in the castle?"

"State of the art, ma'am," she replied. "Dr. Bloodstone designed most of them himself."

"What about cameras?" asked Miss Snow. "Did he install any surveillance cameras anywhere?"

"Yes, ma'am," replied Ms. Steele. "The inspectors will review the cameras when they arrive."

"Don't you think it would be in all of our best interests for us to have a first look at them? To know what they'll be seeing when they arrive?" Priestess Amaranth asked. The robotic woman looked from the witches to the mummy.

"Affirmative," she said. "Though I must insist that the three of you observe *only*. I must preserve the integrity of the evidence. Follow me."

The three of them followed Ms. Steele to a corner of Dr. Bloodstone's laboratory. She opened a panel in the wall revealing a keypad and entered in a code. The mummy and the witches stood in amazement as the stone wall before them swung open to reveal a much smaller room, dimly lit with a wall of monitors.

They entered the room and looked from screen to screen. Most of them showed empty rooms and corridors from the castle, but a few showed movements from the bots. Priestess Amaranth stopped at one that showed Mr. Mist talking in the main entrance, presumably to the vampires.

"Ms. Steele! Did you know this was here the whole time?" asked Miss Snow.

"I did, ma'am."

"Was Dr. Bloodstone spying on us?" asked the mummy, still looking at the screens.

"Dr. Bloodstone did what he had to do to fortify the castle," Ms. Steele replied evenly, sitting down at a control panel in front of the screens. She began working with the controls and suddenly, all of the monitors started rewinding.

"If you'll direct your attention to screen H7, I believe that will offer the clearest look into the laboratory."

Miss Pumpkin, Miss Snow, and Priestess Amaranth stared intently at the screen. They could see Dr. Bloodstone working at his desk, scribbling quickly on a pad of paper. Without warning, the image distorted into static.

"Odd," said Ms. Steele. She sped the tape up, quicker and quicker, but the video did not return for several seconds. When it did, they had a clear image of Dr. Bloodstone, facedown and dead in his lab.

"Very odd," the robotic woman said.

"So someone knew to cut the feed," said Miss Snow.

"But wait!" said Miss Pumpkin. "Look there…" Her voice trailed off as she pointed toward a shelf just barely visible on the right side of the image. It was covered with overgrown plants of all sizes, with large flowers and vines cascading down to the floor.

"What are we looking at?" asked Priestess Amaranth.

"Those plants weren't like that before the feed cut," said Miss Pumpkin.

"She is correct," said Ms. Steele. "It would appear that those plants in particular experienced a period of exponential growth in the time that the video feed was interrupted."

"Was that one of the doctor's experiments?" asked Miss Snow.

"Unknown," said Ms. Steele.

"I want to take a closer look at them," said Miss Pumpkin.

They quickly filed out of the control room and back into the lab. Just as they had seen on the surveillance video, the plants had completely overtaken one of Dr. Bloodstone's shelves.

"Did you notice that it's only the ones on this shelf?" asked Miss Snow.

"I did," said Miss Pumpkin. She examined the plants closer, moving vines out of the way to look at the shelf underneath. When she didn't find anything there, she knelt to the floor to look under the unit itself.

"Well, well!" she exclaimed, jumping up with something in her hands. "What have we here?" She held out an elongated black stone that came to a very fine point.

"Is that..." asked Miss Snow.

"It would appear to be gargoyle skin," said Ms. Steele.

"So how did a shard of gargoyle skin wind up in Dr. Bloodstone's laboratory?" asked Miss Snow. "And hidden under a mess of vines, no less?"

"Princess Thistlebush!" Priestess Amaranth said with a gasp. "Dryads can command plant growth!"

"And it's awfully convenient that those plants just so happened to conceal a shard of gargoyle skin," said Miss Pumpkin.

"So you think Obsidian had a hand in it?" asked the mummy.

"Don't you?" asked Miss Pumpkin. "It's obvious the two of them have some sort of connection beyond diplomatic... maybe the doctor here figured it out and was trying to exploit them for his own benefit?"

"But Dr. Bloodstone wasn't stabbed," said Miss Snow.

"Gargoyle skin is one of the hardest known substances," said Ms. Steele. "Though the doctor wasn't stabbed with this shard, it is feasible that this was used to kill him as it does have the weight to cause the blunt force trauma that ended his life."

"I think we have our answer, ladies," said Miss Snow.

"Ms. Steele? Where are all of the others?" Priestess Amaranth asked.

\* \* \*

Across the castle, Captain Shamrock was climbing the stairs of the south tower with Madame Crimson and Sir Tawnywood, who had followed the scent of the witches.

"Never trust the magic folk," said Madame Crimson. "Especially ones from the Coven of the New Moon. They'll always put their own interests above all else."

"Good to know, madam," Captain Shamrock said, his scaly skin shimmering in the candlelight as he tried to keep up with the werewolves.

"I'll guarantee you they had something to do with this," added Sir Tawnywood.

The trio of monsters reached the top of the south tower and entered a large rotunda. The room was mostly empty, except for a few wall tapestries, an old area rug covering most of the floor, and three broomsticks carefully stored off to the side. They could see through the archway to the balcony that it was starting to rain outside.

"Do you smell that?" Sir Tawnywood asked Madame Crimson. She sniffed the air.

"Sulfur," she said.

"Aye," said Captain Shamrock. "Even I can smell that."

"So they definitely did something when they flew in," said Sir Tawnywood.

"What are you talking about?" Captain Shamrock asked.

Madame Crimson looked from Sir Tawnywood to the sea monster.

"We have a theory, Captain," she began, "that the witches somehow orchestrated the murder of Dr. Bloodstone from the minute they landed in this tower. Maybe they cast a spell, maybe they're carrying a charm… but we need to find evidence first."

"Well what are we looking for?"

"Anything that might indicate magic work," said Sir Tawnywood.

"Well that narrows it down," the Captain said with a laugh.

They searched the room carefully, but the only thing they found out of place were a few stray straws of hay from the broomsticks. While the werewolves searched the room again, the sea monster stepped out onto the balcony; the rain was falling harder.

"A-ha!" he shouted, running back into the rotunda with a vial of glowing blue vapor in his webbed fingers. "Crimson! Tawnywood! Have a look at this!"

"What is that?" asked Madame Crimson.

"Haven't a clue," said Captain Shamrock. "But it was hanging off the edge of the balcony out there!"

Sir Tawnywood took the vial and examined it closely.

"If I didn't know any better, I'd say these were the tears of a ghost," he said.

Captain Shamrock gasped, his gills flaring.

"The tears of a ghost, you say?"

"Yes," said Sir Tawnywood. "Why?"

The sea monster looked around the room and then down to the floor.

"Help me move this rug," he commanded. Sir Tawnywood carefully put the vial in his waistcoat, and the three of them worked to roll up the rug in the center of the room. As they rolled it, the sulfur smell in the room grew stronger. When the floor was exposed, the three of them took a step back.

"I knew it," said Captain Shamrock as Madame Crimson quietly gasped. Underneath the rug were markings and runes made in ash.

"Obviously this is a casting circle," said Sir Tawnywood, "but what are we looking at?"

"These would be the necessary markings for a weather spell," the sea monster said.

"A weather spell?" asked Madame Crimson.

"Aye," said Captain Shamrock. "You fare as many years against the open seas as I have, you hear of a few tricks to get by when the weather turns nasty. They say the magic folk have a way of controlling it, but it's a tricky spell and not at all easy to perform. The ghost tears tipped me off… I'd never seen 'em in person before, that's why I didn't recognize 'em."

"Why would the ghost tears tip you off?" asked Sir Tawnywood.

"It's the element needed to foolproof the spell," said Captain Shamrock. "Without them, weather spells can be tricky, volatile even, but if a witch or wizard can get their hands on some ghost tears... well, they could do just about whatever they wanted."

"And there just so happens to be a ghost on hand to supply the tears," Madame Crimson said.

"So the three of them meet the Sapphire Lady up here," Sir Tawnywood said. "She hands over the tears, they perform the spell to summon the storm. It isolates the castle, giving them enough time to finish off Dr. Bloodstone and escape."

"But they didn't expect Ms. Steele to be on hand to notify the B.S.A. and detain us until the inspectors arrived," said Madame Crimson.

"I'd say we found what you were looking for," Captain Shamrock said.

Just then, a speaker mounted over the door to the stairs started to crackle.

"Attention," came the voice of Ms. Steele. "Attention. I need all guests to join me in the Great Hall immediately."

\* \* \*

"Ladies and gentlemen, may I have your attention," said Ms. Steele. All of Dr. Bloodstone's guests had gathered in the Great Hall, just as she'd asked. As soon as they did, accusations began to fly and arguments erupted.

"You snuck in through the passage from the harbor!"

"We found your casting circle, we know you did it!"

"It was you! You made those plants in the lab grow!"

"Well, one of you three had to track that griffin smell in there!"

"Those footprints lead right to the crypt!"

"Then how else did a shard of your skin wind up in there?"

"They were your tears! They couldn't have done the spell without them!"

"All of you. Listen to me," Ms. Steele called, the volume of her modulated voice increasing until a silence fell over the room.

"I have analyzed the evidence from each of you and have come to the conclusion that you all had a hand in Dr. Bloodstone's murder."

The room erupted again.

"Silence," Ms. Steele said, the volume of her voice rattling paintings on the wall. The guests slowly sat in their chairs around the table.

"Miss Snow, Miss Pumpkin, and Mr. Mist. The three of you arrived shortly after 9 o'clock to the south tower," began Ms. Steele. "There you were met by the Sapphire Lady, who refused to confirm her arrival time so as not to arouse suspicion should she be delayed in providing her tears for your weather spell. You successfully summoned the storm, resulting in the delay of the investigators from the Bureau of Supernatural Affairs.

"Captain Shamrock, upon your arrival you snuck into the castle through the passage into the crypt," Ms. Steele continued. "There you met Count Darknoire and Mr. Gold and the three of you went to the lab. Priestess Amaranth, Sir Tawnywood, and Madame Crimson came from the stables, intending for the scent of the Priestess' griffins to throw off the investigators.

"Earlier today, Obsidian Leatherwing was delivered to the castle in stone form," she went on. "When the sun set, he shed his stone skin as gargoyles do, however in this particular instance, Princess Thistlebush was on hand to procure a shard to be used as a murder weapon.

"The group of you descended upon Dr. Bloodstone's lab before the welcome reception while I was finishing preparations for the midnight feast," Ms. Steele concluded. "An altercation took place, as evidenced by the exponential plant growth caused by a dryad flaring her powers, and ultimately, Dr. Bloodstone fell prey to all of you."

The group sat in a stunned silence.

"Objections?" asked Ms. Steele.

"Just one," said a man, stepping out from behind one of the tapestries. Each guest turned quickly to face the man.

"Brilliantly deduced, Ms. Steele, but I'm afraid that's not exactly what happened this evening," said Dr. Bloodstone.

\*\*\*

Part 6: The Denouement

"When I invited all of you here, I had intended to showcase my latest scientific breakthrough," Dr. Bloodstone said, standing in front of the guests. "We were going to enjoy this meal together before going up to my lab where I was to share my work.

"Unfortunately, that work had other plans."

"What do you mean by that?" asked Priestess Amaranth.

"My darling Priestess, I have branched into a new field of science," Dr. Bloodstone replied. "In short, I've begun experimenting with cloning."

The guests gasped.

"What?" asked Count Darknoire.

"Now before any of you rush to any more conclusions," Dr. Bloodstone said, glancing at Ms. Steele, "I want to let you all know that as quickly as I entered this field of science, I have left it behind."

"Why?" asked Miss Snow. "What happened?"

"Well, three days ago, the clone I created of myself made an attempt on my life," Dr. Bloodstone said. "He caught me off guard and held me prisoner. Fortunately, I was able to escape earlier today.

"I first ran to the south tower where I was able to cast the spell to bring the storm," Dr. Bloodstone continued.

"But how?" asked Mr. Mist. "You haven't any magic!"

"It wasn't I that cast the spell, you see," he said. "I must apologize here, but I used the bot that met the three of you in the tower to subliminally plant a message in your minds to cast the spell using a low soundwave frequency. I also arranged for the three of you to be supplied with a vial of ghost tears from my personal supply to ensure the spell worked. I'd hoped the storm would knock out the power, essentially blinding my clone from monitoring the castle, and allowing me to move about freely.

"From there, I grabbed a shard of Obsidian's skin from the

chamber where he awoke and ran to the stables to hide while the rest of you arrived," he continued.

"And while you all were in the library, I snuck in through the passage from the harbor and up to the lab. I must have stepped in some of Captain Shamrock's slime, which I believe left footprints leading you, Obsidian, back to the crypt.

"The first thing I needed to do when I confronted him was secure my notes. I had to be sure he wouldn't destroy my work. He could have taken years of research with him if I hadn't acted as quickly as I did.

"The clone put up a fight," Dr. Bloodstone said, gesturing towards his bruised face and swollen lip, "but I was ultimately able to overpower him."

The mad scientist took a seat at the head of the table.

"I do find it peculiar that there was still a touch of dryad magic in the shard of gargoyle skin that made the plants in my lab start growing like mad," he noted. "Princess Thistlebush, Obsidian - let's chat more sometime this weekend; I'd love to study those effects further."

Again, the group sat in silence.

"It would appear that I owe all of you an apology," Ms. Steele finally said.

"Think nothing of it, my dear," Count Darknoire said, smiling. "These are... fantastic circumstances, at the very least."

The others nodded in agreement, their minds racing to make sense of everything they'd experienced since arriving at the castle as well as the chain of events that Dr. Bloodstone had just laid before them.

"Ms. Steele, could you summon the kitchen bots?" asked Dr. Bloodstone. "I believe there are two inspectors due to arrive any moment from the B.S.A. that are going to have a lot of questions for me, so I will unfortunately not be joining you all for dessert tonight."

Dr. Bloodstone stayed for a few minutes to visit, but excused himself just as the line of bots entered the room. Before they could serve anything, Ms. Steele stood and faced the guests.

"Dessert, anyone?" she asked.

# THE HAUNTED HOUSE

At the edge of town stands a big, old house. It's set quite a way back from the road at the end of a winding gravel driveway which circles a fountain that's long since dried up. The house is three stories tall; it's gray with dark shutters that are hanging from rusted hinges. Gloomy trees with gnarled branches sit throughout the grounds. The front porch wraps around on the west side of the house, looking across an overgrown garden that runs right up to the woods. No one has lived here for a very long time.

But even though the house is abandoned, it is not empty.

At five minutes to midnight, the pendulum in the grandfather clock on the main floor starts to swing. It ticks and tocks until the hands strike twelve. And as the clock tolls its deep, booming knell, the big, old house comes alive with the arrival of another Halloween.

*Brong. Brong. Brong.* Lights throughout the house flicker to life, their dim bulbs casting an eerie glow through the years of grime that covers them, while a door creaks and swings open on the third floor.

*Brong. Brong. Brong.* The rush of air from the door kicks up a plume of dust from the stained and faded red carpet, swirling through the moonbeams that stream in from the windows.

*Brong. Brong. Brong.* The dust specks take the shape of a woman. She wears an old-fashioned dress with a long, ruffled skirt and a high collar; her hair is piled on top of her translucent head. As she materializes into focus, she looks around with vague recognition.

*Brong. Brong. Brong.* The ghost of Agatha Willowyck has returned to walk the halls of the house that was built for her over a century ago. She moves very slowly, taking one careful step after the next. She pauses for a moment near the railing at the top of the stairs, her hands resting gently on the rotted wooden banister. She looks down into the dimly lit corridors below before continuing on without a word, an ethereal glow following her as she walks.

Downstairs, a tall, thin man has appeared at the kitchen table. He stands and walks over to the window, looking out over the moonlit yard for just a moment before he disappears.

As the night goes on, various creatures move about the house. In the basement, a spindly spider crawls up a stone wall, creeping carefully onto a window sill before starting to weave its web. Upstairs, a rat scurries through the kitchen, squeaking as it runs. Outside, a bat flits around the garden on its nightly hunt for food as clouds roll in over the starry sky, harbingers of an approaching storm.

A little before 2:00 a.m., the warped record on an old phonograph in the parlor starts to turn, filling the silence with crackling music. As the song plays, four ghostly figures materialize in the dimly lit room, two couples dancing in pairs. The women are in gowns and the men are in suits, the last vestiges of a time in the late 1940s when the house served as an exclusive gathering place for the nearby town's wealthier residents.

The dancing spirits leave a faint odor of smoke in the stale air as they twirl and dip around the room. Though the damages to this part of the house were repaired after the fire, the wooden floor underneath the now-worn carpet still carries the burn marks from the night they died. After a few songs, the record slows to a halt and the spirits spin through the parlor until they disappear completely.

Outside, the flashes of lightning and rumbles of thunder that follow in the distance grow closer and closer to the house, while the spirit of Agatha Willowyck watches from a dark window on the third floor. The bat from the garden returns to its roost under the patio roofing, while the spider downstairs finishes working on its web.

At exactly 3:00 a.m., a man's voice shrieks from a corner of the basement.

"NO! NO!" the man wails. "DON'T LET THEM TAKE ME! I DON'T WANT TO -"

The voice stops suddenly without so much as an echo. Across the room, the spider lays in wait for its web to trap its next meal.

An hour or so later, the old man in the kitchen again appears at the table. He stands and walks to the stove. As he reaches for the knob to turn on a burner, he vanishes once again.

Just before daybreak, a soft rain gives way to a steady downpour as the clouds unleash a furious storm. For the next hour, the storm rages outside, with wind and rain beating against the exterior of the old house. In the attic, the wind sneaks in through an old vent. Rainwater is dripping under the crumbling shingles, falling between the cracks in the floor and puddling in the hall below. Eventually the winds die down and the rain stops; the storm passes and though the sun has risen, the clouds in the sky ensure this will be a dreary Halloween.

As the day continues on, the roof in the attic stops leaking, though the wind from the storm has blown the corner of a tattered sheet from an ornate, old mirror. The rat from the kitchen has made its way up here and is darting from one corner of the room to the next. When it runs past the mirror, its foot catches a corner and the sheet flies off, sending a puff of dust into the air before the sheet gently falls to the floor.

Downstairs, the giggles of a group of children who once knew this house as home burst from the corners of an old playroom on the second floor as the rocking chair in the corner starts lurching back and forth. The wallpaper, once bright and cheery, is dirty and peeling. Though most of their toys were destroyed when the orphanage closed for fear of the fever spreading, a rusted doll carriage and a ball remain. The ball rolls around the room while the carriage rattles back and forth along the wall with windows that look out over the fountain in the circle drive.

Suddenly the door flings open and a flurry of pattering feet are heard running out into the hall and down the house's main staircase.

"No fair!" cries a small voice. "Come back here! Willa! Arthur!" More footsteps follow the first; the doll carriage stands still and the ball settles into a corner of the room, both waiting for the spectral children to grow tired of chasing each other around the house and return to their old playroom.

At noon, the man in the kitchen appears once again. He raises his fists and bangs them on the table. He holds his head in his hands and slowly fades away.

The house is quiet for the next few hours except for the creaks and groans in the floors and the walls, noises that are characteristic of a building its age. The spider in the basement is feasting on three flies that have gotten stuck in its web; the bat is fast asleep in its roost outside. A crow lands on the eastern peak of the house, and stays perched there for quite some time, cawing into the gray afternoon.

In the early evening, a woman appears on the bench in the garden. A lost soul with no connection to the old house, she made her way to its grounds after losing her way in the woods long ago. She sits on the bench, shivering as she watches the sun descend lower in the sky. Her clothes are wet and caked in mud, her hair is soaked and matted to her forehead; she can't stop wringing her pruny hands.

The woman turns her focus to the bat as it takes off from its post on the porch to begin its nightly hunt. A grunt from the woods breaks her focus, and she turns her head to look, hopeful that her companions may emerge. After a few minutes of silence, she looks sadly to her feet. The animal that made the noise moves on.

"Trevor... Jed... where are you..." she tries to say, but her voice fails her, as it has for so many years since the accident.

When the sun sinks below the trees, the woman vanishes. She leaves no markings on the bench, no footprints in the dirt. It's as though she was never there.

Miles away, crowds of costumed children descend upon their neighborhoods, cheerfully shouting "Trick-or-treat!" as doors are opened. The warm, autumnal glow of the town can be felt from far away, though it falls just short of the old house. As quickly as they came, the children return to their homes to inspect their bounty. The lights die down and the town goes to sleep.

With only a few hours left of Halloween night, the man in the kitchen materializes once more at the table. He immediately stands and walks toward the doorway that leads to the hall, pausing at the threshold. With a determined look on his face, he reaches toward the defunct telephone mounted on the wall, but he fades from view before his hand reaches its target.

The ghost of Agatha Willowyck reappears at the window where she watched the approaching storm. She looks out over the grounds of the house that was once hers. A whispering noise swirls around her and floats throughout the house, until it's so intertwined with the rustling of the leaves on the driveway that it's hard to tell where one ends and the other begins.

In the basement, the rat has found its way onto the window sill where the spider has built its web. Careless to the spider's intricate design, the rat runs right through the web, clawing at its head to rid itself of the stickiness. The rat falls to the floor and scampers away to another dark corner of the house. The spider climbs the stone wall to begin building its web anew.

The crow outside has moved from its perch on the east peak to a tree in the woods. It watches the bat fly around the garden and without warning, it attacks. The roost on the porch will be empty tonight.

In the main hall, the grandfather clock ticks away the last few minutes of Halloween.

*Tick. 11:56 p.m.* The man in the kitchen appears once more.

This time, he remains seated at the table, his hands folded peacefully as he waits for midnight. Maybe next year, and with some practice, he'll be able to hold his form for longer periods of time.

*Tock. 11:57 p.m.* The door to the playroom on the second floor closes.

*Tick. 11:58 p.m.* The phonograph in the parlor crackles as the record starts to spin, though it stops before it can make a full turn.

*Tock. 11:59 p.m.* The lights throughout the house dim to nothing, plunging the halls and rooms into darkness once again. The ghost of Agatha Willowyck, still standing at the window, slowly fades away into the shadows.

*Brong. Brong. Brong.* The grandfather clock's thunderous chimes ring through the old house, though they don't quite make it to twelve. Another Halloween has come and gone, and the old house at the edge of town, abandoned but not empty, will stand quietly for another year.

# THEY CALLED ME LUCY

They called me Lucy when I was born, a good English name that means "light". It's as if fate played a cruel joke, being named for light but enveloped in the darkness the way I was destined to be. But all my life, I certainly *was* the light for which I was named; from as early as I could remember, people were drawn to me.

"Fair Lucy," they'd call me. "Sweet little Lucy."

And they weren't wrong; I was fair, and I was certainly sweet. And even in the face of unspeakable tragedy - the untimely death of my beloved father - I stayed my course. Good-hearted and kind, pure. One does truly catch more flies with honey than vinegar, as I often heard the maids say.

And then it all ended. I died.

Or rather, I was killed. The tale of that ship was horrible... no crew save for the dead captain. He'd tied himself to the wheel to ensure he went down with his ship, the ropes cutting his wrists to the bone. It blew in with that storm, the likes of which Whitby had never seen, and with that ship came the undead monster that ended my life.

I had not been dead but two days, and yet there I was. Awake. Confused. Lying in my coffin and, as odd as it seemed, feeling better than I'd felt in at least a month. I felt powerful, strong. And parched beyond any thirst I had experienced in life.

I laid in that box for what felt like an eternity, wondering if salvation would ever come. How was I alive? Had a mistake been made on the part of the doctors? Or dare I ask… was I damned? Then, without warning, I heard him speak.

"Come to me."

I felt a rush of cool air and all at once found myself standing in my tomb, outside the coffin, face to face with the wicked creature responsible for my death. He was tall and slim, with a high, aquiline nose. He wore a top hat and stared at me intently from behind darkened spectacles.

"I am the Count," he said, his accent thick with a strange intonation.

"I demand to know what - " I began to say, but he held up his hand and my voice suddenly failed me.

"Quiet, my dear," he said slowly. "You are young, weak. You need to build your strength over the coming days. I will return for you in five nights' time."

Without another word, he backed toward the door of the tomb, his corporeal form fading from view as he tipped his hat. And again, I was alone.

"If it is the last thing I do in this life," I said aloud and with resolve, "I will destroy that creature."

\* \* \*

I spent the entirety of that first night in the tomb pacing back and forth. The air in my stone prison was dry and stale; I was surrounded by death and decay. And when I was not trying to make sense of my predicament, I wept over my mamma's coffin. We had died mere days apart from each other, but somehow I had awoken when she did not.

Only when I could sense the coming dawn did a powerful force come over me. I felt strangely drawn to my coffin, which remained nailed shut. I still did not know how I had escaped to face my murderer, but could not shake the sense that I needed to return to where I had first awoken from death.

*Go back to your coffin,* spoke a firm, feminine voice in my mind.

It was unlike any I'd ever heard, like several women speaking at once and in unison. Stranger yet, they spoke with a similar intonation as the Count.

"Who's there?" I spun around in the empty tomb.

*Go, get back inside. You're safe inside.*

"I-I don't know how," I admitted.

*The space under the lid,* the voice said. *Move toward it, young one. Nothing shall stand between you and where you want to go, where you need to go. Not anymore.*

I walked toward the coffin, my eyes focused on the narrow space like the voice had instructed. Defying all reason, I found that as I went, my form began to dissolve just as the Count had done. I found myself lying back where I'd first awoken, and a great paralysis came over me.

*Did you find your way?* the voice asked.

*Yes,* I answered in my mind, for my voice again failed me.

*Good,* said the voice. *You must return before the sun rises each morning. Now rest, young one… rest.*

I fell asleep soon after and when I awoke at dusk, I found I could move again. I focused on getting out of that cramped coffin, and just as I had the night before, I suddenly found myself standing in the tomb. My mouth was so dry it made my throat burn, and I knew I couldn't go another night without quenching that thirst.

I walked toward the locked door of the tomb, focused on the space between the door and the wall, and just as I had done to return to my resting place, I began to dissolve as I approached the door. I continued my stride until I was standing outside. I took a deep breath, gulping in the cool night air.

*Very good,* the voice in my mind said. *Now for your first hunt.*

"My what?" I asked aloud.

*A child, Lucy… find a child. You're not strong enough to hunt the fully grown yet. You'll know what to do.*

I looked around the churchyard to ensure I was alone and set out into the night. That voice might have been telling me to find a child, but I had another mission in mind.

\* \* \*

I stood outside of the Berkeley Hotel, hoping that the man I was looking for was still inside. One of my suitors, the dear sweet Doctor, had sent for him when I first fell ill. He was a professor from a faraway land, and it seemed to me that he had known the truth of what was happening to me all along; if anyone could help in my quest to put an end to that monster, it was him.

I was looking at the building trying to figure out my next course of action when, to my amazement, the Professor walked out of the front door and right toward me.

"I have been expecting you, my dear," he said sadly. He gestured back toward the hotel and said, "Please come inside, quickly. We have much to discuss."

A little while later, I sat in the parlour of his suite, dazed while the professor scribbled furiously in his little book. It seemed hours had passed while the Professor explained the particulars of my… situation. At first, I was hesitant to even give his theory credence, but as he explained more, I was faced with my doomed truth.

I had risen from death, a member of the undead.

"So you knew," I said. "All along, you knew what was happening to me."

"I'm afraid so," he said, looking up. He sighed. "I have failed you, dear Lucy. All of the knowledge from this world and the next, medicinal and myth alike, could not stop what happened to you. And I am so incredibly sorry for that."

"Oh, Professor," I said, trying to reassure him as best I could. "You tried everything you knew to do! I remember it all… one transfusion after the next. Even your final attempt to put an end to this curse, placing that crucifix on my dead lips only for it to be stolen in the night. There was precious little anyone could do to stop this; I see that now. But all is not lost."

He looked at me, his brow furrowed.

"I have seen the one that did this. The Count, the undead monster. He was in my tomb just last night and in four nights' time, he will return to collect me… and when he does, I want you to help me trap him there. He will be without the safety of his coffin, and when the sun rises, he will be paralyzed as I am during the day. You can put a stop to the horrors he intends to unleash upon London."

"My dear," he said, a smile spreading across his face. "Yes, I… I think that just might work!"

Something in the window caught my attention.

"Dawn approaches," I said. "I must return to my coffin." The Professor gave me a cloak so as to cover my burial dress and avoid suspicion from anyone I passed. He walked me out of the hotel and down to the street to see me off.

"Contact my Beloved," I told him before leaving. "Ask to read through my diaries and notes. See if there's anything in them that can aid in our hunt."

"I will," he said.

"And you must promise me you won't speak a word of this," I said. "Not to my Beloved, nor the Doctor, nor the American. They mustn't know!"

"I promise," he said.

"Thank you, Professor," I said, taking his hands in mine. "I will return tomorrow night."

"I'll see you then, my dear." I left him there and started my journey back to that crumbling churchyard.

I had been ignoring the terrible thirst all night as well as a feeling of dread over what that voice had told me earlier about needing to hunt. Undead or not, I was firm in my resolve that I would do nothing of the sort. But as I neared the graveyard, I heard something that caught my attention.

A soft, quiet whimper from a grove of trees.

I walked closer to investigate, and to my surprise found a small child, huddled under the brush.

"Out so late after playtime… are you lost?" I asked. The child looked up at me; he could not have been older than a few years.

"What a bloofer lady you are, miss," he said, sniffling. I stood transfixed, suddenly noticing a pulsating vein in the child's neck.

The Professor had offered me both water and coffee as well as his finest tea, but none had quenched that unrelenting thirst. But at that moment, with the small child looking up at me from the ground, I knew what I needed: blood.

"Come, child," I said as I held out my hand, my voice a stranger to myself. "Take a walk with me."

\* \* \*

I awoke violently in my coffin the next night, the taste of that child's blood still on my lips. I wiped it away as quickly as I could, horrified at the memories that came rushing back from the previous night's outing. I'd left the child by the side of the road, barely conscious but still far from death, hoping that someone would find him in the day.

I shuddered with disgust as I lay there motionless. That voice was right… when the time came, I knew what to do.

*We sense your strength growing, young one,* the voice said, piercing the silence in my mind. *You must feed again tonight.*

"Enough!" I screamed into my coffin lid. "I demand to know who you are!"

*We are like you,* the voice whispered, with a wicked laugh. *We are three from far away, but we are bound by the bloodlines between us, our minds linked with you. And we are to show you the way until the Count can return you to the castle.*

At the mention of the castle, a flood of images poured into my mind: a strange land, dangerous and rocky terrain. Wolves howling in the distance and blue flames in the night. A large bat flapped its wings as an ancient castle rose into view; I saw three women bathed in moonlight, slowly surrounding a man sleeping on a couch in a cobwebbed corridor. His head turned to view and I screamed.

"Jonathan!"

The images stopped and all was quiet. I had to get to the Berkeley Hotel at once.

\* \* \*

"Professor, it was Jonathan," I said, flushed as I finished telling him of the ghastly things I had seen. "My dear Mina's beloved, he was in that evil place!"

"But Madam Mina left to retrieve her darling Jonathan some weeks ago from hospital in Buda-pesth, did she not?" the Professor asked. He sat at his desk just as he did the night before, my diaries and memoranda that he had obtained from my Beloved spread about.

"Y-yes," I said slowly. "The nun that wrote to her said he was recovering from a brain fever."

"Maybe these things you've seen are… memories?" he asked.

"Perhaps," I replied. "But you should contact Mina. I think this evil Count's influence has spread farther than we already know."

He closed his notebook and turned to face me.

"I will, Miss Lucy," he said. "But I must ask… where do you think these images came from? Who do you think is speaking into your mind?"

I sat for a moment, thinking carefully about his question.

"It has to be those three women," I finally said. "In the castle, the ones I saw surrounding Jonathan… I don't know how, but the voice said we were the same, and that our minds were linked by the bloodlines between us - "

"Aha!" the Professor shouted, jumping to his feet.

"Professor?"

"You are linked by the bloodlines between you, your minds and more," he said to himself, shuffling through the books and papers on his desk. "And through those bloodlines, I would posit that you are also linked to this insidious Count!"

I gasped and buried my face in my hands, fighting tears.

"No, no, my dear," the Professor said, rushing toward me. "This is a most important breakthrough! Because if they are able to share those images with you, through a stream of thought… perhaps that current flows both ways - and thus, we can invade the Count's mind!"

He returned to his desk and sat quietly for a moment.

"We have three nights until the Count returns to your tomb," he finally said. "I have much research to do tonight, and tomorrow I will send a letter to Madam Mina. Perhaps she and Jonathan can provide details we have overlooked in our efforts to thwart this evil."

As I returned to the churchyard that night, my mind was preoccupied with so many things. The Professor was working tirelessly to ensure the ones I loved would no longer be threatened by the evil that had claimed my life, and for that I was eternally grateful.

But what was to come of me? I was undead, much like that wicked Count. When this all was over… where would I go?

Without realizing how far I had strayed from my route while lost in thought, I found myself standing on a quiet street in Hampstead with several darkened homes. One in particular caught my attention with its sweet, enticing smell. I approached the cottage to find that one of the windows around back was open, curtains idly flapping in the nighttime air. Inside, two children slept.

They must have sensed my presence, for at the same moment, both awoke and looked toward the window where I stood.

"It's the bloofer lady!" the one child whispered excitedly to the other. I smiled at them, feeling my sharpened canine teeth over my lower lip.

\* \* \*

"Miss Lucy, what's this about?" the Professor demanded, slamming a copy of *The Westminster Gazette* down in front of me in his hotel sitting room the next night. "Is this your doing?"

I looked from the paper, its headline screaming about a mystery in Hampstead and a "Bloofer Lady", to the Professor's face. He stared at me, his lips pursed with an expression of both anger and sadness. I looked away.

"Yes," I said quietly. "I am afraid that that is about me."

"I was worried this would happen," he said, sitting at his desk. "I can tell a war is being waged inside you, even now. Your old self is dying away, and your new, undead self is assuming control. Each night I have seen you, you have looked more beautiful and stronger than the last. I had hoped it was not because you had started to hunt, but it's clear to me now..."

His voice trailed off and I felt a fury rising from deep within my stomach... anger and rage the likes of which I had never known in life.

"I can no longer allow you to roam freely in the night."

In a flash, I sprung from my chair and was across the room, a guttural snarl escaping my throat as I bared my fangs. The Professor recoiled and in his eyes, for the first time, I could see fear. It was as though I was again sleepwalking along the cliffs in Whitby; I could see through my eyes, but my actions were not my own. I reached for his throat, only to be stopped by a searing pain that started in the tips of my fingers and ran up my arm.

I jumped back, yelping in pain, as the Professor stood over me. Another second, and I would have torn his throat open.

"I'm sorry my dear," he said sadly, as he pulled a small crucifix on a chain out from under his collar. "I had to... for my own protection."

I sank to the floor, devastated at both what I had done and what I had tried to do.

"You are correct," I admitted. "I'm losing the fight, the battle between my old self and these... these new instincts. And when this is all done, once we defeat the Count, Professor, I... you will have to kill me."

The Professor stood quietly, the air in the silent room hanging thick between us.

"You have my word, dear Lucy," he finally said. "Once we have seen to it that the Count has been stopped, I will personally ensure that your soul is saved from the damnation he has cast upon you. My word."

He escorted me back to the tomb soon after, ensuring that no child would go walking with the "Bloofer Lady" that night. We agreed that he would meet me in the churchyard the following night so we could review our plan once more before the Count was to return.

"You were right, you know," he said to me just before he departed the churchyard.

"About what?" I asked.

"Madam Mina and Jonathan," he said. "I have read his journals from his time abroad, and you were right about everything that happened to him at that horrible castle."

"It brings me no joy to know the terrors he experienced," I said. "How is he?"

"Recovering," he said. "It will be some time, but I expect he'll be alright. I'll be meeting with Madam Mina again to discuss everything in further detail."

"Good," I said with a faint smile. "If Mina and Jonathan can live out their days, then this was all for something at least."

As I lay in my coffin near daybreak, I had two unsettling thoughts, the first being that it was unlikely I would see the Berkeley Hotel again. And as I faced that sad realization, I was again fighting a growing thirst for blood, though now with less revulsion than I had felt only a few nights prior.

\* \* \*

I awoke the next night ravenous for blood.

I paced the churchyard erratically, doing everything I could think of to distract myself. The Professor was supposed to meet me there, and if only I could hold off until he had come and gone… I found a bench a short distance from my tomb and sat.

The bench reminded me of the hills at Whitby, where Mina and I had sat for so many afternoons in the sun; while that was only two months ago, it felt like a lifetime had passed since then. I looked up at the moon, and in that moment, I understood I would never see the sun again.

*What are you waiting for, young one?* that voice spoke into my mind. *You know what you need, you know how to get it. Why delay?*

"No," I whispered to myself. "I can't."

*You have to,* the voice said.

"I know."

I stood from the bench and looked around the churchyard;

there was no sign of the Professor. He would never know if I could return before he arrived. I had only taken just enough blood from the other children to satisfy my need. I had left them where they would be found and cared for.

And yet... and yet I needed more.

It was in that moment that I gave in to the undead urges I had been fighting. I was still horrified at what I was becoming, but I knew what I needed to do to survive long enough to put an end to the Count. And after he was gone, the Professor would put an end to me, and those children would be fine.

I left the churchyard quickly and wandered through the surrounding streets. I did not know where I was going, but without realizing it, I arrived at another row of darkened homes. I was almost gliding as I walked past them until I came upon one with a lit window. I looked up and the face of a child returned my gaze.

"Come little one," I whispered into the night. "Come walk with me."

I could see the child's eyes glazing over as it came under my influence, and it soon walked around from the back of the house. The child took my hand and we walked down the street. There were clouds rolling in over the moon, and I heard a distant clock strike two. I had been away from my tomb for longer than I had meant to be, and needed to return before the Professor arrived. I resolved to hide the child among the yew trees on the far side of the churchyard until our tasks for the night were completed and I could feed.

As we neared the churchyard, the child grew drowsy and its steps became heavy, so I picked it up to carry the rest of the way. I had just walked past the first few gravestones when I heard a voice hissing from the darkness.

"Miss Lucy!" the Professor cried out.

I had been caught.

"Give me that child!" he commanded, holding a crucifix toward me. I was powerless but to comply. I dropped the child to the ground and stood still while he scooped it up.

"I haven't fed on it yet," I said.

"I see that," he said abruptly. "And I see that I went against my better judgement by not sealing you in your tomb last night."

I could say nothing in reply, but again felt the same anger rising up within me that I'd felt the previous night. Who was this weak man to say he would lock me up?

*No,* I suddenly thought. *No, he is right. This... this is for the best.*

"Professor, I'm sorry," I finally said. "I cannot fight this much longer."

"The Count is returning for you tomorrow night," he said. "Are you able to complete our task?"

"Of course," I said. "But I will need you to seal me in tonight."

"That, I will do," he said. From afar, I heard a rustling in the leaves.

"What's that?" I asked. The Professor looked worried.

"Miss Lucy, I... I'm afraid I had to enlist some assistance."

"What?!" I screamed, the wind kicking up around us. "Who did you tell!"

"With your decline and the tasks at hand, I decided to tell friend John."

"So the Doctor knows."

"He knows," confessed the Professor. "He has seen your empty coffin. But he does not yet believe."

That dear, sweet Doctor... I never wanted him to know what had become of me in death. But if the Professor felt this had to be done, then a part of me knew that it was the correct course of action to take.

"Do what you need to do, Professor," I finally said as the child in his arms stirred. "Seal me into that tomb, so that I may not harm another soul. And return tomorrow night so that we may end this once and for all."

\* \* \*

The Professor was waiting in my tomb the next night as I slipped out of my coffin. My need for blood was so intense that I only noticed him when he spoke.

"Good evening, Miss Lucy," he said. "Are you ready for tonight?"

I looked him up and down, the intoxicating smell of his blood commanding attention from all of my senses.

"Miss Lucy?"

I licked my lips and stared at his neck with wide eyes, the big vein in his neck pulsating just under his flesh with every breath.

"I thought this might happen," he said, brandishing a crucifix as he reached into his bag. He produced a small pouch.

"What's that?" I said, salivating.

"Blood," he answered simply. "I was able to obtain this pouch from the hospital to satiate your appetite for tonight."

*Bless him,* I thought. He pushed the pouch toward me on the ground, and I practically pounced on it. Once I had satiated my thirst, I wiped my mouth as delicately as I could. I barely felt human anymore.

"The Count comes for you tonight, my dear," said the Professor. "Are you prepared to face him?"

"Yes."

"Good," he said. "I have brought an abundance of garlic flowers and several crucifixes with which I will seal the entrance once he has entered."

"He has no idea the wrath that awaits him in this tomb," I said with menace. "And what of the Doctor?"

"Friend John does not join me tonight," he said, to my relief. I did not want him to face the Count with the Professor. "I have left a letter addressed to him with my papers and effects, everything connected to this case in the event that I do not return to the Berkeley Hotel."

I looked at him and nodded, tears welling in my eyes. Here was an intelligent man, a good and kind-hearted man, who was willing to sacrifice his own life to aid in the quest to avenge my own, and, most important, protect those that I loved. At that moment, I made peace with the particulars of the situation.

My life was over, but the lives of so many that were dear to my heart depended on what I was able to accomplish that night.

"Take this," the Professor said, handing me a wooden stake.

"You now have strength beyond what you did in life. Draw upon that strength to drive it through the Count's heart to incapacitate him until the morning."

I took it and nodded. It felt light in my hand, a small weapon to take down such an enormous evil.

"I will wait outside until the dawn," he said. "He will seek shelter with you, but once the sun rises, he will be powerless to stop me from ensuring he does not rise again."

"And once the deed is finished?"

"I will do the same for you," he said quietly.

"Good."

With that, the Professor tipped his hat toward me and made his exit, the heavy door creaking as it closed behind him.

While I awaited the Count's arrival, I paced the length of the tomb. I felt the same rage that I had felt over the last few nights boiling deep within me once again. I was about to face the monster who was responsible for so much pain, so much suffering. He'd ended my life, and with that, cast a dark shadow over the lives of my Beloved, Mina and Jonathan, even the Doctor and the American. And of course, the Professor who, even now, waited outside knowing that he too may meet his end this cursed night.

When I could walk no more around the tomb, I jumped on top of my coffin and sat with my legs crossed over the side, staring intently at the entrance.

"No," I said to myself with a snarl, "that Count has no idea."

Before long, a fog started to seep through the space around the door. It spilled into the tomb and swirled around the ground, kicking up specks of dust until a form rose from within and took his shape. I was again facing the Count.

"You do not bow before your new master?" he asked, his accent as thick as I remembered.

"I bow to no one," I said, jumping off my coffin so that I could look him in the eye. "Least of all to you."

"Ahh," he said with amusement. "They told me you had... spirit."

"They?"

"The ones I left in the castle," he said. "I trust they have shown you the way over the last several nights? I see in the local papers that you have already learned to feed. That's good."

I was repulsed; he had been watching me and receiving reports from whoever that was that had been speaking in my mind.

"And now, you will join me at Carfax Abbey," he said, walking toward me. "I will send for your coffin so you can rest beside me. You will no longer have to call this cramped tomb your home."

I felt frozen where I stood; he was close enough that I could feel his icy, dead breath on my neck. He was so fixated on me, that he didn't notice the sounds of the Professor filling the gap in the door with the items that would trap him inside. As he moved closer, I could feel that anger again building inside of me.

"How about another taste?" he whispered, the points of his canine fangs grazing the skin of my neck, sending a shiver to the base of my spine.

"I would rather burn," I said, my rage exploding through whatever restraints he had placed upon me. He jerked away, but I grabbed him by the arm, my nails digging into his wrist.

"What is this?!" he shouted.

While I still had him in my grasp, I pulled him close and landed two solid hits to the chest before I brought him to the ground with a kick behind the knee. And once he was down, my fists rained on him with an undead fury that frightened and exhilarated me.

I hissed and growled, giving in to the beastly urges I had been fighting since I awoke in that tomb only a few short nights ago. The Count had made me a monster, and if this was to be my last night, as either living or undead, I was taking him with me.

"And now to keep you still until the morning," I said, pulling out the wooden stake the Professor had given me.

The Count rolled over on the ground, and as he did, I kicked him so hard in the ribs, there was a sickening crack. He gasped, but as he caught his breath, started to laugh, his bloodied teeth bared.

"You fool," he said. "You really think you accomplish anything by such violence against the one who made you?"

"That doesn't matter," I said. "The fact remains - you won't be leaving this tomb."

"That's where you are wrong, young one."

"What?"

"Do you think the garlic flowers and whatever else is now stuffed along that door will keep me here? That little man hiding outside? I have been undead for far longer than you, and such puerile defenses cannot contain me when my life hangs in the balance."

I stopped.

"Oh yes," he said. "Precious little beyond a consecrated Host can hold the most powerful of our kind. But I expect that will not make much of an impact in what fleeting time you have left."

He knew of our plan. It was over.

"I had so hoped to have you by my side here in London," he said, staring up at me. "But alas, it was not to be."

His form again began to dissolve into a mist along the ground.

"No!" I screamed. I tried to stab the Count's chest with the stake, but I was too late. It went right through his form, and he grinned at me with a wicked smile.

"Good luck, my dear," he said, his voice echoing around me. "We shall not meet again."

And with that, he was gone. I ran to the door of the tomb, beating on the metal and screaming for the Professor. The acrid smell of the garlic burned my nostrils and the crucifixes he had placed around the door made the metal sting when I touched it, but I did not care. We had failed in our mission.

Suddenly, the door swung open and a burst of fresh, nighttime air flooded in. The Professor stood there.

"Sweet Lucy!" he yelled. "The fog has come from the tomb and gone. What happened?"

"He knew," I said, my senses flooded with emotion. "He knew what we had planned and he knew that he could escape."

I recounted my interaction with the Count.

"We failed, Professor," I finished. "We failed."

He thought for a moment.

"My dear," the Professor began, "can you not see? While we may not have vanquished the undead evil this night, he has provided us with ample information that will prove useful in the days and weeks ahead.

"His strength cannot be bound by garlic and a crucifix alone," he said. "But something more powerful. Through this communication with your mind, from the ones far away and his knowing what is in your thoughts, we have also seen the power of the bond between the minds of the undead.

"So you see, Miss Lucy," he concluded. "We have not failed, as we can walk away with what I surmise to be information that will be crucial to bring about the Count's eventual demise."

I smiled, feeling my fangs on my lips.

"You have shown great prowess in the fight against this evil Count," he said. "However, I expect your undead consciousness to be fully asserted by this time tomorrow night."

"Even now, I feel the lust for blood returning," I admitted. "There is not much time before I lose what little of myself I have left."

"It's alright, my child," he said. "You have done all you can do. I will seal you in the tomb one last night, and return tomorrow morning to free you from the - "

"No," I said. "I've thought about it, and I want my Beloved to do it."

The Professor looked at me, confused.

"I want him to know what happened to me, that it was beyond his control, so that he does not live out his days wondering if there was more he could have done," I said. "You all fought so hard to save me, and I... I want him to see me when I am set free from this curse."

"Very well, Miss Lucy," said the Professor, nodding. "I will see to that. For you."

\* \* \*

I awoke the next night as though I was in a dream. I could see through my eyes and hear through my ears; I could smell through my nose and feel every sensation on my skin - but I was no longer myself.

I was running on instinct, and my first priority was to procure fresh blood.

Either the Professor had removed the barriers on the door or I was strong enough to pass them, but regardless I had no trouble slipping out of my tomb. I breathed in the night air and felt it filling my lungs, as though I could breathe for the first time. My every sense was heightened as though I was experiencing the world again for the first time. The stars in the sky, the scents on the breeze… it was all foreign to me in its lush beauty. I had been reborn.

It did not take long for me to make my way to a quiet street, where I again found a child willing to walk with me in the moonlight. And while a part of me was still reviled by what I had become, I found I was no longer in control of my body; I was barely in control of my mind.

I took the child back to the churchyard and fed on it, each drop of blood giving me renewed strength and vitality. Only the crunching of leaves in the distance broke my concentration.

I looked up to see the Professor with my Beloved. The Doctor and the American stood a little way behind them. In a flash, I threw the child to the ground and found myself drawn to my Beloved.

"Come to me, Arthur. Leave these others and come to me," I heard myself say, my voice again strange and unknown to me; deep and sensual. He stood transfixed, staring at me in horror, and I hoped he could see behind the malice in my eyes.

*I'm sorry,* I wanted to scream. *I did everything I could, my love.*

He moved closer to my outstretched arms; I was like an animal waiting to pounce, horrified at what I knew would happen if he came within my grasp.

And then there was the Professor, standing between us holding a crucifix in my direction. I retreated toward my tomb, but again found it sealed so that I may not reenter. He had sealed it this time with consecrated Host, and even standing this near such a holy object caused spikes of pain to surge through my body. I turned to face them as the moonlight caught my face, rage twisting it beyond recognition, so much so that I heard the Doctor gasp in the distance.

I stood for a moment, trapped between two forces that held me in place. The Professor spoke to my Beloved, and then removed the seals that kept me from entering. I retreated quickly to the safety of my tomb, though just before I was fully inside, the Professor's eye caught mine. I knew he saw through the wicked fire that burnt in them, if only for a moment, my unending gratitude. For though I had come to the end of my days, I knew that our tasks over the last few nights would be instrumental in destroying that evil Count once and for all.

The Professor again sealed my tomb, and the party departed.

* * *

They returned the next afternoon.

I was paralyzed by the daylight, but I could hear them enter the tomb from within my coffin. I could hear the Professor explain to my Beloved what was to happen when he drove the stake through my heart. And though my undead self was screaming in my mind, cursing them for what they were to do, there was a calm in my soul knowing that I had come to the end of it all.

I could hear the coffin lid opening. I felt the point of the stake pressing against my flesh. And with the clank of a hammer, the crunch of wood breaking bone, it was over.

They called me Lucy when they set me free, and my spirit departed that dark place to wait until they came to me again.

# WHO WAS THAT GUY?

You know how these parties go... Your parents are going out of town for the weekend to watch your brother's college football game, so you tell a few people, who tell a few people, who tell a few more people, and the next thing you know your house is full of kids from your school and the surrounding area, some of whom you don't even know. But it's the Friday before Halloween and everyone's in costume, and we're all having such a great time that I'm not even mad about it.

It doesn't take long for the party to spill out to the backyard. A few kids brought a table and have a game of pong going and that's where I first notice him. He's taller than everyone else on the deck and I'm creeped out by his overalls that are stained with fake blood. I can't see his face because he's wearing a burlap mask with two dots of red paint and a grin that looks like he painted it on himself with his fingers. I can hear him breathing from here, and he smells weird. A mix of sweat and... something metallic. He's standing by himself, watching the game play out.

"Hey," I say, walking over to him. "Having fun?"

He nods slowly.

I stand next to him, putting my elbows on the rail behind me. My little witch capelet flutters in the breeze, and I take a drink.

"Do I know you?"

He looks toward me and then back at the game.

"Oh, okay," I say. "I get it… playing creepy, huh?"

No response.

"Well, have fun." I push off from the rail and head back inside. I find Cass and Rachel in the kitchen and jerk my head toward the backyard.

"Have you guys seen the tall guy out back?"

"In the scarecrow mask?" Rachel asks.

"If you could call it that," I say. "He's wearing overalls."

"Yeah," says Cass. "I'm pretty sure that's Jeremy Walker."

"Well, whoever it is, he's kind of creeping me out."

"Really?" Rachel asks.

"I was out there watching the guys play pong and he's just standing off to the side. He didn't say two words to me."

"Creeper," says Cass.

"You know how guys get around Halloween, Kat," Rachel says. "He probably thinks he's being cool."

"Whatever," I say. "If he doesn't cut it out, we'll have Corey and Dave kick him out."

"Forget him," says Cass. She pops open another bottle and hands it over. "Cheers!"

\* \* \*

An hour or so later, I'm in the backyard sitting around the fire pit with a few kids from my fourth hour. Two of them are telling the group about some scary movie they saw a few weeks ago when I notice him again.

He's standing near the treeline, his hands at his sides, looking at the house. He hasn't taken off that stupid burlap bag he's trying to pass off as a mask yet.

"Hey!" I call out, interrupting the story. Everyone turns to look. "You just gonna stand there or are you gonna come hang out?"

His head slowly turns toward the fire pit, then back to the house. He doesn't say anything.

"Who is that?" Mark Cooper asks the group.

"Rachel thinks it's Jeremy Walker and he's just trying to be creepy," I say.

"Wait," Lizzy Martin says. "Isn't Jeremy Walker out of town this weekend?"

"Is he?!" I ask.

"Yeah," she says. "I think he's on a college visit. Maybe it's Noah Burgess?"

"But that guy's taller than Noah," I say.

"What about Bobby Vaughn? He's pretty tall?" Alicia Hale says.

"Well whoever he is, he's not over there anymore," Mark says.

I spin around as fast as I can in my chair and see that Mark's right - the guy's gone. I hear the conversation around the fire pit pick back up while I'm still looking at the trees. I'm running through a list in my head of all of the kids at our school and I'm honestly having a hard time figuring out who that guy might be.

\* \* \*

After a while, I go inside to track down Rachel and Cass again. The party's been going on for a little while at this point, and I'm feeling pretty good, but for some reason I just can't shake this uneasy feeling about the guy in the overalls.

*If Jeremy's really out of town, who is that?* I think. *Maybe it's Jeff Kennerly. He's pretty tall... come to think of it, he'd be the kind to try and freak everyone out.*

I find the girls hanging out with a bunch of our other friends in the basement.

"Rach," I yell. "I figured it out!"

"Figured what out?"

"Who the guy is!"

"What guy?"

"The one in the overalls," I say, getting annoyed.

"Oh... who is it?"

"It's Jeff Kennerly!"

"Oh," says Rachel. "I could see that."

"Yeah," agrees Cass. "I bet it's him."

"He did say he was gonna come," I say, remembering just then that he had mentioned it in passing earlier today. "What a jerk, though, right? Trying to freak everyone out?"

"I mean, I'm not really worried about him," Rachel says, raising her eyebrows and tilting her head toward Troy Klein. He's sitting on a couch on the opposite side of the basement with a few of his teammates from the football team; they're all wearing their jerseys as costumes.

"Yeah," says Cass. "It's your party, Kat, and you're not even having fun!"

"Whatever," I say, standing up. "I've gotta go to the bathroom."

If the girls aren't worried about who this guy is, maybe I shouldn't be either.

Everyone is either in the kitchen or outside, so I go upstairs to use my parents' bathroom because no one else is up there. I stop on the landing and send Jeff Kennerly a text.

*Hey! You still coming by the party?*

I'm walking down the hall when I hear a noise like something being dropped from my parents' bathroom.

"Hello?" I call out, immediately shaking my head at how stupid that was of me to do. Isn't it funny how people do that in situations like this? Like, in the movies - if there's a monster or a serial killer hiding somewhere, what are they gonna do... answer me?

I walk through my parents' room and get to their bathroom door to find that it's closed and locked.

"Huh?" I say aloud.

The toilet flushes and whoever is in there turns on the sink. I knock on the door.

"Who's in there?"

No answer. I start breathing faster and my heart starts racing. *It's that guy, I know it's that guy,* I think, my mind racing.

The lock on the handle clicks and I hold my breath. My hands start to shake. The handle turns, the door opens, and there he stands.

I try to maintain my composure, but I'll admit: I'm terrified.

"Hey, Jeff," I say casually. He doesn't move.

I walk up closer to him. I can hear him breathing from underneath that burlap bag on his head. It might just be because we're in a dark room, but it seems like the painted face is a little darker than it was when I first saw him on the deck. Was that only a few hours ago?

"I told everyone not to come up here."

He says nothing, and looks me up and down.

"I know it's you, Jeff. You're not scaring anyone."

He continues to breathe heavily under that mask in reply. He starts walking toward the bedroom door, and as he passes, I again smell that mix of sweat and metal. He keeps walking into the hall and from where I'm standing, I hear him go downstairs.

It's taking everything in me not to freak out while I go to the bathroom. My hands tremble while I wash them, and I'm trying my best to slow my breathing; I'm almost lightheaded. On my way back downstairs, I check my phone. Still no reply from Jeff.

\* \* \*

Later in the night, I'm standing on the deck watching another game of pong when I hear a noise in the yard. There's no one tending to the fire pit, so it's burnt down to a glowing pile of embers. I'm about to turn back to the game when I see him in the flickering light; he's looking right at me.

I don't say anything, waiting for him to say or do something.

After what feels like an eternity but was probably only a minute, he slowly raises his hand to me, waves, and puts it back down to his side. He turns and walks away from my house and into the Hendersons' yard. He doesn't stop and continues on into the Barretts' yard. I watch until I can't see him anymore.

A chill starts at the base of my neck and runs down my back. I still have no idea who that guy was, though most of my friends seem pretty convinced it was Jeff Kennerly playing a joke. He wandered from group to group all night, even got in a few pictures with people, but he never spoke a word.

I'm not so convinced it was Jeff, so I keep checking my phone. He hasn't replied to my text yet, so who knows?

Not long after, the party starts to wind down. The fire in the pit is out, the table on the deck stands empty; there's just a handful of us left and we're in the living room watching a movie. I try to stay focused, but I can't stop thinking about that guy.

"You guys, where did he go?"

"He left, Kat," says Rachel. "Now watch the movie!"

When the movie ends, everyone but Rachel and Cass are leaving since the two of them are staying the night.

"G'night," I say as they leave. I watch the others drive off and stand for a minute by myself on the porch watching the leaves spinning in a circle on the street. The girls come out to check on me, and after a few minutes, we go back inside and get ready for bed.

Rachel and Cass fall asleep pretty quickly, but I toss and turn for a while. It's after 4:00 a.m. and I can't sleep, so I go to the kitchen for a glass of water. I clean up a bit while I listen to the quiet house. Once everything's tidy, I go upstairs to use the bathroom before going back to bed.

*Maybe that guy was Jeff*, I think to myself. After washing my hands, I open the cabinet door to replace the toilet paper. I reach in to grab a roll and jump when something clangs to the bottom of the cabinet. I drop the toilet paper and reach around feeling for it when my fingers touch something smooth. I carefully pick it up and pull it out.

"What the..." I say, my voice trailing off as my mind races. It's a pretty big pocketknife and the blade itself is tucked into the handle. Curious, I push the button and it swings out, splattering a dark fluid all over the counter. I look closer and my eyes go wide, horrified at the realization that the knife is covered in blood.

And that's when the smell hits me: a mix of sweat and metal, just like that guy at the party and everything clicks. The guy had been in this bathroom, the red paint on his mask got darker as the night went on, and that weird metallic smell... the smell of blood. He was covered in it, his mask was painted with it, and here I was, holding a knife with it dripping all over the counter.

I throw the knife down and scream until lights flash in my eyes, my temples ache, and I'm red in the face. And by the time the girls come flying in to check on me, I've collapsed in a heap on the floor, sobbing hysterically into both hands.

\* \* \*

I run into Jeff Kennerly at school on Monday morning.

The sun had come up before Rachel and Cass had calmed me down enough to fall asleep. I'd spent most of Saturday cleaning up and then catching up on sleep. I didn't even hear my parents come home that evening.

By Sunday afternoon, Rachel and Cass had me convinced that it was all an elaborate prank that Jeff had pulled on us. I mean, what other explanation was there? I felt ridiculous for getting so worked up over the whole thing, and didn't tell my parents anything about it.

"Nice job on Friday night, jerk," I say as I walk up to Jeff's locker. "You really got me with that stupid knife. What did you put on it, like a rusty syrup or something?"

"Hey Kat," he says. He's congested and his voice is hoarse; his eyes look glassy. He closes his locker and throws his backpack over his shoulder. "What are you talking about?"

"You know, the knife," I say. "At the party? I threw it away, by the way."

"Oh yeah, I'm sorry I didn't make it."

"What?"

"Yeah, I started feeling sick after school on Friday, so I took some cold medicine and passed out early. I'm still getting over this stupid sinus infection. It was awful, especially the weekend before Halloween, you know? Anyway, how was your party?"

I could feel the blood draining from my face.

"You okay, Kat?"

"But… if you were at home sick on Friday," I say, trying not to scream as my hands start trembling, "then *who* was that guy?!"

# MARCELINE STARLINGTON

It was about midday on a Friday and there hadn't been a passing car for what felt like hours when that beat-up, old truck came puttering down the road. I exhaled slowly and held out my hand, my thumb outstretched and hoping for the best. The guy pulled over right away.

"Where ya headin', sweetheart?" he asked me, looking me up and down. He was older than me, but not by much; somewhere between thirty and forty and definitely old enough to know better. A little unkept, greasy, but nothing a shower and a good night of sleep couldn't take care of. His attitude, however... well, I had a hunch it would go this way. It almost always does.

"Town," I said, holding up my hand. His eyes glazed over, and he sat quietly, transfixed on my palm. "And you're going to take me there without incident."

"Yes, ma'am," he said slowly, his eyes focusing. "Hop on in."

"In silence," I added. Men like this are always so easy to control.

I threw my duffel in the back and kept the other bag on my lap. I was heading into town for Halloween, just like I always had with my mom, but he didn't need to know that. The ride was quiet except for the drone of the road against his crackly radio, some twangy country sound going in and out of reception.

His collection of keys jangled against a metal keychain shaped like an electric guitar that said "Nomad Life" in sharp letters. He was attentive to the road, and behaving himself at that, so I decided it would be alright to strike up a little conversation. Truth be told, I was starting to get bored.

"What's that from?" I asked, pointing to the keychain. He struck me more as the type of guy who never made it out of his hometown than a nomad. He looked at me and then back to the road.

"Oh, right," I said, waving my hand and allowing him to speak.

"It's from my days on the road running lighting for touring concerts," he said, finding his voice again. "I've seen almost every part of this country, north and south, east to west. It was fun while it lasted, but then I settled down… came back home." He paused. "What about you?"

"Me?"

"Where d'you call home?"

"I guess… I don't really have one," I said. "Not one that most people would call a home, anyway."

"You do strike me as a girl with a story," he said.

I laughed.

"Well, I suppose with a name like 'Marceline Starlington', you can't help but have a story," I said, looking out the window.

"Oh," he said. "So that's your name?" I could tell he was fishing for more conversation, and he seemed nice enough.

*Why not*, I thought to myself.

"You know, it's funny," I said, watching the drooping trees covered with Spanish moss pass in a blur. "You never think there's anything… peculiar about yourself, or off. You're just you, plain and simple. But only when you look back, does it all come together… and it starts to make sense. Life, I mean.

"It's all about how people look at you," I said, looking at him. "It's just… they look at you funny, you know? The neighbors across the street when you go to get the mail, the other girls in class on the playground when they won't let you join the group, the boys in the bars when they bring you a drink, stumbling back when they get that one, good look at who you are…

"My mom moved us around a lot. She always said we followed the autumn wind, but I figured there was something more to it. And my dad was never around, you see, and everywhere we went, every new town, every new school… it was only a matter of time before they all looked at us with that same, funny look. People have a way of knowing.

"She passed a few years ago, so I've been on my own more or less ever since. Still following that autumn wind, but in my own way… moving around from place to place, seeing the world," I said. I nodded toward his keychain. "So in a way, I guess, I've had my own nomad life."

He bobbed his head sympathetically and we drove for a while longer in silence again. After another half hour or so, we were just outside of the city limits and he pulled into a gas station.

"Don't you ever get lonely?" he asked, putting the truck in park. "I mean, I know when I was on the road…"

"Oh, all the time. But I've still got enough of her grave dust with me, so…" my voice trailed off as I gently patted the bag in my lap.

"What'dya mean by that?" he asked, confused.

"Well, so long as I have grave dust, I can still conjure her spirit from time to time for a chat or a check in," I explained. "Really, it's all you need to summon anyone's ghost."

"W-what?" he asked.

"Oh, didn't you guess? I'm surprised," I said with a smirk. "I'm a witch, sugar. A sorceress… An enchantress. A daughter of darkness, if you will. I thought for sure you'd figured it out. But I guess not… you haven't looked at me like all the others."

"I-I… what?!"

I raised my hand and his eyes again glazed over as he fell under my power. He was silent.

"Don't worry 'bout it," I said, calmly. "You won't remember a thing."

A few minutes later, he drove out of the parking lot without so much as a glance back in my direction. I smiled; he was nicer than I'd expected him to be. I guess people can still surprise you.

I tossed my bag over my shoulder, his "Nomad Life" keychain clanging against the others I'd collected from the strangers kind enough to give me a lift over the last few years. Right now, I was just a fuzzy memory, like someone in a dream you can't quite place, and by tomorrow, he'd have no memory of me whatsoever... just like all the rest.

\* \* \*

That night, once I was settled in the little two-bedroom bungalow I'd be calling home for the next week or so at least, I decided I was overdue for a talk with my mother, and an important one at that. I set the candles in a circle on a low coffee table and drew the symbols in white chalk, just like the ritual called for, humming quietly to myself. I lit the candles one by one, and it wasn't long before the room was bathed in a warm, flickering glow.

"Well, let's get this over with," I said to myself, carefully retrieving the pouch of grave dust from my bag. I sat down next to the table and began to mutter the spell, which I'd memorized long ago.

Once I finished with the incantation, I reached deep into the black leather pouch, my fingers scraping the bottom through what little remained of the dust inside. I closed my fist and drew my hand back out, tossing a small handful into the air. I waited a moment in silence, listening to the wind in the trees outside and the subtle crack of the burning candlewicks.

Suddenly there came a familiar breeze through the room and the dancing flames shrunk, the candles on the table remaining just barely lit. I looked up as the dust in the air began to swirl around, faster and faster. She was on her way.

"Hello, Marceline," the ghost of my mother, Viviane Starlington, said once she came into view atop the table. She looked around the room with a raised eyebrow. "Where do you have me now?"

"Take a look around... can't you tell? It's almost Halloween," I said. She was just as beautiful as a ghost as she was when she was alive: tall, statuesque, and now swathed in an ethereal, blue glow that lit up the room like her smile did when she was among the living.

"I thought this felt familiar," she said, floating down from the table. "What can I do for you, dear heart?"

"We need to talk," I said. She looked at me in the cold way ghosts can look at you when they're trying to be attentive. "I'm done with all this... this moving around, having to go from place to place. I'm tired of being the girl everyone whispers about, I'm tired of not being able to have friends, a community, being able to put down some roots... and it all comes from the magic, Ma."

"What are you saying?" she asked.

"What I'm saying is this," I began, taking a deep breath. "After Halloween, I'm done. I'm renouncing my magic."

The candle flames flared and a violent wind kicked up, blowing my hair every which way and a chair in the corner blew back against the wall, splintering against the exposed brick. I knew she wouldn't take it well.

"No!" my mom's ghost shouted. "You are Marceline Starlington - the last of the Starlington witches! Magic is who you are! You are descended from one of the great lineages of witchcraft, and a founder of the Coven of the New Moon. Don't turn your back on all of that!"

"Like they turned their backs on us?"

"Come on now, Marceline," she pleaded with me. "You know it wasn't that simple..."

"And where were they all those years, Ma?" I demanded. "Truthfully."

She again looked at me with that cold, ghostly stare; it almost rivaled the glares I got as a little girl whenever I found myself in trouble, which, as it was, happened on more than a few occasions.

"I've thought this through," I continued. "And I know that magic's like a muscle. If I stop using it, it'll eventually..."

I trailed off, and she was quiet.

"You won't be able to conjure me anymore," she said quietly.

I looked at her sadly.

"Look," I said. "I didn't call you here tonight just to deliver news I knew you wouldn't want to hear. I'm in town for Halloween! I thought we could carve our pumpkins... like old times."

She nodded and I made a circular motion with my hands, drawing two large, bright orange pumpkins into being. I pulled our old carving kit out of my bag and she sat beside me.

For the next hour and a half, it was just like the Halloweens I used to know. We listened to a few of our favorite old records and carved pumpkins like we did every year around that time. I told her about the guy I'd hitched a ride into town with, and we laughed about some of our old adventures. But as the candles burned down low, she started to fade from view... just as she always does when the spell has about run its course.

"It's almost time," I finally said.

"I know," she said. "I've enjoyed this. I'm so glad you still wanted to celebrate Halloween, even though..."

"Listen, I - "

"Don't give up on your magic just yet, Marceline," she said, her voice little more than a whisper. The candles on the table had started to burn out, one by one. "There is something entirely special about you. You bring out the best in people, and you never know when you're just on the cusp of..."

The last candle extinguished with a puff of smoke, and she was gone.

"Something great," I finished. She used to say that to me all the time when I was little. "I know, I know."

I sat in the dark room collecting my thoughts for a good while before I cleaned up our mess from the pumpkins and went to bed.

\* \* \*

The next day, I put on a loose minidress with a sheer cardigan and grabbed my favorite wide-brimmed hat, all in black of course. I pulled on my boots and finished the ensemble with an amethyst pendant necklace, tossing a kiss to the jack-o-lanterns still sitting on the table from the night before as I walked out the door. I hadn't bothered too much with fixing my hair, figuring the humidity, even this late in the season, would unleash my natural waves no matter what effort I put into taming them.

Halloween was in just a few days and I was heading out to explore all of the festivities that were kicking off around town. The irony wasn't lost on me that I was more or less dressed as a typical "modern witch", something I would have desperately tried to avoid even just a few years ago in an effort to be seen as normal. But trends come and go, and the best way to fit in these days was my witchy best; I'm usually pretty good at blending in.

I was lagging about a half a block behind a walking tour in the Cobblestone District, half listening to the yarn of history the guide was unraveling with my thoughts wandering, when an old woman carrying a stack of books rushed right into me. I jumped back as the books went flying, my arms outstretched in an effort to keep her from falling. The books were scattered everywhere.

"Oh, I'm so sorry!" I said, quickly. "Let me get these for you." I knelt to the ground and started stacking the books. They were old, heavy books that were bound in leather.

"Pardon me, dear," she said, looking up to my face. "It's all my fault, really! I was rushing and... not watching where I was going. Are you new in town?"

I stood to assess her, cradling the stack of books in my arms. She was short with an old, embroidered shawl draped over her shoulders and a dress with flowers on it; her hair was gray and stringy, sticking out under a black straw gardening hat and I was immediately intrigued by the bejeweled spectacles that rested on her hooked nose. If I didn't know better...

"Just here for the holiday," I said. "Here's your books."

"I hate to ask, dearie," she began slowly, "but would you be so kind as to help me get these to a bookshop down the road? I was just heading to drop them off, and they were getting so heavy... if it's not too much trouble?"

She batted her eyelashes at me over those sparkling glasses. I looked over her head to see if I could still catch the tour group, but they were gone.

"Sure," I said with a smile, hoping it looked genuine. "Lead the way."

"Ohh, excellent! Spellbound Books is only about a block or two this way, follow me!" she said, clapping her hands quickly and scampering off down the street.

She turned this way and that, darting in and out of the crowds while I did my best to keep up with her. I was trying to keep an eye on where she was going while also making sure not to drop the books again. They were pretty heavy already, and I found myself wondering how she'd managed to lug them by herself from wherever she'd come from.

I stopped a moment to shift the weight of the books from one arm to the other, and when I looked up she was gone.

"Ma'am?" I said aloud, though no one walking by stopped. "Where'd you go?"

I peered up and down the street, and was just about convinced she'd disappeared entirely when I caught the faintest glimpse of her floral print dress sweeping past a large wooden door into a book shop about six stores away. I shook my head in disbelief that she'd managed to get so far so quickly; she was a spritely old thing, that was for sure!

I walked toward that book store with purpose, eager to drop those books off and get on with my day. With any luck, I'd still have time to get to the town square to watch the start of the annual Halloween bake-off. I reached the steps and looked up to the sign.

"Spellbound Books" the old wood sign read in carefully painted lettering over a large book opened down the middle, with purple swirls coming from its pages.

"Well I guess this is the place," I said to myself, walking up the steps. I pushed the heavy door open with my shoulder, and stepped inside, a bell ringing to announce my presence.

"Hello?" I called. No one answered.

The shelves that lined the walls and the display tables scattered about were filled to the brim with books. Halloween banners hung from the ceiling with trinkets spaced throughout, and there was instrumental music playing softly from a speaker on the counter. To the right of the register, a short flight of stairs led to an upper area in the back that was just visible from the entrance. Light streamed in through a wide, industrial window along that back wall that had had a few of its panes replaced with stained glass in vibrant colors.

There was no sign of that old woman.

I stood for a moment, unsure of what to do and again shifting the books from one arm to the other, when I heard footsteps coming down the stairs along the wall from the second story. A girl with long, colorful braids came down first, her shoes clacking loudly on the wooden steps. She was followed by another, this one blonde with a tight ponytail and looking like she'd just smelled something foul. Neither of them could have been much older than me, and I could tell they had both gotten the memo about dressing the part of a modern witch: all in black, with a free-spirited style that was impeccably chic and accessorized just so.

"Hi there," the first one said cheerfully as she reached the main floor. "Thanks for coming in! Is there anything we can help you with today?"

"I was helping somebody actually, an older woman... She was bringing these books here and asked that I help her carry them... Did either of you see her? Flower-print dress, bedazzled glasses..."

The two of them looked at each other and then back to me.

"Mirabella," the second girl said, rolling her eyes as she walked to the counter, messing with her ponytail.

"I-I'm sorry?"

"Here," the first girl said, reaching out to take the books. "Let me take these for you. I'm Mary, by the way. Mary Ellis. And we call that one Elizabeth."

The second girl smirked at her from behind the counter.

"What's your name?" Mary asked.

"Marceline Starlington."

"That's beautiful," she said warmly.

"What is this place?" I asked as Mary placed the books in front of Elizabeth, her bracelets clanking. "Who's Mirabella?"

"Mirabella Honeycutt is a bored old witch with not much else to do but tinker around in her gardens at the Caldwell Estate and pop into town whenever it strikes her fancy to pester those of us who have a job to do," Elizabeth said.

"That is a delightful way of saying she is one of the elders of our coven," Mary said, glaring at Elizabeth, who shrugged, and then turning back to me.

"And this is Spellbound Books! We're one of the oldest purveyors of the written word, magical and mortal alike," she added with a wink. "The store was founded and run by the Coven of the Midnight Garden to this very day."

"So you're all, I mean, both of you are witches, too?" I asked carefully.

"Of course," Mary said. "Couldn't you tell?"

"Well, I'd guessed, but…"

"So what's your story?" Elizabeth asked from the register, looking up from the catalog she was flipping through. "You and your coven fly into town for Halloween? Or are you just one of the tourists with a big hat and a couple of crystals in your pocket who's gonna need to forget all about this little talk."

I casually flicked a few of my fingers and the catalog in front of her slammed shut, causing Elizabeth to jump back in surprise.

"Definitely not just a tourist," Mary said to herself quietly.

"No coven," I answered curtly. "Just in town for Halloween."

"Oh!" Mary said with excitement. "Do you have any plans for Halloween night?"

"None at the moment," I said.

"Great!" she said. "You should join us at the Caldwell Estate!"

"What's that?"

Elizabeth had moved on from the catalog to clicking around on the computer.

"It's our covenstead out in the country," she explained. "It's one of those stately old mansions you see in all the movies; it's been in Olympia May's family for generations and home to our coven since our founding."

"Olympia May?"

"Olympia May Caldwell, our High Priestess," Mary clarified. "I know she'd be delighted if you joined us for the evening. Or at least for the lighting of the Garden of a Hundred Pumpkins!"

"You have a garden with a hundred pumpkins?"

"Oh yes," Mary gushed. "It's beautiful! The garden's filled with jack-o-lanterns of all sorts and we light them on Halloween night together as a coven. We carve them with magic, of course."

"I'll think about it," I said.

"I'm sure that's why Mirabella led you here," Mary added. "She doesn't crash into just anyone with those heavy old books, you know, and she's always saying she's on the lookout for new blood..."

"Blessed be, Mary Ellis, let the girl alone!" Elizabeth called from behind the computer screen. "If she wants to do her own thing solo for Halloween, then let her do just that."

"Well, *excuse* me for being the slightest bit welcoming to a new witch in town," Mary spat back to Elizabeth. "Not that you'd know the first thing about being - "

*My own thing solo*, I thought. I had been doing my own thing solo for so long, I'd almost forgotten what it was like to feel included, especially by other witches.

"Actually," I said, interrupting their spat, "I think I will join you ladies for Halloween. That sounds nice."

"Excellent!" Mary said, clasping her hands together and blasting a triumphant smile toward Elizabeth, who had once again cracked open the catalog. "Oh, the others will be so excited! We have such a great time every year with the music and a bonfire and, oh! You'll have to try Etta's mulberry pie; it's award winning!"

"I wouldn't miss it," I said with a smile.

I spent the next hour or so in that book shop getting to know both Mary Ellis and Elizabeth Dautrieve, learning about the other ladies and the history of their coven when they weren't helping other folks who'd wandered in. They showed me a few of their favorite magic books, and I showed them a spell or two of my own.

When I was getting ready to leave, Mary told me to come back to the shop on the afternoon of Halloween in a few days and we could trek out to the countryside together. She also made sure I knew that I was welcome to return before then if I wasn't busy with anything else in town. Elizabeth even mumbled that it was nice to meet me as I pulled the heavy door open to leave.

*Who knows?* I thought to myself. *Maybe I'll win that one over yet.*

And as I walked back toward one of the town squares to catch whatever was left of the annual Halloween bake-off, it occurred to me that maybe I was nearing the end of my time living a nomad life, just like that guy in the truck did. Maybe I *was* just on the cusp of something great. And maybe I wouldn't be renouncing my magic after all.

My mother was going to be beside herself.

# MADNESS! AT CASTLE BLOODSTONE

"Good evening, Dr. Bloodstone," the mechanical woman known as Ms. Steele said, entering the third-floor laboratory in the eastern turret of the castle. The stars were shining outside the window in the dark, night sky. "You summoned me?"

"Correct," the mad scientist said, focused from behind his thick goggles on the small device he was tinkering with in his hands. Ms. Steele stood attentively, her eyes glowing blue against her brushed metal face while a collection of intricately designed and placed gears worked quietly throughout her body. Dr. Bloodstone finished his work and looked toward her, raising his goggles to sit atop the wild hair on his head.

"I've decided to host a little feast at Castle Bloodstone for some of our friends in a few days' time on Halloween night," he told her. It had been a little over a year since the incident with his murderous clone and the subsequent inquiry by the Bureau of Supernatural Affairs, which was the last time they had taken guests in the castle.

"Who can we expect to be in attendance, sir?" she asked, her electronically synthesized voice even and matter-of-fact.

Dr. Bloodstone thought for a moment.

"A delegate or two from the Coven of the New Moon will be joining us," he said. "And Priestess Amaranth. She insists things are frightfully dull in the mummy tombs around Halloween, and was quite eager to visit again."

"Noted, sir."

"Count Darknoire will be attending solo - I hear he's on the prowl for a new Mr. Gold," he said. "Captain Shamrock would also like to take part in our little fête, which will give us an excellent opportunity to show off the upgrades we've made in the harbor."

Ms. Steele nodded.

"And I believe Sir Tawnywood will be joining us," Dr. Bloodstone finished. "Madame Crimson was invited to be a guest at the annual Ghost Ball by the Sapphire Lady, and I would hazard to guess that he hasn't made plans of his own."

"Noted, sir," Ms. Steele repeated. "When should we anticipate their arrival?"

"They're all to send word the day before Halloween," he said.

"Excellent," Ms. Steele said. "I'll begin making preparations immediately."

"Thank you, Ms. Steele," Dr. Bloodstone said, picking the screwdriver on his table up and looking back toward the device before him. "That will be all."

She nodded and turned to leave, her metallic footfall echoing throughout the lab.

"Ms. Steele," Dr. Bloodstone called as she reached the door. She stopped and looked back at him. "One more thing, I - "

Suddenly, the robotic woman found herself powering back on in her charging station deep within the castle.

As her systems came online, her internal clock logged an alert that twelve hours had elapsed from the time she had been in Dr. Bloodstone's lab, and she had missed her morning duties for the first time ever recorded.

"Peculiar," she said aloud. She attempted to access her memory banks, but found there was nothing recorded in the last twelve hours. She had no recollection of what else Dr. Bloodstone had needed when he stopped her at the door, no memory of leaving his lab or how she had returned to her quarters. The last twelve hours were simply gone.

"If this continues," she said to herself, "I may need to run a full system analysis." She disconnected from her power source and accessed her work routines for the day.

* * *

When she entered the kitchen, Ms. Steele was surprised to find that a majority of her tasks had already been completed. The kitchen was spotless, the fires were roaring, and preparations were underway for the Halloween feast by the kitchen bots. Most curious of all, everything had been completed in line with her standards, which no other of Dr. Bloodstone's robotic creations had been programmed to do.

Ms. Steele walked over to the bot designated KIT-822, one of the most advanced among the kitchen bots, who was busy slicing something wriggling on the counter with a modular knife apparatus.

"If I may interrupt you for a moment," she said. KIT-822 stopped slicing and turned toward her. "Who is responsible for the state of the kitchen today?"

The kitchen bot made a series of beeps and buzzes in response, telling Ms. Steele that she was.

"I'm aware that overseeing the start of the day-to-day operations in the kitchen is one of my responsibilities, particularly as we begin preparations for the Halloween feast," Ms. Steele said. "But who specifically was in charge today in my absence? I wish to commend them on a job well done."

Again, KIT-822 made a series of noises to answer Ms. Steele's question, repeating that she had been responsible for the kitchen that day.

"You must be mistaken," she said. "I have not yet been in the kitchen today, my day has just begun."

The kitchen bot made another noise and resumed working on preparations for the Halloween feast.

"Concerning," Ms. Steele said. "If I was indeed already in the kitchen completing my morning tasks, then there must be a recording error in my memory banks."

She surveyed the work of the kitchen bots, and found their progress satisfactory.

"Attention," she said, the volume of her modulated voice increasing as she made her announcement to the bots in the kitchen. "The work you have completed so far today has exceeded expectations, and Dr. Bloodstone is most appreciative. I will now be going to oversee the setting of the feasting table in the Great Hall. Please send word if you require any additional assistance."

The bots resumed their tasks, and Ms. Steele left the kitchen, attempting to ignore a growing sense of concern over the twelve hours that were missing from her memory banks. If KIT-822 was correct, she had been in the kitchen that morning, going about her tasks as usual so that the kitchen bots may conduct their activities, but she had no recollection of such events.

* * *

From outside of the Great Hall, Ms. Steele summoned the two automatons that would be assembling the feasting table via the castle's intercom system. She could, of course, handle the entire set up on her own, but Dr. Bloodstone had assembled these two for just such the task to avoid any undue stress on her mechanical joints.

Ms. Steele stood outside of the Great Hall for ten minutes waiting for the automatons to arrive, and after five more minutes with no sign of them, she decided to handle the placement of the table herself. She opened the doors to the Great Hall to begin cleaning, and was surprised to see the feasting table in place and the two automatons finishing their task.

"How did you complete this so quickly?" Ms. Steele asked, approaching them.

"We've been working for the last two hours, ma'am," the first automaton said slowly, his voice tinny as it echoed through the speaker in his chest. Though most of the castle's automatons didn't speak, much like the task-focused bots in the kitchen and the stables, Dr. Bloodstone had installed rudimentary processing units in these two, with a simple speaker setup through which they could speak in short bursts to aid in their tasks around the castle.

"Very good," Ms. Steele said. "But who summoned you?"

"You did, ma'am."

The blue light in Ms. Steele's eyes flared brighter for just a moment. For the second time in one day, she found herself with no recollection of events she had allegedly been a part of.

"This morning?"

The automaton nodded.

"And when you saw me this morning, when I called you to the Great Hall, how was my demeanor? Did I appear lucid? Were any of my systems noticeably malfunctioning? Any information you can share with me about our encounter this morning is of great importance," she said. She knew there was only a marginal chance the automatons would be able to help, as their memory banks were far more limited than her own.

"She's a fair bit more talkative now, eh?" the second automaton said to the first.

"What do you mean by that?" Ms. Steele asked him.

"Only that you didn't speak to us this morning, ma'am," the first automaton answered. "We arrived in the Great Hall and you handed us a note with instructions."

"Do you have this note?"

"Here," the second automaton said, producing a slip of paper and handing it to her.

Ms. Steele examined it closely. Though she had no memory log of writing this note or giving it to the automatons, it was undeniable that the penmanship was her own, programmed handwriting that was always the same.

"Thank you, gentlemen," she said to the automatons. "That will be all."

They both nodded toward her in unison, the gears in their necks spinning, and left the Great Hall. She stood staring at the paper in her hands wondering what was going on for eight minutes, as her internal clock had logged it. Suddenly, she heard the sound of footsteps approaching the room. She looked up to the door and listened carefully; they were getting closer, and though she had no reason to believe she was in danger, she started to power on her defense systems as a precaution. The handle unlatched with a groan and the creaking door started to swing open -

Ms. Steele powered on in her charging station, and as her systems came back online, she was alerted that five hours had passed from the time she had dismissed the automatons in the Great Hall. And again, there was no record of anything from those hours in her memory banks.

"I need to run that full system analysis," she said aloud. "Immediately."

An hour later, Ms. Steele unhooked herself from the diagnostic device that Dr. Bloodstone had created for her to maintain her own systems. Though she had made sure the device had pored over every circuit and system throughout her body, the conclusion was the same both times she ran the program: She was operating at optimal capacity with no reportable errors or malfunctions.

"It must have been a glitch," she said aloud. "Just a simple system glitch."

She powered down the diagnostic machine, and set out to complete the remainder of the day's tasks. Since the machine had concluded there was nothing wrong with her, there was no need to bring any of this to Dr. Bloodstone's attention. The Halloween feast was only two days away, after all, and there was much to be done.

\* \* \*

The following day, Ms. Steele powered on at her normal time and began her work around the castle as she usually did without incident. She made sure the kitchen bots were prepared to execute their daily tasks before finishing the preparations for the Halloween feast in the Great Hall. Later in the morning, she began receiving confirmation notices with arrival times from a few of the guests. Things had seemingly returned to normal, but in the early afternoon, the strange occurrences of the previous few days slowly crept their way back to her attention.

Her first hint that something was amiss was when she came upon a team of cleaning bots in the crypts when they should have been in the western turret.

"Pardon me, but what are all of you doing down here?" Ms. Steele asked. The lead bot broke away from the others and beeped in reply.

"Oh, my mistake," Ms. Steele said abruptly. "I must have… forgotten that I asked you to make sure these crypts were cleaned today in preparation for Count Darknoire's arrival tomorrow. Carry on."

She turned and quickly left the crypt. It was happening again, she was starting to get that sense of concern that something was going wrong with her systems. If it continued, she would have to bring the matter to Dr Bloodstone's attention.

Ms. Steele was en route to the stables to ensure they were in order to house the griffins that would be pulling Priestess Amaranth's chariot when she came upon one of the automatons from the day before.

"Hello again, ma'am," he said, his voice crackling through the speaker in his chest. "I'm glad to see you've been able to address the issue with your eyes."

"My eyes?" Ms. Steele asked, confused.

"Yes, ma'am," the automaton said. "When I saw you this morning, your eyes were flickering and then they turned red. Don't you remember?"

Ms. Steele had no memory of seeing the automaton that day, nor any record of a malfunction with her visual systems; they were programmed to flash red whenever there was an error in one of her systems, though she had no logged occurrence of it happening that morning.

"My apologies," Ms. Steele said. "I appear to be experiencing a lapse in my memory matrix."

"Best to have Dr. Bloodstone take a look at you, ma'am," he said. "He'll have you fixed up in no time at all!"

"Your concern is noted," she said. "Good day."

The automaton nodded as Ms. Steele walked on. Maybe he was right? Perhaps it was time to alert Dr. Bloodstone to the malfunctions that had befallen her over the past few days.

She continued on toward the stables via the main entrance, which had always been one of her favorite spots in all of Castle Bloodstone. From there, one could see all the way down to the harbor and across the distant hills from the safety of the castle, and when the moon was shining just right...

Footsteps. She heard those strange footsteps ahead, the same as she'd heard approaching the Great Hall the day before. She stopped and stood, listening.

Ms. Steele couldn't place it, but there was something strangely familiar about the footsteps as she heard them pacing in the entryway. She had to know who, or what, they belonged to, so she resumed her walk, taking care to step as carefully and quietly as she could so as not to scare whatever was ahead. She rounded the corner into the entryway and -

Ms. Steele was powering back on, though as her visual systems came online, she realized she was not in her charging station as she should have been; she was in the large circular room at the top of the western turret. Her internal clock noted that thirty-six minutes had elapsed.

"I need to report to Dr. Bloodstone," she said aloud, her synthesized words hanging in the air.

She set out for his lab at once. Dr. Bloodstone was sure to be hard at work still at this time of day, but enough of these incidents had warranted what Ms. Steele could classify as an emergency. Along the way, she stopped twice, sure that she'd heard those footsteps again, only this time they were walking quickly away from her.

Thoughts shot from her central processing unit through her circuits and back again. The missing time, the interactions she had no memory of, and the mysteriously familiar footsteps she was starting to hear everywhere she went in the castle... what was going on? Was her hardware breaking down? Was there some sudden and rapid degradation in her systems that she was unaware of? Or was her mind simply... going?

She could think of nothing else, neither her duties nor the preparations for the Halloween feast as she trekked toward Dr. Bloodstone's third floor lab. She hadn't even bothered to check for any updated communications from the guests that were expected the next night. She knew only that she had to get to Dr. Bloodstone, he would know what to do.

Ms. Steele reached the door to Dr. Bloodstone's lab and was surprised to find it locked. She knocked twice and waited for him to answer. She could hear him approach from behind the heavy metal door.

"Uhhm, just a minute," Dr. Bloodstone shouted.

Ms. Steele realized from the clamoring behind the door that Dr. Bloodstone wasn't alone in his lab; she could again hear those mysterious footsteps echoing in there with him. The sound surrounded her, the oddly familiar, metallic footfall, that almost reminded her of... the latch on the inside of the door clicked as it was unlocked.

"Ahh, Ms. Steele," Dr. Bloodstone said breathlessly, grinning a wicked grin as he pulled the heavy door open. "I was just about to send for you. If you'll - "

Suddenly, Ms. Steele was standing in a dark, damp room, her systems again powering back on. She had no idea where she was or how long it had been since she had been ushered into Dr. Bloodstone's lab. From afar, she could hear a dripping pipe, and as her visual processors came online, she realized from the dimly-lit brick arches that she was in one of the cellars beneath the kitchen.

"Hello?" she called, her voice echoing. There was no answer, and though she was not restrained, she felt a sense of urgency about leaving the cellar and started walking toward the stairs at a brisker pace than she would have under a normal circumstance.

Once again, she found herself in a part of the castle with no idea how she'd gotten there or what she was doing, and the increasing frequency of these episodes was becoming cause for great concern. She had almost reached the stairs when she noticed a spark in the shadows from the far corner of the cellar.

"Hello," she said again. In the light from the sparks, she could see that her hands were covered in the residue of a dark substance. She raised a hand to her nose and inhaled; her scent processors identified the substance as a motor oil.

Ms. Steele stepped cautiously toward the corner of the cellar, increasing the brightness of her eyes to cast as much light on the scene as she could. Whatever was there was continuing to emit showers of sparks. She could just make out a shape in the corner when she slipped and had to steady herself. Looking down, she saw that she was standing in a pool of oil, the same that was all over her hands.

"Concerning," she said. She stood in place and continued to survey the scene. There were machine parts strewn about: gears, wires, and circuits... the inner workings of one of Dr. Bloodstone's bots. Without warning, another wire emitted a shower of sparks and in the light, she was able to identify the twisted, metal remains of the kitchen bot, KIT-822.

* * *

Ms. Steele was on hand the next evening to greet the guests for the Halloween feast as they began to arrive. She had gathered KIT-822's parts in a corner of the cellar and sealed it off before returning to her charging station for the night, resolving to handle the matter the next morning.

After a full recharging cycle, she awoke ready to bring everything to Dr. Bloodstone's attention, but he had immediately sent a list of items for her to complete as the day was starting. Perhaps he was already aware of the situation and was keeping her busy to avoid another episode? One task led to another, and before she realized it, Ms. Steele was standing in the castle's entrance waiting to greet the guests; one of the automatons was also on hand with a tray of drinks.

She had spent a good portion of the morning assisting the bots in the kitchen, as the absence of KIT-822 left them short handed and behind on their final preparations for the feast. None of the others had paid much mind to KIT-822 being gone, as Dr. Bloodstone would frequently pull the bots for diagnostics and upgrades, but that didn't stop Ms. Steele from compulsively checking over her shoulder to ensure no one was looking at her with suspicion.

Priestess Amaranth was the first to arrive, escorted by one of the stable bots, who promptly returned to tend to her griffins. She was wearing the ornate wrappings customary of a mummy with her status and a beaded headdress that was black and orange in the spirit of the holiday.

"Ms. Steele!" she called, holding out her delicately bandaged hand with metal bracelets jangling around her bony wrist. "Happy Halloween! How lovely to see you again!"

"And the same to you, Priestess," the robotic woman replied. "Dr. Bloodstone will be joining us shortly for a reception before dinner."

"Excellent, my dear," the mummy said before walking on to grab a drink from the automaton.

Mummies had a way of interpreting signs and knowing things… could she sense something was amiss with her hardware and programming? Ms. Steele barely had time to think about it before the next guest arrived.

"Good evening, Sir Tawnywood," she greeted him. "Welcome back to Castle Bloodstone."

The werewolf smiled, his sharp teeth bared, and shook hands with her before moving to greet Priestess Amaranth. Had he brushed her off? With his keen sense of smell, was he able to sniff out the residual scent of oil on her hand as he held it in his own, thus deducing what she'd done to KIT-822?

A few minutes later, Count Darknoire arrived in bat form, quickly changing to his humanoid appearance with grandeur. As Dr. Bloodstone always said, vampires do like to make an entrance.

"Greetings, everyone!" he said loudly with cheer, his black satin cape swirling behind him as he strode toward the automaton to grab a drink. "Do you have any O negative this evening? Ahh, fantastic!"

Though she was usually not amused by the Count's

showboating antics, Ms. Steele was quietly grateful that he was drawing most of the attention in the room to himself and away from her. She was on high alert for the sound of those footsteps, and worried about slipping into another episode of whatever mania she'd been experiencing. Fortunately, she'd been able to maintain her wits about her so far that day.

Miss Pumpkin from the Coven of the New Moon was the next to arrive, holding onto her wide-brimmed hat as she landed her broom in the courtyard; the embroidered constellations on her deep purple cape matched those in the night sky. She was followed shortly after by Captain Shamrock, who was escorted from the harbor by another of the castle's bots.

"Aye, it's a pleasure to see all of you again," said the sea monster, his scaly skin shimmering in the light. The group mingled and chatted while Ms. Steele watched them carefully. It felt as though no time at all had passed from the last time they and several other of their friends in the mystical community had been in the castle a year ago.

Ms. Steele found she could remember every detail of that fateful gathering, but was at a loss to account for any of the time missing from her memory banks over the last few days. All she'd been able to glean was what the other bots and creations of Dr. Bloodstone had let slip to her about her actions and whereabouts. She wondered if she'd eventually be powered down for good or if she'd snap and go on a rampage, destroying everything in the castle the way she had KIT-822.

"Ms. Steele?" asked Miss Pumpkin, pulling her from her thoughts. She'd stepped away from the other guests.

"Yes, ma'am?" she answered, hoping she wasn't able to read her thoughts.

"Would you care to join us all over here?"

It became clear to Ms. Steele that Miss Pumpkin, at least, must not have had an idea of what had been happening over the last few days. The witch wouldn't have invited her to join them all if she knew what she'd done.

"Certainly," she said, and followed Miss Pumpkin to join the others. While she did her best to stay attentive to the conversation, she couldn't help but let her mind wander. Dr. Bloodstone was sure to deactivate her once he knew she'd become one of those homicidal robots the bots in the castle told stories of. Or worse, he'd call the Bureau of Supernatural Affairs, and who knew what they'd -

"Good evening, everyone," Dr. Bloodstone said, walking into the room. "And Happy Halloween to you all! I'm glad you could join us at Castle Bloodstone tonight. Apologies for my tardiness - I was working in my lab, and time just got away from me! I assure you all, though, I am myself, not a deranged clone."

The others laughed while Ms. Steele stood silent.

"Actually, before we head to the Great Hall for dinner, I'd like you all to follow me to my robotics lab," Dr. Bloodstone said. The guests followed him out of the entrance, but Ms. Steele lagged a little behind.

According to the timeline that Dr. Bloodstone had prepared for the evening, they were to be on their way to the Great Hall for the feast right now, not one of his labs, especially his laboratory devoted to his work in robotics. He must have wanted to have her deactivated before dinner, before she had the chance to cause any more damage than she'd already done.

She quickly assessed the situation: Dr. Bloodstone, a mummy, a vampire, a werewolf, a witch, and a sea monster... she could handle them each individually if absolutely necessary, but together? They could easily work to subdue her. There was another option, though, another way. She could make a run for it now, leave the castle, start anew...

"Ms. Steele," Dr. Bloodstone called. "That includes you, please. There's something there I want you especially to see."

\* \* \*

Ms. Steele stood quietly staring at the five glass pods in Dr. Bloodstone's robotics lab. They were identical, each cylinder tall enough to hold a grown adult and filled with a thick, swirling smoke. The guests seemed anxious to hear what the mad scientist was about to announce, eager even. But Ms. Steele hadn't ruled out making a quick exit in the interest of self-preservation.

"As you all know," Dr. Bloodstone began, "we had a most regrettable incident last year when a clone of myself went rogue and attempted to end my life. But thanks to some ingenious sleuthing on the part of all of you, not the least of which was thanks to my dear companion, Ms. Steele here, I am alive and well today!"

The guests clapped politely.

"And cleared of all charges by the Bureau of Supernatural Affairs, I'd like to note," he added, making them laugh.

"But what really struck me after the incident with the clone was how many of you contacted me commending the actions of Ms. Steele that night. She was forthright and true to her programming, holding her own against all of you and the others in attendance while defending me and protecting the castle."

Ms. Steele stood in the lab, speechless as the guests again erupted in a round of applause. What was the meaning of all of this?

"In fact, at one point or another, each of you asked about the possibility of having a Ms. Steele of your own," Dr. Bloodstone concluded. "Of course, I could never replicate her completely, given how her personality has evolved over time, but I did still have the blueprints on hand, so without further ado…"

Dr. Bloodstone flipped a lever and the pods began to rise into the ceiling, the smoke inside them dissipating into the lab. And as the smoke cleared, Ms. Steele found herself looking at five replicas of herself standing in a row. In unison, their eyes lit up and they powered on with a series of beeps and whirs.

"Ladies and gentlemen, I'd like you to meet Alumina, Chromia, Crystalline, Titania, and Heather," Dr. Bloodstone announced. "Ms. Steele… say hello to your sisters!"

She stared at them, assessing one and then the next. Each looked just like her, though the markings on their faces and the shades of their plating differed slightly. They were the same height and their eyes all had a similar glow.

"They're wonderful!" Priestess Amaranth said.

"Amazing," echoed Sir Tawnywood. "The pack will be glad to have her home!"

"Aye, and you took care of the solar mobile charging request?" Captain Shamrock asked.

"Of course," Dr. Bloodstone answered. "Even on your ship, Captain, she'll be able to maintain a charge."

The guests turned back to the bots, while Dr. Bloodstone walked toward Ms. Steele.

"Sir, this is..." she began, but was unable to find the appropriate words for the occasion. So much had happened over the last few days, so many things to process.

"I do owe you a bit of an apology," Dr. Bloodstone cut in. "I've been working on them for quite some time, but I couldn't let you know until now. A few days ago, I had to install a new subroutine in your programming as I was running final tests on them; you probably noticed when you were offline for such a long time. Essentially, it caused you to power down any time you came near them until I was able to circumvent a glitch that would have resulted in a total system failure had you encountered one of them. And fortunately, everything is working in top shape now!"

Suddenly, it all made sense. The mysterious footsteps must have belonged to her sisters and she'd been powering down whenever she got too close to one of them to avoid a catastrophic system failure. And whenever the other bots in the castle mentioned interactions she was not able to account for, they must have been talking about one of the others, not her. She wasn't losing her mind after all...

"Thankfully, I was able to install a new safety protocol in your central processing unit last night when you came to my lab in the eastern turret," he continued. "So now, as you can see, you're able to be in the same vicinity with them and not suffer any undue glitches."

"Remarkable," Ms. Steele said, looking from one of her sisters to the next and back to Dr. Bloodstone. "So I'm not to be deactivated?"

"Deactivated?! Not at all! Why, that's quite preposterous," Dr. Bloodstone said. "What would have given you that idea?"

"Well, sir," Ms. Steele began, "I was concerned that my systems were in a sudden and rapid decline, and that there would be no other choice. And after finding KIT-822 in the cellar…"

"Ahh yes," he said. "There was a bit of a regrettable incident with Chromia and one of the kitchen bots, but I'll have KIT-822 up and running again within the week."

"An incident?" Count Darknoire said from across the room, his eyebrow raised.

"Nothing to worry about," Dr. Bloodstone said. "Her programming has been corrected, and everything is running as it should. I don't want another brush with the B.S.A. for letting a homicidal robot loose in the world, you know."

The Count nodded and turned back to his conversation.

"Alright everyone," Dr. Bloodstone said. "Your bots will be ready to return home with you at the end of the evening. I think it's time we head down for the Halloween Feast!"

The others filed out of the laboratory, with Dr. Bloodstone and Ms. Steele staying behind to make sure everything was properly shut down.

"I can't believe you thought I was going to deactivate you," Dr. Bloodstone said to her quietly. "I couldn't have accomplished a fraction of the things I've accomplished in this castle without you! You keep everything running, and masterfully at that."

"Thank you, sir," Ms. Steele said, her voice steady.

"And you've done a fantastic job preparing for tonight's feast, even with all of the madness of the past few days," he continued. "So much so that I'd like you to take the next few days for a full system recharge. The automatons can handle the cleanup from tonight."

"Of course, sir," Ms. Steele said with gratitude. "Happy Halloween."

"Happy Halloween, Ms. Steele," he said. "Now come on, let's join the others."

# A TRICK-OR-TREATING THEY WILL GO

When I was a kid, one of my favorite days of the entire year was the day we'd decorate for Halloween. The air was crisp, the leaves were changing, and I'd wake up on that Saturday morning excited to see all of my favorite decorations being put up throughout the house. Of course, we'd decorate for other seasons and holidays, too, but there was just something special about decorating for Halloween.

We always started with the big plastic bag full of cardboard die-cuts. I'd run from window to window, carefully hanging them with suction cup hooks, each one in its designated spot. Once those were in place, we'd get up the blue storage bins and change over the dining room table. We'd carefully lay out the pumpkin patch tablecloth, one of the most beautiful I'd ever seen, and the centerpiece would be swapped for an ornate candelabra with bats on each arm. Window clings would go on the bathroom mirrors and strands of lights would be carefully placed around each room to cast an enchanting glow.

Next, we'd pull up the big stuff, like the tin Frankenstein candy holder that was almost as tall as I was, and the whimsical haunted house with several spooky inhabitants that sat on a table next to him. It was also made of tin and just about the same height, so it stood extra tall. From there, it was all about the finer details: wooden signs here, battery powered candles there, and little things that just made the house feel magical. And though it was hard to pick a favorite piece, I loved them all so much, it was undeniable that there was something extra special about the four Halloween kids that would go on the coffee table in the living room.

They were each about a foot tall, and dressed in Halloween costumes. One of the boys was a scarecrow with overalls and a big floppy hat, another a ghost wrapped in a white sheet. The girl was a witch, her curly hair sticking out from under her pointed hat, and the last boy was a dapper vampire with a cape lined in orange. They all held little jack-o-lanterns in one hand and little bags to collect their Halloween candy in the other.

Together, this quartet of trick-or-treaters would stand perched on the coffee table, waiting day after day for the chance to go and collect their candy. And on the Eve of Halloween, once we'd all gone to bed, they'd awake for their yearly trip around the house and a trick-or-treating they would go.

\* \* \*

As the clock on top of the old console TV in the living room strikes midnight within its glass dome, the Halloween kids stretch and come to life, looking to each other with wide smiles.

"It's time!" the scarecrow says.

"It's here!" says the ghost.

"There's not a moment to waste," the vampire says.

"Let's go! Let's go!" adds the witch. "Our candy awaits!"

Together, the four kids help one another climb off of their bases and down from the coffee table to embark on this mission they've waited for the whole year.

On their way to the foyer, they stop to visit with a pair of skeletons that sit on the small chairs next to the old console TV. One is dressed in a classic tuxedo while the other wears a white, satin gown.

"Trick-or-treat!" they say, approaching the skeleton couple and holding out their little brown candy bags. The skeletons have a strand of orange lights wrapped around their chairs that sends a warm glow throughout the room.

"Hello, kids!" says Mr. Skeleton, his plastic jaw bone flapping up and down.

"Happy Halloween!" says Mrs. Skeleton, carefully dropping a small candy bar in each of the kids' bags. "Do you have your jokes ready to go? You know how the other decorations enjoy a good joke on Halloween!"

"We do!" says the witch. "Want to hear one?"

"Sure!" the skeletons say.

"What do you call a witch on the beach?" she asks.

"I don't know," Mr. Skeleton says.

"A sand-witch!" the witch says as everyone dissolves into a fit of giggles.

"Oh, you little ones have fun tonight," says Mrs. Skeleton. "And mind that you're back before dawn - we don't want you out and about when the humans wake up!"

"Don't worry," says the vampire. "We'll be back before first light!"

\* \* \*

The four trick-or-treaters head for the foyer, where the tin Frankenstein candy bowl stands tall next to the whimsical haunted house on the entry table. They step carefully so they don't make too much noise on the hardwood floor.

"Trick-or-treat!" they call to the Frankenstein that towers above them. "Happy Halloween!"

"Oh! It's the kids!" he says cheerfully, quietly tapping an arm against the purple-hued haunted house. "Hey look everyone, the kids are here!"

The witch at the end of the thin rod sticking out of the top of the house flies around in her circle, her dress the same shade of purple as the house's exterior, while the metal ghosts along the front wave hello.

"Happy Halloween, little ones!" says the metal witch, still flying around. "Have you brought us a joke again this year?"

"Oh, I've got one!" says the ghost. The others giggle, knowing what he's about to say. "What do ghosts get in their nose?"

"What?" the metal Frankenstein asks.

"I'm stumped!" the little witch says from atop the haunted house.

"BOO-gers!" the ghost says, and all four of the kids erupt into laughter. The little witch cackles while the metal ghosts along the front laugh, too.

"Good one, kiddo," the tin Frankenstein says as he tosses some candy down from his bowl to the trick-or-treaters. They catch the candy, piece by piece, and graciously say their thanks.

"Hey kids - before you go, you'll want to listen to this," the tall Frankenstein says. "There's a new decoration in the family room!"

"A new friend?" asks the scarecrow.

"It must be!" says the witch, jumping up and down, her curly hair bouncing as the others join in.

"It's possible," Frankenstein says. "But no one's really sure."

The kids stop, confused.

"I saw them setting him out when they carried up our house," the little metal witch explains, slowing to a halt. "I couldn't really tell what he was, but he's just about as tall as all of you and wearing a long, dark cloak."

"A long, dark cloak? That doesn't sound so scary!" the ghost says. "We'll have to say hello."

"And welcome him to the house!" adds the vampire.

"Whatever you do, be mindful," says the Frankenstein candy bowl. "Perhaps some of the other decorations around the house know more, but that's all that we've heard about this new, cloaked gentleman."

The ghosts on the haunted house murmur in agreement.

"And of course," Frankenstein says warmly, "have yourselves a Happy Halloween!"

\* \* \*

The kids say their goodbyes to the Frankenstein candy stand and the inhabitants of the big haunted house. They file out of the foyer and continue on their quest for candy, heading toward the dining room.

The pumpkins in the patch on the tablecloth spring to life as they enter, their carved smiling faces breaking into even wider grins, while the bats on the candelabra in the middle of the table flap their wings in greeting.

"Hello!" they say. "Happy Halloween, kids!"

"Hello, pumpkins!" the scarecrow says back. "Happy Halloween to you, too!"

The four trick-or-treaters walk past the dining room table to the far side of the room, where the haunted Halloween village is set up on a buffet over a bright green cloth that's covered with a tattered, spooky fabric. A tractor hauling pumpkins counts down the days to Halloween out front, while a collection of houses and shops light up the room with their green and purple shine. A large haunted house rises out of the back, carefully positioned on an elevated platform overlooking the village, with trees and pumpkins placed throughout the scene. The little figures that live there - monsters, ghosts, witches and more - come and go as they please, waving to each other as they pass while eerie music plays softly in the background.

"They're here!" their little voices shout as the trick-or-treaters approach the display. "The trick-or-treaters are here!"

"Trick-or-treat!" they say softly, so as not to startle the little figures gathering at the front of the buffet.

"Tell us a joke!" the figurines say. "Tell us a joke!"

"Oh, you'll like this one," says the scarecrow. "Why did the scarecrow get an award?"

"Why?" they ask.

"Because he was out-standing in his field!" he says, sending a roar of laughs through the little Halloween town. The kids hold out their bags as the residents of the spooky village drop little pieces of candy for them to catch, giggling as they make a game out of it.

"My, what great costumes you all have," the witch from the

costume shop says sweetly once all the candy is passed out.

"Top notch," agrees the skeleton from the bell tower.

"Thank you," says the vampire. "We're having so much fun this year - and we hear there's even a new decoration in the family room for us to meet!"

"Oh," the scarecrow that drives the tractor says, walking over. "I've heard about him."

"You have?" asks the ghost.

"Yes," he says. "The ghosts in the graveyard say he carries a strange lantern unlike any they've seen before with a candle lit inside... isn't that right?"

The ghosts in the back of the village float to the edge of the display as the costume shop witch shudders.

"Beware..." one of the miniature ghosts says softly. "Beware..."

The four trick-or-treaters look from one to another before the vampire turns back toward the figures from the village.

"A dark cloak and a strange lantern? That doesn't sound so scary," he says confidently. "He might even be expecting us!"

"Yeah," says the witch. "After all, it's Halloween!"

"And speaking of," says the scarecrow, "we'd better be moving on. There's more candy to be had!"

The trick-or-treaters wave goodbye to the residents of the spooky village, thanking them for their treats as they go. And though most of the figures shout "Goodbye" and "Happy Halloween", one of the ghosts in the graveyard keeps saying "Beware..." long after the kids have gone.

\* \* \*

The next stop on their trek for treats is the kitchen, which is home to a collection of cardboard die-cut decorations: a trio of ghosts spin slowly from where they're hanging over the back door while a smaller ghost rides a broom over the kitchen table from where he's attached to the light fixture above; a black bat with crepe paper wings hangs in front of the hutch. Strands of Halloween lights with ghosts and pumpkins on them line the plant stand in front of the window and light up the room with a cozy radiance as the smell of a pumpkin medley candle lingers in the air.

"Trick-or-treat!" the kids say cheerfully, approaching the other decorations.

"Ohhhh, kids! Hello," says one of the ghosts over the back door, the one holding the candle.

"Happy Halloween!" says the ghost over the table while the bat over the china cabinet rustles his tissue paper wings. "What jokes do you have for us this year?"

"I've got one you'll really like," says the vampire. "What does a famous vampire get in the mail?"

"We don't know," the ghost with the candle says after checking with the others. "What?"

"Fang-mail!" the vampire says before the kids and die-cuts all burst into laughter.

"You kids are too cute," one of the ghosts says, dropping a few pieces of candy into each of the trick-or-treaters' open bags. "Are you having a great Halloween?"

"By the looks of those bags, I'd say so!" the third ghost says, with a laugh.

"Oh yes," says the witch. "We've already had great fun!"

"We visited with our friends in the foyer," says the ghost.

"And the dining room!" adds the vampire.

"Fantastic!" the bat on the china cabinet says.

"And we heard about the new decoration, too!" the scarecrow says excitedly. The die-cut ghosts stop spinning and face the kids at once.

"You've heard about him?" the long ghost says, to which the kids nod eagerly.

"We're excited to meet him!" says the witch.

"Then you've heard he doesn't have a face," says the ghost with the candle.

"W-what?" asks the scarecrow.

"Ah yes," says the bat. "It's true. I saw them bringing him in a few weeks ago... they said they got him at the market. And there's no face that I could see - only the hood of his cloak!"

The kids exchange an uncertain look between themselves before turning back to the die-cuts.

"Well," begins the vampire, "there's lots of decorations without faces! Like pumpkins before they're carved or spooky trees or - "

"That's true, little one," the bat cuts in, his voice squeaky. "But where there are bony hands, like the ones I saw he had, you'd think there'd be a face!"

"Hmm," the scarecrow says, looking at the others. "A long, dark cloak, a strange lantern, and he doesn't have a face? Maybe he *does* sound a little scary…"

"Now, now," the smallest ghost over the back door says to the others. "We don't want to frighten them!"

"Just be careful, is all," says the bat. From a few rooms away, they hear the chiming of the clock in the living room.

"Come on, friends," the witch says quickly. "We'd better keep going."

The trick-or-treaters thank the die-cuts for their candy and turn to leave the kitchen, with the cardboard ghosts and the bat calling "Happy Halloween" behind them as they go.

\* \* \*

The trick-or-treaters next make a stop in the first-floor powder room, which has a long strand of purple lights running up and down the vanity that bathes the little room in a mysterious shimmer. The lights illuminate a set of window clings that are carefully placed around the bathroom's mirror: a smiling jack-o-lantern in a pointed hat with stars, a witch on a broom, and a ghost leaping out of a pumpkin with stars and crescent moons of varying size scattered around the edge of the mirror.

"Trick-or-treat!" the kids say, entering the room.

"Oh, I thought I heard them coming!" the witch on the mirror says excitedly. "Happy Halloween, kids! Tell us a joke!"

"Knock, knock," says the ghost.

"Who's there?" asks the witch.

"Orange," he says.

"Orange, who?" she asks.

"Orange you glad it's Halloween!" he says with a chuckle. The clings pass out their candy, and the kids politely thank them. The jack-o-lantern can't help but notice something seems off.

"Everything alright, little ones?" he asks gently.

"Oh yes," begins the ghost, "we're having lots of fun!"

"It's just…" the vampire starts to say, but his voice trails off.

"Have you heard about the new decoration in the family room?" asks the ghost.

The clings lock eyes then look back to the kids.

"We have," the jack-o-lantern says. "And we were going to say something, but we didn't want to frighten you."

"Is he that scary?" asks the scarecrow.

"We haven't met him," the ghost in the pumpkin says, "but… oh, I'm not sure if we should say!"

"Say what?" asks the witch, clutching the pumpkin in her hand.

"Well," begins the jack-o-lantern, "he has a large scythe resting on his shoulder."

"A what?" asks the ghost.

"It's a big, hooked blade," explains the jack-o-lantern. The kids' eyes open wide.

"A long, dark cloak, a strange lantern, no face and he's carrying a scythe," the witch says. "The new decoration definitely sounds scary."

"M-maybe we should skip the family room this year," says the vampire. "I don't know if I like the sound of that."

"We've gotta stop and see Midnight," says the scarecrow. "But after that, maybe it's best if we return to the living room." The others nod their heads.

"Thanks for the treats," the ghost says as the kids leave the room. "And a Happy Halloween to all of you!"

\* \* \*

The last stop on the kids' trick-or-treat trail is the family room, home of the stuffed black cat with orange-striped socks and bright green tennis shoes known as Midnight as well as some decorative odds and ends. They enter the room quietly, looking nervously toward the mantle above the fireplace, but they don't see the new decoration. Luckily, Midnight sits right inside the entrance, flanked by two flickering lanterns.

"Trick-or-treat, Midnight," the kids say quietly.

"Happy Halloween, kids!" the black cat says, handing them their candy. "You may want to be getting a move on, I don't know if you've heard about…"

"We've heard about the new decoration on the fireplace," says the scarecrow. "That he wears a long, dark cloak."

"And he carries a strange lantern!" adds the ghost.

"We've heard he doesn't have a face," says the witch.

"And that he's got a big, curved blade that rests on his shoulder!" finishes the vampire.

Midnight nods solemnly.

"It's all true," says Midnight. "I'll tell you all, though, I haven't seen too much of him, he mostly keeps to himself up there."

"Well, these bags are getting pretty heavy," says the scarecrow, jostling his candy bag about. "I think we're gonna head back to the living room."

"That sounds like a good idea," agrees Midnight, and as he nods toward the mantel, the kids see a cloaked figure looking out from behind a plant.

"That must be him!" the scarecrow whispers quickly, the kids all grabbing one another's hands in fright. And though it was true that he didn't have a face, each of the four trick-or-treaters could feel him staring directly at them from across the room.

"Wait," says the ghost as the figure looks down, his shoulders slumping. "He… he almost looks kinda sad."

"Yeah," agrees the witch. "He does."

"Do you think he's sad we were about to go back to the living room without stopping to trick-or-treat at the fireplace?" asks the vampire.

"Maybe," says the scarecrow. "But there's only one way to find out… Halloween's for all of us, and that includes him!"

"We'll have to be brave!" adds the witch.

The others nod in agreement and hand-in-hand, the four costumed kids march across the family room toward the cloaked figure on top of the fireplace mantel, determined to make one last stop. Behind them, Midnight sits in his chair covering his face with his paws.

"Trick-or-treat!" the kids yell together when they reach the fireplace, while up on the mantel, the cloaked figure watches from behind the plant. For just a second, he keeps looking in their direction, then slowly ducks behind the leaves and out of sight.

"Maybe this was a bad idea?" the ghost whispers.

"Let's try it one more time," suggests the vampire. "We'll see if he comes back."

"Trick-or-treat!" the kids yell again, a little louder than before.

There's another shuffling in the leaves on the mantel, and the figure slowly emerges. His cloak is as dark as the metal witch in the foyer said, his lantern as strange as the scarecrow from the village warned. He has no face, just like the die-cut bat in the kitchen told them, and on his shoulder rests a menacing scythe, as the jack-o-lantern cling on the bathroom mirror said there'd be. He stands at the edge of the mantel, looking in their direction and just as they're about to turn and run, he jumps down to the hearth.

"Happy Halloween!" he says to the kids, his arms full of candy. "Oh, I was so worried I wasn't going to get any trick-or-treaters! Here, don't be shy!"

The figure passes out candy, treats, and more to each of the kids, filling their bags to the brim with all sorts of Halloween goodies.

"It's nice to meet you," says the ghost.

"Welcome to the house!" adds the vampire.

"Your black cloak matches my dress," the witch says.

"Do you want to hear a joke?" the scarecrow asks.

"Of course," he says. "I love a good joke!"

"What do birds say on Halloween?" he asks.

"Hmm... I don't know!" the new decoration says. "What?"

"Trick or tweet!" the scarecrow says, giggling as the new decoration doubles over with laughter. He laughs so much that the other kids join in; they can even hear Midnight nervously laughing from across the room.

"Thank you for the warm welcome, kids," he says, between laughs. "My name is Mr. Grim and I know I look scary, but I love Halloween just as much as all of you! It gets awfully lonely up there, so I'm extra glad you came to see me tonight."

"We're glad, too," says the vampire, struggling to hold his heavy candy bag.

"In fact," says the scarecrow, "wait right here. We'll be back in a few minutes!"

He grabs the other kids' hands and pulls them aside.

"I've got an idea," he says. "Let's get everyone together so they can meet Mr. Grim, too! Once they see how nice he is, they won't be so scared!"

The others agree, excited for the rest of the decorations to meet their new friend. They run from room to room, calling to the others to join them. And fortunately, with the kids' encouragement, the others don't need much convincing.

In no time at all, all of the Halloween decorations are gathered to meet Mr. Grim. From the skeletons in the living room to the Frankenstein candy dish, who carries all of the little figures from the Halloween village in his bowl, they all make their way to the family room. Midnight even helps bring the cardboard die-cuts from the kitchen and the clings on the bathroom mirror in to meet the new decoration.

"Attention everybody," says the scarecrow. "We'd like to introduce you to... Mr. Grim!"

A chorus of greetings rises from the group as Mr. Grim steps out from behind the plant on the mantel. and before long, he's been introduced to everyone. They spend the next few hours celebrating Halloween together, and just as dawn's first light starts to rise from the horizon, they all make their way back to their places until only the trick-or-treaters are left with Mr. Grim.

"Well, I have to say, you kids restored my Halloween spirit

tonight," Mr. Grim tells them. "I had just about given up on ever getting to celebrate with any of the others when you four showed up at the fireplace… so thank you. Tonight was everything I've ever hoped for in a Halloween celebration!"

The trick-or-treaters shout hooray before surrounding Mr. Grim in a big, group hug.

"Halloween *is* for all of us," says the vampire. "No matter if you're scary or not!"

"That's very true," Mr. Grim says with a smile. "And I hope you won't be strangers!"

"Of course not, Mr. Grim," says the ghost. "You're part of the family now! We'll come and see you all the time."

"Happy Halloween!" the witch says as they start back toward the coffee table in the living room. "This was our favorite Halloween yet, and we're glad to have met you."

"Yeah, we hope it was your best Halloween ever!" says the scarecrow. "Until next year, that is!"

# THE THIRTEENTH STORY

"Well, here we go... 'The Thirteenth Story'. The last story of the book," I say aloud. "Let's see what lies ahead in this one."

It's the night before Halloween, and, as so often happens when I get wrapped up in my books, I've lost track of the time and it's getting late. I shift a little, adjusting the fuzzy blanket that's covered in jack-o-lanterns so it's draped over my shoulders while taking care to hold my place in the book. The wind is picking up outside, and the clock on the wall says that it's a few minutes before midnight.

The three flames in the Pumpkin Harvest candle on the coffee table have burnt pretty low to the wick, and the wax is pooling at least an inch deep in the glass jar, so I blow them out. Wisps of smoke rise into the air, and I watch until the embers go out and the smoke stops, grabbing my mug of apple cider for a drink; it's lukewarm at best.

I'm sitting up in my chair, flipping from the first page of this last story to the cover of the book and back again.

*I've got time for one more,* I decide, sinking back into a comfortable reading position and finding my place on the page. *Besides, it's almost Halloween, and what better way to kick off my favorite holiday than by reading one last spooky story before bed. Now, let's see what this one is all about...*

"The Thirteenth Story" starts with a poem.

"On the eve of Halloween,
when the moon is at its peak,
three knocks will strike against your door
to embark on the 'venture you seek."

*Knock. Knock. Knock.*
"What?!" I say, snapping my head to face the door, still holding the book in my hands. I quickly glance down to the words on the page then lift my eyes back toward the door. The silence in the room is broken only by the occasional rustle of wind from outside.

"It can't be," I say, my voice hanging in the air. "I mean, it's late, I'm tired… it's getting windy outside, maybe… maybe that had something to do with what I heard- what I *think* I heard…"

I sit for a moment, getting lost in thought with the book resting in my lap, and I've just about convinced myself that I didn't hear what I heard and I should probably go ahead and call it a night when I hear it again.

*Knock. Knock. Knock.*
The unmistakable sound of three knocks at my door, just like the opening verse of the poem in "The Thirteenth Story".

"It's not possible," I say, jumping up from the chair. I toss the book behind me and walk toward the door. When I get there, my hand starts to tremble as I reach to open it.

In one quick motion, I unlock the handle, twist it, and fling the door open. There's no one there, so I step over the threshold and into the cool, night air. I'm barefoot and still wrapped in the fuzzy blanket.

"Hello?" I call softly; it's almost midnight after all, I'm not trying to wake anyone up. "Who's there?"

I stand for a minute and look around, to the left and the right, but I see no one.

*Oh Lord,* I finally think to myself, shaking my head. *You've become one of those people in a scary movie: totally exposed, standing at the door and asking 'Who's there?' like an idiot. It's time to go to bed.*

And just as I'm about to go back inside, something on the ground catches my eye. It's small, like a little paper scroll, and I would have missed it entirely if not for the glimmer of the string it's tied with.

"What's this?" I mutter, kneeling to pick it up. I carefully untie the string, jamming it into my pocket before unrolling the note, and reading aloud:

> "On the eve of Halloween,
> when the moon is at its peak - "

I inhale sharply as my mouth drops open and I stop reading the handwritten note.

"No way!" I whisper, my heart racing as I frantically look around. Still, I am alone. "This has to be some kind of prank! It's the poem from the book but... but.... how?!"

I hold the paper taut in my trembling hands; I look down and keep reading.

> "On the eve of Halloween,
> when the moon is at its peak,
> three knocks will strike against your door
> to embark on the 'venture you seek.
>
> With a midnight stone to guard you
> and a guide to lead the way,
> you'll collect the wares together
> that deliver this hallow'd day:
>
> A ticket to the midway
> and a flower most blood-red,
> a piece of crumbling headstone,
> and a spellbook page well-tread.
> Then last a spectral talisman
> and before the night's complete,
> bind them all with once-charmed thread,
> 'else there be neither trick nor treat."

I flip the weathered paper over, but there's nothing else written on it. I pull the blanket tighter around myself, and though it offers a momentary sense of safety, the relief it brings is fleeting.

"'To embark on the 'venture I seek'?" I reread to myself slowly. "What's going on? Who put this here?"

Again, I find myself about to turn around and go inside, convinced that all of this, whatever *this* is, is just a figment of a tired mind with an overactive imagination that's been stimulated by one too many spooky short stories on the night before Halloween. But as I turn back to the door, I kick something on the ground with my left foot. Whatever it was makes a clunking noise against the door.

"Ow!" I yelp, jumping back, the note still clinched in my hand. It didn't really hurt and what little pain there was from stubbing my toe is gone as quickly as it hit. I screamed more from surprise than anything. "What was that?"

I look around to see if I can figure out what it was that I kicked, and after a quick scan of the area, I see it: a drawstring, black velvet pouch.

*Now what's this?* I think, picking it up and looking at it closely. I open the pouch and hold it upside down; a strange, dark blue stone falls into my hand. The oddly-shaped stone is covered in tiny crystals, with rough edges that sparkle even in the darkness of the night. With the stone in one hand and the note still in the other, the clock inside begins to chime. It's midnight...

"A midnight stone!" I say in shock. "W-what..."

A gust of wind rises and I hear a curious murmur from down the way. I spin around to see what's going on, and when I see it, I jump, my breath catching in my chest as my hands go numb. There's a person standing in the glow of the streetlight at the corner wearing a dark, hooded cloak. They're no taller than me and they're facing my direction.

I breathe quick, shallow breaths and inch toward the door, afraid to take my eyes off of whoever this is staring me down. Slowly, the figure nods their head toward me and holds out an arm, gesturing toward itself.

"Is this yours?" I call, holding out the pouch. The cloaked figure doesn't answer, just standing there, slowly beckoning me to come closer. I'm not sure who's under that cloak, but it starts to dawn on me that it's gotta be someone I know, one of my friends pulling a prank or maybe even a neighbor or someone I mentioned reading this book to.

"Okay, very funny," I say. "If the bag and the stone are yours, you can have them back. This note, too."

Again, the person in the cloak says nothing.

"Hold on, I'll be right back."

I run inside to grab a pair of shoes and my drawstring bag before throwing on a jacket. I step out into the night and pull the door shut behind me, eager to return everything and get back inside. But when I look toward the corner, my heart skips a beat as I see that the cloaked figure is now turned away from me.

*Oh, come on,* I think. *What am I doing?! I'm going back inside and going to bed right n -*

"This way," a whisper of words interrupts my train of thought, almost as if they were spoken by the wind itself.

"W-what is going on?!" I yell to the cloaked figure, no longer worrying about who hears me.

"This way," I hear the words repeated. "Follow me."

"Absolutely not," I say. "I'm done with this."

The wind picks up again, blowing the leaves around. It's hard to explain, but with it, I feel something in my chest, like a rising sense of... courage? Adventure? Or maybe just bold stupidity.

*This feels like something out of that book,* I think excitedly. *Besides, there's no way I'm falling asleep now, and if I need it, my cell's got enough of a charge.* I reach into my bag to make sure my phone's there.

"Alright," I say, slipping the bag over my shoulders. "Where are we going?"

For a moment, there's silence, and then I hear it again as the figure starts walking away.

"Follow me."

*Well, here goes nothing...*

I follow the figure up the street and out of the neighborhood. I try to quicken my pace to catch up, but whoever's in the cloak increases theirs in time with my own so that we're always a good distance from each other. We wind through the maze of neighborhoods, each as dimly lit as the next, marching past one dark house after another until I start to wonder if they have a destination in mind at all.

The night is quiet except for the sound of the wind through the trees. No cars pass, no dogs bark. It's as though the whole world has gone to sleep.

The figure turns a corner and I realize where we're heading: the neighborhood grade school a few blocks over that sits right on the edge of the town square.

I stop for a moment to catch my breath. With a deep inhale, I set off again, but when I reach the corner and turn toward the school, I don't see the person in the cloak anywhere.

"Hello?" I whisper as loudly as I can, straining to see through the chain link fence that surrounds the school. No one answers, so I walk a little closer, and as I approach the parking lot, I realize the school has a carnival set up.

Striped tents rise from the black-topped pavement with flickering light strands zig-zagging between them. Beyond the lot, a collection of carnival rides glow from the soccer field, their bulbs twinkling like a welcoming invitation for riders. An old calliope plays over a crackly speaker from deep within the carnival and I can just make out the sugary smells of caramel corn and funnel cakes.

"Must be getting ready for their Halloween carnival," I say quietly. "I wonder what we're doing here?"

As if on cue, the wind gusts again and I hear that whispery voice.

"Get the ticket."

I spin around, but there's no one there. The hair on the back of my neck stands up and I shiver.

"What ticket?" I say into the night.

"Get the ticket."

I stand for a moment, trying to figure out what ticket I'm supposed to be getting when I remember something... something from the poem. I grab the rolled-up piece of paper from my bag, skimming through the poem written on it until I reach the line I'm looking for.

"'Then collect the wares together that deliver this hallow'd day'," I read aloud. And the first item on that list?

"A ticket to the midway," I say, nodding. I look up to the carnival and back down to the paper in my hands. "I guess I'm on some kind of a scavenger hunt... and I know just where I can get that first item."

I set off toward the ticket booth at the entrance to the parking lot, carefully rolling the paper and putting it away.

*It's so late... I wonder if anyone's even going to be here.*

As I get closer to the booth, I realize that there's a dingy light on inside with someone sitting behind the counter.

"Hello," I say, walking up to the booth. Through the plexiglass front, I take a look at the man inside. He sits leaned back on a folding chair, one leg crossed over the other and holding up a newspaper that blocks his entire head and torso. He doesn't move or react to me at all.

"Hello?" I say again, this time a little louder in case he's hard of hearing.

"We're not open," the man says in a gruff voice from behind the newspaper.

"Oh, that's okay," I say. "I was actually wondering - "

"I said we're not open," he growls, rustling the paper. "Come back tomorrow."

"Sure thing, yeah, it's just... I was actually wondering if I would be able to, uhm... get a ticket?" I sputter.

The man uncrosses his legs and sits up, still holding the newspaper in front of his face.

"A ticket," he repeats in a low, throaty growl.

"Yeah," I say. "A ticket to the midway."

The man slowly lowers the newspaper to reveal his greasepaint-smeared face. He's wearing tattered, striped overalls with a stained shirt underneath and a grimy blue wig on his head.

*A clown!* I think, suddenly becoming acutely aware of just how quickly my heart is beating. *I didn't think these little school carnivals usually had clowns.*

The clown carefully folds his newspaper and sets it on the counter in front of him. He straightens his wig and slowly looks me up and down before meeting my gaze.

"A ticket to the midway, huh?" he finally asks, and I nod in response. The song playing over the speakers ends and the few seconds before the music starts again stretch on for what feels like hours of silence. I do my best to smile at the clown in the booth, but I can't ignore the uneasy feeling in my stomach.

"Wait right here," he finally says, breaking into a yellowed, toothy grin that causes his makeup to crack further. He steps backward, deeper into the booth and the light inside flickers before going out altogether.

*Where is he going?* I think, confused and unsettled by the whole interaction.

I stand for a few minutes outside of the booth, waiting for the clown to come back. The night air gets cooler, and I zip up my jacket. The music playing over the speakers ends and another song begins, this one slower and somehow even more unnerving.

I walk around to the back of the ticket booth to see if I can find anyone else, but there's no one there. Looking around the dimly lit midway, I come to realize that I am alone; it seems there's no one else at this carnival.

*Well if they're closed, and there's no one here... then what was that guy doing in the ticket booth?* I think.

I breathe out a deep sigh and fold my arms across my chest, shifting my weight from one leg to the other. For whatever reason, I can't shake that uneasy feeling and just when I've about convinced myself to turn around, run home, and forget this whole thing, I hear it: the laughter.

It starts as a single, low chuckle coming from behind the ticket booth that's quickly joined by others: a high-pitched giggle, an ominous snicker, a wicked guffaw. They get louder and louder until I'm surrounded by a symphony of this diabolical laughter, though I can't see anyone around me.

"Hello," I say firmly, hoping I sound braver than I feel.

A loud metal clanking rings out, like something heavy fell to the pavement, and I see sparks low to the ground in the distant shadows.

"Okay, I'm out of here," I say, but before I can take a single step, the bulbs strung up all over the carnival jump to their full brightness with a jolt, the air buzzing with electricity. And as my eyes adjust, I see the line of clowns in the distance.

There are at least five, maybe six, and I can just make out their paint-smeared faces that are twisted into evil grins. One of them is bald except for a pile of lime green hair on top of his head like scoops from an ice cream cone; another has rainbow pigtails and has an oversized mallet resting on her shoulder. There's a tall one wearing a dirty polka-dotted jumpsuit that's dragging a shovel with a trail of sparks flying behind him as the group advances toward me. And with a shock, I recognize the clown from the ticket booth leading the way.

"Forget this!" I yell, turning to run back down the street, but when I get to the ticket booth's side, there are two more clowns walking toward me from the entrance to the school's parking lot. They're dressed identically, twin girls with ruffled skirts and oversized bows sitting askew in their tangled wigs. Their arms are linked side-by-side and each is twirling one end of a chain with their free hand; they're staring right at me, laughing through the same devilish grin as the others. I slowly back away from them, and the realization that I might be backing right into the other group of clowns sends a sour taste from the back of my tongue down through my throat.

I steal a glance over my shoulder and see that the line of clowns is picking up their pace. They're far enough away, but they'll be at the ticket booth within the minute, by which point the twins will have me tied up with that chain. I decide to run.

I have no destination in mind, only needing to get as far from this carnival and these freaky clowns as fast as I can. My shoes beat the pavement, one foot down and then the other; I'm running faster than I ever have in my life, dodging tent after tent, hoping to have lost the clowns. I decide to head toward the field with the rides, hoping I'll be able to slip out of the carnival on the far side of the school.

I race down the midway, the lights streaming by overhead, and stop to catch my breath on the field, listening carefully as I'm crouched behind a carousel. In the distance, I hear shouts among the old carnival music that continues to play over the speakers.

"Which way?"

"This way!"

"Come on!"

*I've gotta get out of here,* I think, looking around. Just as I had thought, the school's far field does butt right up to one of the town's squares, but as I quickly take stock of the situation, my heart sinks. The field is surrounded by a tall fence, and the clowns are getting closer.

*I'll hide until they go back,* I think, turning to run. *The train? Too small... the funhouse? No, I'd be trapped in there if they found me... what about...*

My thoughts stop abruptly as I catch sight of something standing next to the Ferris wheel. Something... or someone!

The cloaked figure!

My heart skips a beat as I take off toward the Ferris wheel at the far edge of the field, hoping to catch whoever is in that cloak before they disappear again. I'm almost there when I peek over my shoulder to make sure the clowns haven't spotted me yet, and when I turn back the figure has vanished.

*No!* I think desperately.

As the clowns reach the field, I slide underneath the Ferris wheel's operator perch and try to slow my breathing. Listening intently, I can just make out their shouts.

"Spread out..."

"...can't have gone far..."

Just then, the wind picks up and I hear that familiar whisper.

"Get the ticket."

I try to look out from under the ride, but I don't see anyone - no clowns and no mysterious figure either. I decide my best bet is to make a run for it and climb over the school's fence. I carefully poke my head out from under the Ferris wheel, looking in every direction to make sure the coast is clear when something catches my eye from across the street.

*How'd they get over there so fast?* I think, my eyes just able to make out the person in the dark cloak standing across the street from the carnival. *And how'd they get over the fence?!*

"Hey," I whisper as urgently as I can, waving to get their attention. "Over here! Help!"

The figure stands there.

"Get the ticket."

*What's so important about this stupid ticket,* I think. *I need to get out of here! How am I supposed to get away from these maniacs, I...* my thoughts trail off when I notice the Ferris wheel's ticket collection canister.

"I wonder..." I say aloud.

I slowly rise to my feet and sneak toward the bucket as quietly as I can. I lift the lid and peer inside, seeing nothing but ripped and discarded ride tickets. But right when I'm about to replace the lid, a reflection of something in the tube catches my eye. I brush a few of the ripped ones aside, revealing an ornate, gilded ticket that's at least triple the size of the rest with the words "Admit One" written across the front in old, curlicue writing.

"This must be it," I whisper to myself, reaching to grab it. It's heavy, like thick cardboard, and almost warm to the touch. And just as I pull the ticket from the can, I feel a vibration start in my bag.

*What's going on?!* I think, frantically trying to make sense of the situation. I pull open the drawstring bag, carefully placing the ticket inside. Something is still rattling around in there, so I reach in and am surprised to find the vibrations are coming from the midnight stone.

"What *is* this thing?!" I say, pulling it out for a closer look. It continues to pulsate in my hand, increasing in frequency until I can barely hold it.

"Ahh!" I yelp in surprise as the stone suddenly leaps from my hand toward the nearby fence. Through the darkness, I hear the sounds of metal grinding and the links of the fence popping apart. I hurry over to see what's going on and am surprised to find a fresh cut in the fence, just big enough for me to get through, and the midnight stone on the ground, no longer pulsing.

"Thank you, whatever you are," I say, picking up the stone and dropping it back into my bag. I squeeze through the fence, being careful not to jostle the chain-link too much. Once I'm on the other side, I waste no time running after the person in the cloak, being careful to stay in the shadows and out of the clowns' line of vision.

After I've made it a good distance away, I stop to look back at the carnival. The clowns have reached the Ferris wheel, but none are looking toward the fence, none are looking in my direction at all. Soon after, they disappear from view, retreating toward the midway.

*They must not see where it's cut,* I think with relief. *They don't know I'm gone.*

I continue on, wanting to put as much distance between myself and that horrible carnival as I can.

"That's enough excitement for one night," I say to myself with every intention of going home, but then I hear a fresh round of sinister laughter erupting into the night followed by a loud clanking. With a sick feeling in my stomach, I realize the clowns must have found the opening in the fence and it won't be long before they're after me again.

Before I can even think of a plan, I catch a glimpse of that person in the cloak ducking into the old theater across the square.

"This way," I hear in the wind. "Follow me."

There's still time before the clowns catch up to where I'm at now, and the theater's dark; they won't know I'm there.

*Why not,* I think. *Seems as good a place to hide as any.*

With a quick look around to make sure I'm in the clear, I make a beeline for the old theater, hoping I won't need to hide out there for too long. I cut through the center of the square, up the sidewalk and under the marquee, stopping only to yank open the door the figure had used to enter, quickly jumping inside.

As the door closes, an odd silence descends around me. It's as though the entire outside world has been blocked out, sounds and all. I struggle to look through the tinted glass; it's so dark but I don't think any of the clowns saw me come in. I turn around to look for the person in the cloak and assess my musty surroundings.

The theater's lobby is dimly lit by a few wall sconces. The old carpet is worn, the striped wallpaper is peeling, and at the far end of the lobby is an old snack stand that's covered in cobwebs. There's no sign of the cloaked figure.

*This place is pretty rundown,* I think. *Actually... how long has it been here? I... I don't think I've ever noticed it before tonight.*

From somewhere deep within the theater, I hear the muffled sound of applause followed by the haunting melodies of an orchestra warming up.

"Is there a show going on?" I wonder aloud. "At this time of night?"

I start to walk toward the double doors at the far end of the room when a woman's voice calls out through the silence.

"What are you doing out here?!"

I freeze, my heart pounding.

"Hello," she says. "I'm talking to you!"

I slowly turn around and see a short woman, dressed in black from head to toe with a stern look on her face and a clipboard at her side.

"I'll ask you once more... *what* are you doing out here?!"

"I... uh... got lost?" I hear myself saying, hoping that the less I say will be to my benefit.

She quickly looks me up and down and then sighs.

"Oh," she finally says with a light chuckle. "It happens. This is a big, old theater... lots of corridors and corners, all the new blood gets lost! Don't fret, it happens."

I force a smile.

"Now, come with me," she says. "The show's starting and we've got work to do."

*The show?* I think. *Work?*

She leads me through the double doors at the far end of the lobby, shaking her head at the state of the snack counter as we rush past. She asks me my name, so I make one up and then she introduces herself to me as Mrs. Babington-Whitby.

"I'm the house manager," she explains. "So I'm responsible for making sure tonight's show goes off without a hitch! Which, as I'm sure you can imagine, is *quite* the undertaking…"

"The… show?" I ask.

"Yes," she says, stopping and turning around to face me so quickly I almost bump into her. "The show! The annual Eve of Halloween performance… and our *special* task? We covered this at the pre-show?"

"Oh," I say, trying to laugh it off. "That's right. I, uh, forgot."

"Honestly, I don't know where they find these people," she mutters to herself, shaking her head as she looks me up and down. She sighs and turns around. "No matter! We have to get downstairs; the first act will be finishing up soon enough."

I follow her through another door and down a set of winding stairs, deeper into the theater. After two, maybe three flights, the steps end at a gloomy landing with old marble floors and we reach what I'm guessing is the basement of the theater.

"Hey," I start, "I must have gotten a little mixed up when I got lost. Sorry, um, if you don't mind going over it again… w-what's going on here tonight?"

She turns to face me, her annoyed expression breaking into a soft smile.

"You weren't at the pre-show lineup, were you?" she asks.

"No," I admit. "I'm sorry, I got pretty turned around as soon as I got here."

"It's okay," she says, patting my shoulder. "Well, it's the Eve of Halloween, you know. The night when the veil between the worlds of the mortal and supernatural is at its thinnest… when one can spill into the other? I'm sure you know all about it…"

I nod as she keeps talking, though I'm starting to think she's making it all up.

"But of course, there's the ritual… and the five enchanted wares that reinforces the barrier to keep that from happening. Which is *why* we have to protect the blood-red flower…"

*Wait… wares? Flower?! That's… that's… from the poem! But if she knows about all of that, then that would mean…*

"Right?" she asks with a threatening sweetness, her fingertips now digging into my shoulder and snapping me from my thoughts. "You haven't seen anyone suspicious around that could be here to steal it, do you? The one chosen to collect the items and perform the ritual... keep the veil between the worlds strong enough to preserve Halloween for the mortals? Because it so rarely happens that the Countess Dragavei finds the flower in her possession from the Delegation and so help me, if I'm the one responsible for its loss, I... I... I don't know what she would do!"

Mrs. Babington-Whitby lets go of my shoulder with an almost hysterical squeak and continues on.

Suddenly, everything starts to make sense. The knock at the door, the figure, what happened at the carnival... *I* must be the person she's talking about! The one chosen to gather the items in the poem and keep the supernatural world from spilling into our own and, apparently, saving Halloween in the process.

I subtly shrug my shoulders to adjust the drawstring bag on my back, feeling for both the midnight stone in its pouch and the ticket for reassurance before taking a quick look back up the stairs. I'm trying to remember the route we've taken in case I need to double back to the lobby on my own. Suddenly, I can hear the low rumble of applause from far away.

*She's not kidding,* I think. *There must be a ton of people up there!*

"Well, that'll be the first intermission," Mrs. Babington-Whitby says just as the thunderous sound of footsteps erupts above us. "She'll be waiting for us, come on."

She takes off again, leading me down one hall after another until I'm so turned around in this maze of a basement that I'm not sure I could find my back to the lobby without a trail of breadcrumbs. We finally reach a door with a sign that reads "Authorized Personnel Only", which she pushes open without hesitation and barrels through.

*I guess we're authorized,* I think, though I'm still keenly aware of the surroundings.

Behind the door feels like another world entirely. Where the theater's basement was almost cozy between the low lights and lush carpeting, the backstage area is sterile with nothing but concrete floors and cinder block walls, though it's as dimly lit as the rest of the theater with low level fluorescent lights lining the ceiling. I continue in her wake as she flips from one page of her clipboard to the next, muttering to herself, until we stop at a door with a man, also dressed all in black, sitting next to it on a stool.

"Is she in there?" Mrs. Babington-Whitby asks.

The man grunts in reply, nodding as he opens the door.

"You're dismissed," she says to him before turning back to me. "You can come in with me, but stand just inside the door. We shouldn't be in here too long."

Stepping into what I assume to be Countess Dragavei's dressing room is like moving from one part of a dream to the next. The air is heavy with the scent of an old perfume and there are tall racks of gowns scattered about the space which make it hard to see the other side of the room. I can just make out a woman in a sheer black dressing robe with feathers along the trim. She's sprawled across a velvet chaise with a heavy looking goblet in her hand, though I can't see her face. Mrs. Babington-Whitby slips around one of the racks, and I decide to heed her advice and stay just inside the door.

"How was the first act?" she asks quietly.

"Don't talk to me about the show until the show is over," the woman says slowly, her voice deep with a heavy accent. She swirls whatever liquid is in the goblet. "We've been over this, pet."

"Yes, Countess Dragavei," Mrs. Babington-Whitby replies quickly. "My apologies."

"Stop sniveling," the Countess says. "We have a magpie in our midst."

"A-a magpie?"

"Yes," says the Countess, sitting up. "I have received word that the ticket has been collected. Those clowns failed like I knew they would, and whoever got it would feasibly be on their way here to get the flower."

"But, i-it's so well guarded, ma'am," Mrs. Babington-Whitby

says. "How would anyone be able to..."

"Quiet," Countess Dragavei says, raising her hand. "Do I smell fresh blood?"

*Me! She must be smelling me!* I think, panicked.

"Yes, I have one of the stage hands with me, to, uhm, help with..."

"Shh," the Countess says, quieting the house manager. "Bring the little lamb to me."

Mrs. Babington-Whitby emerges from around the dress racks, looking at me sorrowfully before she pushes one of them aside, and suddenly I'm staring at Countess Dragavei. Though her face is half hidden by the metallic glass she's drinking from, her eyes are locked intently on me. She is deathly pale with raven black hair, and as she finally lowers the goblet, I see that she has two fangs that protrude over her lower lip. Whatever she's drinking has left a red stain around her mouth.

"Well, hello there," she says, smiling. "Is this your first experience with the vampire theater?"

Transfixed by her gaze and suddenly feeling lethargic, I nod slowly.

"Ahh... I thought as much. Come closer, pet."

My eyelids start to feel heavy and my legs move on instinct alone, one and then the other to get me across the room. My breathing is slow and methodical.

I'm sitting, my lips parted and my hands resting in my lap.

I'm sinking into the plush furniture, the chaise; the Countess is grinning at me, her pointed fangs bared.

*What... what's going... on?* I think. It's as though my body's moving in slow motion, even my thoughts.

Countess Dragavei sets the goblet on the small table next to the lounge and turns to me, her ice cold hand grazing my cheek.

"Is it smart to... snack before the second act, ma'am?" Mrs. Babington-Whitby says, her voice cutting through the room. The Countess whips her face toward her.

"I will do as I please," she says threateningly. "Besides, I'm not due back on stage until the fourth number of the second act... and there's plenty of time before the feast at the grand finale. There's nothing wrong with… a sip."

I'm paralyzed to move as she turns back to face me, a beastly grin stretched across her pale face.

*She's a vampire!* I think with panic rising in my brain though my body is powerless to react. *And I… I'm not gonna make it out of here!*

"Shh," she coos to me. "You won't feel a thing, little lamb… a quick sting, perhaps, a lingering tingle…"

Countess Dragavei gently pushes my face to the side, exposing my neck and facing me toward her vanity. I try to focus on the items scattered around it to distract my mind from what's about to happen. There are several mannequin heads with wigs in various colors and styles, ornate bottles of perfume, brushes, combs… and a beautiful flower in the middle of it all, delicately positioned with petals I could only describe as the deepest blood-red.

*A flower… most blood-red,* I think slowly. *A flower most blood red!*

"Take the flower," I hear a voice whisper.

I strain my eyes to look, but neither Countess Dragavei nor Mrs. Babington-Whitby heard what I heard. The Countess is breathing on my neck and I'm suddenly very aware of my surroundings. The feeling returns to my limbs and whatever trance I was under starts to break.

*The flower is* right *there! If I could just…*

"Grrraaah!" I finally shout. Breaking free of my stupor, I raise my arms and shove the Countess away, knocking her into the goblet on the side table, splashing what I now see to be blood across her dressing gown and onto the carpet. Without stopping to look, I leap from the chaise and grab the flower from the vanity. Mrs. Babington-Whitby has rushed to help the Countess up, though they're still in the way for me to make a break for the door.

"No!" she roars. "The flower! Secure the flower!"

Mrs. Babington-Whitby opens her mouth, hissing as fangs slide down from her gums.

"I should have known when I found you in the lobby," she says with menace. "Now give me that flower and we'll let you go…"

As she's talking, I again start to feel a strange vibration in my drawstring bag.

"You need to keep this safe, right?" I say.

"It's of no use to us," the Countess says.

"You're lying," I say, mustering all the courage I can. "I know you're lying… if all you needed to do was keep me from getting this flower, you could come and take it. But that's not all there is to it, is there… once I've got it, you *can't* take it, can you?"

Countess Dragavei growls, shooting a furious look toward Mrs. Babington-Whitby.

I slowly grab my bag, not taking my eyes off of either of the vampires in the room. I open it and softly push the flower inside, being careful to keep it intact. I feel around in the bag for the vibrating midnight stone and wrap my hand around it.

"No," the Countess says, "but we can get you!"

She nods to Mrs. Babington-Whitby, who leaps toward me with a snarl, her hands outstretched like claws. Instinctively, I pull my hand out of the bag to shield my face, but as I open my fingers, an incredible light bursts forth, causing Mrs. Babington-Whitby to recoil, screeching. I clench my hand around the stone and the light disappears.

*The midnight stone!* I think, looking at my fist. *It cut the fence, and now… and now…*

I face the vampires.

"Get out of my way," I say.

Countess Dragavei stands to face me, blood now smeared across her mouth.

"You're in no position to make demands down he - "

I open my hand and again the incredible light explodes from the midnight stone. Both vampires howl as they retreat from the light, their fangs bared as they try to cover their faces, the skin on the back of their hands blistering in the light.

"I think I am," I say. I back toward the door as quickly as I can, holding the stone in my hand to aim the light toward the vampires. I feel for the handle behind me and with a last burst of energy, fling the door to jump out.

After it shuts, I can still hear the two vampires shrieking in the dressing room.

*They should know better than to pursue,* I reassure myself. I quickly assess my surroundings. *I could go back the way I came, and risk getting lost in the maze of hallways that make up this theater, not to mention who knows what I'd run into...*

I look the other way, where the hallway extends into darkness.

*I could always take my chances down there,* I think, feeling the midnight stone in my hand. *If I could just -*

My thoughts are interrupted by the sudden, chilling sound of several footsteps approaching from where only a short time ago Mrs. Babington-Whitby had led me to what was almost my doom. I can't make out what they're saying, but there's a good number of them... and they sound angry.

"I'm taking my chances," I say, and start to run further down the hall. I look at the stone in my palm and am relieved to see it's still emitting a little bit of light.

*I guess it dims the further I get from the vampires,* I deduce. I raise my hand and hold up the stone to light the way as I round one corner and then another, the lights in this subterranean tunnel getting dimmer as I go. I can still hear a bit of the commotion behind me; whoever was coming to their aid had probably found the Countess and Mrs. Babington-Whitby by now.

*I need to find some stairs and get out of here,* I think. I keep running until the light from the stone goes out and I find myself barely able to see through the darkness. I stop to put the stone back in my bag and when I do, I remember that I've got my cell phone with me. I grab it out, but just as I figured, I have no service.

"At least the light still works," I say, turning on the phone's flashlight and continuing down the hall. It's been quite some time since I turned the last corner and this hallway has continued on for much longer than I thought it would, but I keep going. I can't stop thinking about what happened in that dressing room, but then my mind races back to the carnival! That already feels like it happened days, if not weeks, ago.

And even though I'm thoroughly freaked out by everything

that's happened so far tonight, I can't deny there's a little part of me that's excited by the prospect of it all.

*I mean, who gets to say they've had an adventure like this?* I think to myself. *And save Halloween in the process? It's seriously like something out of that book!*

I keep walking. Once or twice, I think I see the outline of that cloaked figure ahead of me. At one point, I even call out to them to slow down so I can catch up, but there's never anyone there. And just as I start to wonder if I'm even under the theater anymore, I hear a slow, steady dripping noise that stops me in my tracks.

"Where am I?" I say, looking around. I'm unable to see anything clearly beyond the foot or so of light from my phone, so I walk toward the wall and jump back in horror when I realize that the cinder block walls of the theater's basement are now the jagged rock of a pitch-dark cave. When I aim the light to the floor, I'm just as surprised to see that the ground is still the concrete of the hallway, but it's not long after I continue on that the concrete ends and the soft dirt of the cave stretches on into the darkness.

*Nowhere to go but forward,* I think, tightening the drawstring of my bag and again holding up the light.

I continue on into the cave, checking to see if I have any cell phone service every few minutes, but of course, I don't and what little excitement I'd found is giving way to a rising panic in my chest. The air is heavy, damp, and stale at the same time. It's stifling and my pace is slowing with each step.

*What if no one ever finds me?* I think. *What if I never get out of here?*

I'm trying not to, but I'm falling deeper and deeper into my thoughts, so much so that I almost don't notice when the dirt under my shoes becomes a cobblestone pavement.

*This was put here!* I think, jumping up from taking a closer look. Reinvigorated by the prospect of reaching the cave's exit, I again start to run, continuing on until I find myself at the base of a stone staircase. I carefully put my foot on the first step, and then the next to make sure it's safe.

The stone staircase is solid.

Satisfied that I won't fall through, I start going up the stairs, taking one and then two at a time until I reach a landing with a heavy door. I use the light to find the door's handle and then put my phone away, not wanting to immediately announce my presence in whatever room I'm about to walk into.

The latch creaks and the door groans as I push it open, any hope of quietly sneaking into this room now gone. I peek around the corner and am immediately greeted by thick cobwebs. I step into the room and as soon as I take my hand off the door, it slams shut behind me.

*So much for silence,* I think, looking around anxiously. Thankfully, it doesn't seem like the noise has attracted any unwanted attention. Nothing shifts, nothing moves. I look around the room a little more when suddenly the realization hits.

I'm standing in what appears to be a crypt.

"Oh no, no, no, no," I say out loud, rushing toward the door. Thankfully, it's not locked and I'm easily able to slip outside, escaping the mausoleum as quickly as I found myself in it.

Gulping in the fresh air, I see the moon is still high in the sky, casting just enough light that I can make out shapes through the darkness. I'm trying to make sense of my surroundings when it hits me: I'm in the middle of an old graveyard. It's not very big, just a few dozen or so simple headstones, and I can see the spindly, wrought iron fence that surrounds the property.

*How far did that tunnel go?!* I think, panicked. The night is quiet except the occasional rustle of leaves from the breeze. *This must be where I get the next ware.*

I pull the rolled paper from my bag and re-read the poem.

"A piece of crumbling headstone shouldn't be too hard to find around here," I say, putting the scroll away. I walk down the steps from the crypt, standing in place for a moment to make sure I'm alone. After the ordeal with the clowns and then the vampires, I don't know what I'm expecting in this graveyard, but it's almost more unsettling that the night is so still, so quiet.

I can't shake the feeling that something's waiting for me.

Setting out into the graveyard, I don't know if there's a specific headstone I should be looking for or not. I can barely make out any of the markings or names carved on them. They're all very old, weathered by both the elements and time itself. I don't want to vandalize any of them, let alone take a piece from the wrong one.

I wander back and forth through the graveyard, trying to decide what to do. I'm about to give up and just pick one to break a piece off from when I notice one headstone in particular. It's just as worn as the rest, but something about it just shines in the night. I walk over to take a closer look, being careful not to step on any of the graves.

Like all the others, the lettering on the headstone is worn with moss growing all around it. It's about three feet tall with an eroded cross rising from the middle and two spire-like postcaps on either side, though the one on the left is only half as tall as the other.

*Hey wait!* I think. *If that piece is broken off, maybe it's somewhere nearby!*

I use the light from my phone to search the ground near the headstone, and it's not long before I find what I'm looking for.

"Perfect," I say as the light shines on the piece of broken headstone, resting in the dewey grass as though someone carelessly tossed it aside centuries ago.

"I don't know who this guy was," I say, nodding toward the headstone, "but he's sure been helpful tonight!" I kneel down to pick up the broken piece and just as my fingertips touch the old stone, a hand bursts from the ground and grabs my wrist.

"Hey!" I shout as a reflex, trying to pull myself away, but the decayed hand has an ironclad grip. I look around wildly, trying to figure out what's going on, and to my horror, hands like the one that's got a hold on me are popping up all over the graveyard, sending dirt and grass flying in every direction. I can hear low groans coming from deep beneath the ground.

I watch, eyes wide and frozen in horror as the hands around the graveyard push at the ground beneath them. They claw away at the earth, digging themselves from their graves until the rotted faces of the undead are rising, their mouths gasping in the night air as they crawl from the ground.

"Zombies?!" I scream, continuing to struggle against the hand that's gripping my wrist. I yank my arm away using all of my strength and with a sickening crack, I break free and fall backwards to the ground. The hand is still gripping my wrist and it takes a few tries, but I'm able to pry it off, throwing it as far away as I can. From far off, the door to the mausoleum creaks as it opens; I can only imagine how many more are about to come stumbling out.

And like a punch to the gut, I realize that in the chaos of the last few minutes, I've lost both my phone and the piece of headstone.

"Ahh, where'd it go, where'd it go," I shout, feeling around on the ground for either, careful to avoid the other hand that's flailing about just to my left. I can hear the low groans and grunts coming from the other zombies, now fully emerged from their graves and getting closer. Thankfully, it isn't long before I find my phone, but locating the headstone piece is proving to be more difficult.

"Where is it?!" I scream, frantic. I stop for a quick look over my shoulder to see how much time I've got. They're getting closer, their hands outstretched, their gray skin hanging from their rotting faces with empty, hollow sockets. I've got about thirty seconds left to look, at most.

I squint my eyes tight, trying to ignore my growing panic.

*This is it,* I think. *I could try to make a run for it, but they're everywhere. There's no escape… they're just everywhere.*

The groans of the undead are getting louder and louder as they get closer, the hand sticking out of the ground to my left is now working on digging out the rest of its body. I'm feeling around in the grass, fingers stretched as far as I can get them while trying to find the piece of this headstone.

They're closing in. I can smell them now, a mix of muddy grass and the putrid stench of decay. I try to breathe through my mouth to avoid the smell, but it still catches in the back of my throat and I retch once or twice.

*Come on,* I think, refusing to give up the search. *Come on…*

A hand grabs my shoulder from behind and at that exact

moment, my fingers touch the cold piece of crumbling headstone on the ground. All at once, a high-pitched ringing erupts from my drawstring bag.

"The midnight stone!" I yell.

The undead man that had grabbed my shoulder throws his hands to his ears and staggers backward away from me as quickly as he can, and the others follow suit with a hideous, gurgling noise escaping their mouths. The hand to my left has gone back in the ground.

I add the piece of headstone to the collection of items in my bag and pull out the midnight stone. It continues to emit that high pitched ringing while the zombies are stumbling around the graveyard, so I hold the stone over my head and the sound amplifies, bringing the zombies to their knees.

I keep the stone held high as I dart toward the graveyard's gate, and by the time I'm there, the zombies are starting to crawl back into the ground. I quickly open the latch on the gate and run through. It closes behind me with a clang that echoes through the moonlit woods.

As I back away from the graveyard, the ringing from the stone gets quieter and quieter until it stops altogether. I return it to my bag, which is feeling fuller now with everything that's in it, and when I look up, I can't help but feel that someone's watching me. There's no more movement in the graveyard, and the night is quiet once again. But once I turn around, I see the cloaked figure standing across the way between two trees. An arm raises, beckoning me to follow, before they turn and start walking into the woods.

"There you are," I say with a sigh. "Lead the way."

I follow the cloaked figure as best as I can, dodging one low-hanging tree branch after another. It gets darker the further we trek, and the scraggly branches start to feel like fingers reaching from the sky to grab me, scratching my arms as I push through them. The drawstring bag on my back even gets caught on a branch or two, but I'm able to quickly free myself as soon as it does without ripping it open.

We walk this way and that, between the dense trees and up a

little hill then back down again. There's no path to speak of, just occasional clearings in the underbrush.

"Where are we going?" I call ahead. The person in the cloak says nothing.

"How did you find me?" I ask, deciding to take my chances with a different line of questioning. "Did *you* pick me for this... this mission? Why? Does it have something to do with that book? Because I can't be the only one that - "

The figure stops suddenly and I hear the whisper of a muffled *shh* come floating back through the trees that stops me where I'm standing. I take the hint.

The person in the cloak starts walking again and I follow in silence. As we're making our way through a gnarled thicket, I step on a twig that cracks loudly, and I realize that, just like the neighborhood earlier, these woods are unnaturally quiet. There are no night bugs buzzing, no animals making noise from far off. Just this person leading me through these twisted, silent trees to who knows what.

*A spellbook page well-tread,* I think to myself, remembering the poem. *A spellbook... Hmm, that would imply... well, I guess I shouldn't be too surprised after everything else I've seen tonight.*

The trees thin out a bit and I can see something glowing up ahead, an eerie green and purple radiance, with a low crackling that grows louder as we approach.

"What's up there?" I ask as loudly as I can in a whisper. The figure keeps walking, the moonlight brightening the woods a little as continue on.

We've been going in silence for so long that I'm caught off guard when I first hear the singing. Someone up ahead is singing!

And the closer we get, the clearer it all becomes. The moon is again shining through the trees and the silent woods have given way to a chorus of singing, laughing, and shouts. Without realizing it, my eyes become mesmerized by the flickering ahead. I'm no longer following the person in the cloak, instead just walking toward whatever is casting that strange light in the woods.

I inch my way closer, not paying any mind to the branches

that scratch my arms, until I find myself hiding behind a big, old tree and trying to peek around it. The tree is at the edge of a clearing and the glow I've been following is coming from a green-and-purple-flamed bonfire in the center, around which there are seven women in black dancing with their arms outstretched.

"Witches," I whisper to myself, noting their pointed hats and long, flowing capes. Of the seven, there are two that look to be about my age. One's a little younger, one's much older, and I can't quite make out the faces of the rest, but from what I can see, they've all got a jubilant, almost wild look in their eyes as they leap and bound around the bonfire, cackling as they go.

"Find the spellbook."

I jump as I hear the words whispered into my ear, suddenly remembering the cloaked figure. I spin around, looking every which way and being careful to stay hidden, but whoever is in that cloak has again vanished. I resume my position hiding behind the tree, looking intently toward the witches.

On the other side of the clearing, there's a great cauldron suspended from a low-hanging tree branch over a bed of smoldering coals. Nearby, there's a little table with all sorts of strange things scattered about: crystals and herbs, glass vials, candles dripping wax, and what looks to be a very large, leather-bound book.

"Gotcha," I whisper to myself. I look skyward to make sure the moon is still high enough in the sky. It might take me a bit of time, but if I can stick to the treeline, I should be able to get to the other side of the clearing without the witches ever knowing I'm here. Again holding the straps of my bag for reassurance, I set out, all the while the witches in the clearing continue to romp around the fire.

I'm about halfway there, tiptoeing through the darkness, when one of them throws a handful of something into the flames, which explodes with a burst of purple light and a boom that knocks me off my feet. The witches hoot and holler in response.

"It's nearly ready!" I hear the eldest call to the others, her voice sending a shiver down my back. I scramble to my feet as quickly and quietly as I can, intent on getting to the spellbook on that table without making a single noise.

After another few minutes, I'm almost to the other side when a far off howl distracts me, and I step on a leaf, which crunches softly underfoot

"What was that?" says one of the witches in the clearing, turning her head to where I'm standing, paralyzed with fear.

"Oh, 'twas nothing, sister," says another. "An animal, perhaps?"

"Hogwash," says the first. "You know as well as I that no creature will stir tonight."

"Then what do you think it was?" the eldest asks.

"Let's find out," she says, turning and throwing her arms to the side in a motion that sends her cape flying behind her. The others spread out in formation.

I'm about eight feet away from the table so I decide to make a run for it. I just need to grab the book, swipe a page, and get out of here.

*But wait,* I think. *A spellbook page well-tread… that sounds fairly specific, how will I know which page to grab?*

I'm so preoccupied with worrying about not knowing what to do once I get to the table that I almost run right into it. The witches are still spread out, investigating the edge of the woods around the clearing with the bonfire's green flames raging in the center. None of them are looking at the table.

I grab the book and when I do, I feel a small jolt of energy hit my hand, running up my arm until I almost drop it. Careful to keep my grip, I duck back into the woods as quickly as I can, my drawstring bag hanging off of one shoulder as I retreat into the darkness. Once I'm far enough away from the clearing, I stop and open the spellbook.

All of its pages are yellowed and delicate, with handwritten text in languages I don't recognize alongside diagrams, drawings, and the occasional stain. I get about a third of the way through the book before I find what I think I'm looking for: a page that's dog-eared and worn, the ink faded and the paper itself thin from years of handling.

*Seems as well-tread as any,* I think. I look up to make sure that the witches haven't followed, and am relieved to find that I'm alone. I grab hold of the page and start to tear it from the book's binding when a menacing voice calls out.

"*Prohibeo.*"

I stop immediately, one hand holding the spellbook by the spine, the other holding the half-torn page. I look up, my breath catching in my throat.

The witch who heard me step on the leaf is walking toward me with tiny bolts of green energy emanating from her outstretched hand, her cape billowing behind her as she advances. Her eyes are glowing and they're locked on mine.

"I knew I heard you back there," she says calmly, unblinking. "I knew you'd come."

I open my mouth to speak, but no words come out.

"You've made it to this point, to the fourth ware, and that's admirable," she says. "But you have gone as far as you're going to go."

She's almost to me, and I'm still frozen.

"Give me the book," she says and suddenly I can move. She stands in front of me, her lips pursed and hands outstretched.

I pull the book closer to me, unsure of what to do. In my haste, it almost slips from my grasp and as I scramble to catch it, she flinches.

*Wait a minute...* I think, remembering something from earlier. I smile and pull the spellbook closer.

"No," I say firmly. "I won't give you the book."

"What?" she says, scowling.

"I said I won't give it to you," I tell her. "Because I know that once it's in my possession, you can't take it."

The witch exhales angrily, folding her arms.

"Clever," she admits slowly. "Very clever."

I keep my eyes on her while I finish tearing the page from the spellbook, careful not to rip anything else. I fold the page with one hand and reach over my shoulder to slip it into my bag.

"You know I'm not going to let you go," she says. "Even

now that you have the spellbook page."

I smile as I close the book and swing my bag around so that I can access its contents easier.

"Yes, you will," I say knowingly. With my free hand, I reach in and feel around for the midnight stone.

"You're awfully confident," she says.

"It's because I have this!" I shout. I pull out the stone and hold it toward her, unsure of what it's about to do but I'm certain it'll guard me from whatever dark magic this witch is about to unleash.

But nothing happens. And after about thirty seconds, when I'm still holding the stone as a powerless shield against the witch, I feel a knot forming in my stomach.

"What's that?" she asks, laughing. "A piece of azurite?"

"No," I say, inspecting the midnight stone closely. It's not vibrating like it did before, it's not emitting any light or any noise. It's just a dark blue stone, lifeless and cold. "No, it's…"

In my panic I drop the book.

"Aha!" the witch shouts, rising into the air as bolts of green energy again erupt from her fingertips. "Without the spellbook in hand, you've lost its protective barrier! You fool!"

An evil grin comes across the witch's face, her eyes glowing brightly in the night. I swallow hard and look back down just in time to see circles and lines etching themselves into the stone, forming some sort of intricate symbol.

*What's it doing now?!* I think.

I look up just as the witch flies toward me, and as a reflex, I hold my hand up, the midnight stone facing her.

"Arrrgh!" she shouts, her whole body violently flinging backwards from me. I pull the midnight stone down and look at it again, the rune now carved onto it reminding me of something I saw in the spellbook. The witch starts to fly toward me again, but when I raise the stone she stops in midair, staring me down.

After almost a full minute of our silent standoff, I take a cautious step toward her and she glides backward in the air. I take another step, my hand still held high, and she again retreats.

"I'd run away if I were you," the witch says coldly. With a

wave of her hand, the spellbook flies from the ground to her, and she catches it one-handed. She sneers at me before turning and flying back through the trees toward the clearing.

"I got what I needed," I say aloud, looking at the midnight stone in my hand, the runes it carved into itself to repel the witch slowly filling back in with tiny, dark blue crystals. I drop the stone back in before throwing my bag back over my shoulder. "Getting far, far away from here doesn't seem like a bad idea."

I run in the opposite direction the witch flew off from, dodging trees and branches as I go. I keep hoping to round a corner and spot the person in the cloak, but they're nowhere to be found. The deeper I run into these woods, the more alone I feel with only the occasional crunch of leaves or far-off howl breaking the silence.

*I thought no creatures were supposed to be out tonight,* I think, remembering what the witches said with a shiver. *Or creatures like I'd know them, I guess.*

I keep running.

*What if... what if I never get out of here?* I think, my feet pounding the ground as quickly as my legs can go. *What if I'm trapped in some sort of nightmare? And I'm just going to keep running through these woods and... no. No, stop. You can't let yourself think like this. You'll find your way eventually, you're not there yet. You just have to keep going.*

I slow to a jog when I reach the shores of a shallow stream flowing through the woods. I follow the bank for a while until I find a point where I can cross. I jump from one wet rock to the next, taking care to keep my shoes as dry as possible.

On the other side, I'm surprised to find a gravel path that leads away from the water and into the woods. Looking around, I decide it's as good of a route to take as any, and there's still no sign of whoever that is in the dark, hooded cloak.

A short time later, a mist descends upon the path, and I press on through the thick fog, determined to see where this graveled trail that's crunching underfoot leads. Finally, I find myself at an iron gate, behind which I can just make out the shadow of a big, old house.

"And I bet here is where I find that spectral talisman," I say aloud, remembering the poem. I open the gate to let myself onto the grounds of this massive, surely haunted house, and as it comes into better view, I'm no less comforted by the sight.

The house is very rundown, covered with dark shingles and splintered wood. It must have at least two, maybe three floors inside, with a balcony off the center turret that overlooks the grounds. Broken shutters flank the windows and there are no lights on inside that I can see.

"I kinda hope no one's home," I say to myself quietly as I get closer.

The mist lifts a little just as I reach the circle drive, and I gasp when I see the outline of the person in the cloak standing on the porch.

"Hey!" I call as softly as I can in case there's anything in the surrounding woods listening. "Wait there!"

I rush past the dried-up fountain that's overgrown with thorny vines at the center of the driveway, and as I approach the old house, I'm surprised to hear the faint, melancholy sound of a lone piano coming from deep within.

*I know that song,* I think as I reach the stairs to the porch. *I can't place it, but I know it.*

As soon as I reach the stairs to the porch, I look up just in time to catch a glimpse of the cloaked figure sweeping through the front door, which creaks as it closes behind them.

"Why am I not surprised," I say with a sigh. I take the steps two at a time and soon after, I'm standing at the front door. With a deep breath, I reach my arm out and pull the door open, leaping over the threshold before I can change my mind.

*Last stop of the night,* I think to myself while my eyes adjust to the darkness.

I can still hear the piano being played somewhere in the house, and as I expected, whoever's in that cloak is nowhere to be found. Looking around, I realize I'm standing in a grand foyer, with doors on each wall and stairs leading to the house's upper levels. The lower half of the walls are covered in a dark wood wainscoting, while an ornately patterned wallpaper stretches to the ceiling from the point where the wood ends. The wallpaper is peeling away in places, revealing aged wooden slats underneath. Cobwebs hang from every corner and dust floats idly through the stale air.

There is no sign of anyone, and if it wasn't for that haunting melody coming from somewhere in the house, I'd be convinced it was abandoned.

"How old is this place?" I wonder aloud. I stand in the foyer for another minute or two, and finally decide that following the music is my best chance to find that last ware.

*Someone's gotta be playing that piano,* I think.

The music seems to be coming from everywhere at once, so I go past the stairs and into a long, dark hallway full of old portraits hanging on the walls. I'm tempted to grab my phone for extra light, but after using it to see through almost the entire tunnel to the graveyard, I'm worried the battery is getting low. Through the shadows, it feels like the painted faces in the pictures are watching me as I walk by, including an austere older woman, a young boy, and a man with a monocle, among others.

As I walk down the hall, my footsteps muffled by the worn carpet, I glance in the rooms that break off from the corridor: a parlor, an office, and a powder room. Nothing stands out in any of them, so I keep going deeper into the house. The hall ends at the entrance to a large kitchen, through which I find a solarium filled with dead plants and windows from floor to ceiling that overlook the grounds off the back of the house.

I have yet to find the piano, let alone whoever might be playing, so I double back through the kitchen and toward the foyer. Again, I can't shake the chilling feeling that the people in the paintings are watching me as I pass them, their scowls and disapproving glares following my every move.

*Whoever they are, they must have been miserable,* I think.

When I'm again standing at the foot of the grand staircase, I think about going up to see what I might find in the upper levels of the house, but something in my stomach says to keep looking on this floor. Unsure of where to go next, I head toward the doorframe across from the stairs and stand quietly, listening to the music.

After a minute, I walk toward the other and I can tell right away that the music is louder on this side; not by much, but just enough to be noticeable. So I follow the sound down this hall, past a few more closed doors and another room or two, all of which are as silent and empty as the next. The music gets louder and louder until I'm standing at another closed door, behind which there is definitely a piano being played.

I reach my hand toward the handle, and get halfway there before the nerves hit; my fingers are trembling as I close my hand around the knob. I twist slowly, careful to make as little noise as possible. The music is still playing. The handle turns quietly, and I push the door open, silently willing it not to squeak.

The room on the other side is much larger than most of the others I've found in the house so far, with various instruments scattered around: a dusty harp, a tarnished saxophone, and a fiddle covered in etchings, among others. And on the far wall is an old piano, at which a small, translucent figure is seated, coming in and out of focus as he sways with the music, his ghostly blue hands gliding back and forth across the keys.

With a shiver, it hits me that he's the young boy from the painting in the hall.

My mouth hangs open, my breath catches in my chest and once again, I find myself struggling to stay calm as I stand there, watching this ghost boy play the piano. I don't want to move or catch his attention in any way, but if I'm going to find that talisman, I'll need to at least talk to him.

I take a step and the floor creaks beneath me. All at once, the music stops and the boy spins around, his eyes going wide for an instant before he disappears with a gasping whisper in a swirl of mist that floats toward the ceiling.

"Hey!" I shout. "Come back!"

I start to run toward where the boy disappeared, but barely make it two steps before a gust of wind tears through the room. The sheets of music strewn about fly up into the air as I'm pushed with a force that feels as though it's moving me toward the door.

"Stop! Please!" I scream. "I'm not here to - "

The sheets are swirling around me with such intensity that I lose my train of thought. The door to the music room opens as I approach and though I try to stand my ground, I feel a force push on my chest, shoving me back into the hall. The door slams shut in my face.

"Hey!" I yell again, raising a fist to pound on the door but stopping when I hear the bang of opening doors slamming against the walls behind me followed by a symphony of frightening whispers. I spin around and gasp when I see that the empty hall I had only minutes ago walked through is full of spirits drifting back and forth through the walls.

There are men and women alike; some younger, some older, and all dressed in varying styles of clothing from different eras. They nod to each other as they pass and continue on their way. A few of them look vaguely familiar, and with a start I realize I recognize them from the paintings in the hall, just like the ghost boy at the piano.

The spirits pay no attention to me, if they can even sense I'm here at all, and I stop trying to count how many there are when I hit thirteen.

"There's so many of them," I whisper to myself, my voice quaking. They fill the space with that same blue glow as the ghost boy, and their whispers cover my limbs in goosebumps.

I take a step toward the foyer and though the floorboard groans loudly underneath, the ghosts carry on with their business. I take another step, and then another. As I continue, the hall clears out until I'm once again standing alone in the dark, old house.

*One of them* has *to know something about a spectral talisman,* I think, adjusting the bag on my back. I reach the door to the first room, and my heart sinks when I see that there are no ghosts inside. I run to the next, and again, it is empty.

"Hello?" I call, gently. "I know you're here... someone. Anyone? I just... need to talk to you. One of you. Please?"

There is no response.

I continue on until I'm once again standing in the foyer, the house silent around me. I'm no closer to finding that last ware, and while I'm trying to decide where to look next, a noise from outside catches my attention.

It's subtle, but unmistakable: the crunch of gravel.

*What was that?* I think, rushing over to look through the front door's peephole. I close one eye and lean in, looking outside. At first, I don't see anything but as my eye adjusts, a figure comes into view and my mouth goes dry.

It's the blue-haired clown from the carnival.

"It can't be!" I whisper to myself in horror, watching as two more of the clowns from the carnival join him on either side. Further behind them, I can just make out what looks to be the shuffling figures of the zombies from the graveyard coming up the driveway. And as I look at the crowd assembling outside of the house, there's another howl, this one much closer.

*They're all coming here,* I think, backing away from the door. *They're all coming here and I'm no closer to finding that talisman and I doubt the midnight stone can ward them all off at once, what am I -*

A crash interrupts my thoughts and I turn around to find that I've bumped into an end table, knocking over a vase.

"Great," I mutter.

Just then, I hear a faint whisper coming from the top of the grand staircase and I look up as the ghost of an old woman appears on the second-floor landing, floating a few inches off of the floor. I immediately recognize her as the austere woman from the biggest of the paintings in the hall. She's wearing an old dress with a ruffled collar. Her stringy hair is piled on top of her head and just like the boy at the piano, she's going in and out of focus, although she's staring directly at me.

"Do you know where I can find the talisman?" I ask, hoping she'll answer.

She stares at me for another moment then slowly, she starts to nod. The muffled sounds from outside are increasing as, undoubtedly, more of the fiends from the night are arriving.

"Where do I need to go?" I ask.

A resounding clang from outside takes the ghost's attention from me; she looks scornfully toward the front door. After a moment, she returns her gaze to mine and raises a hand, beckoning me toward her just as a witch's cackle erupts through the commotion outside. I glance back at the door, making sure it's latched before going up the stairs, though I have my doubts about what good an old door will do against a mob of monsters.

I take the steps two at a time, and reach the landing where the ghost still floats, staring at me. She doesn't speak. I stare at her for a moment, a strange sense of familiarity coming over me. She's not anyone I've known in person, but she almost reminds me of...

"Do you know where I can find the talisman?" I ask again. The ghost starts to back away from me slowly, gesturing for me to accompany her.

I follow through a doorway and down a hall, and as we traipse these haunted halls, the sounds from outside get quieter and quieter until we're so deep inside the house, I can't hear them at all. We go up another set of stairs and through a few rooms until I'm completely lost and worried I won't be able to find my way out. Finally, we stop near the door at the end of a long, dark hallway.

The door slowly swings open, revealing another set of stairs that go up, presumably to the house's attic.

"Is the talisman up there?" I ask.

The ghost smiles faintly and reaches behind her neck with one hand, the other floating out to the side. She unhooks a clasp and a necklace floats forward from under the ruffled collar of her dress. The necklace is a simple chain that's looped through what looks like a large marble with a swirling vapor inside and delicately set in a handcrafted metal.

"Whoa," I say quietly. The talisman is no bigger than the midnight stone itself, and the whole piece is translucent like she is. It hangs in the air until she cups her hand underneath, and it falls toward her palm, though it stops just short of her ghostly hand, the chain undulating around the talisman itself through the air.

The ghost again looks at me and nods.

Instinctively, I hold out my hand as she reaches hers forward, and just when our fingers are about to touch, the spectral talisman floats through the air, leaving her possession and coming to rest above my own palm. She looks toward the open door and fades from view, closing her eyes as she vanishes.

*I've done it,* I think, looking at the talisman as it floats above my hand. *I've collected all the wares…*

"The attic," a familiar voice whispers. "Get to the attic."

"Alright, I hear you," I say. I open my bag and the talisman again floats through the air, landing gently inside. I pull it shut and keep the bag in hand as I start up the stairs for this old haunted house's attic.

The boards squeak under my feet as I climb the narrow staircase. I reach the top and look around, unsure of where to go, or what to do next.

The attic is like something from a scary movie: large, dusty, and full of old things that cast strange shadows under the low lights in the rafters overhead. I keep walking, hoping that something, anything will show itself to tell me what to do next.

I pass an old dress form and a couch covered in shabby blankets. There's a carriage with a doll, a desk with a typewriter, taxidermy, specimen jars, and stacks of musty cardboard boxes, all at least a foot taller than I am, arranged in labyrinthine rows. I start to wonder if the ghost was wrong to send me up here when I round a corner and stop.

At the end of the aisle of boxes is a large window that looks out over the front of the house, and standing in front of this window that's caked with decades, maybe centuries, of dust is the person in the cloak with their back to me.

"It's you!" I call to them. The person in the cloak doesn't turn around, but nods slowly.

Fighting the urge to break into a run, I walk quickly toward them, holding out the drawstring bag.

"I've got them all," I say. "The ticket, the flower, the piece of headstone… the spellbook page and the talisman. All the wares from the poem."

They don't respond or even move.

"Now what do I need to do with them?" I ask, standing just

behind them. From below, I can hear the muffled shouts of the horrors that have gathered outside.

"What do I need to do with them?" I repeat, growing agitated. "Tell me!"

The person bows their head and turns around to face me as my heart feels like it's going to pump right out of my chest.

*This is it!* I think. *I'm finally going to see who this is!*

Both hands raise to either side of the cloak's hood, pulling it back as the person underneath raises their face to mine. My eyes go wide as the hood falls to the back of the cloak; I clap my free hand to my mouth as my brain attempts to make sense of what's before me.

I'm staring into my own, grinning face.

"I... huh? What?" I ask, barely able to string my thoughts together to speak. "How? What's going on?!"

"This was your story," the person says, their voice my own, as they gesture around the attic. "A story for the reader... *your* Halloween adventure. Tonight was all for you, and I was your guide. 'A guide to lead the way', remember? I couldn't say much more than that until we reached this final step."

My mouth hangs open and I furrow my brow, more confused than ever.

"You read the book," the guide explains gently. "You followed along with the tales of the others, living through them as their stories progressed.

"But you... what sets you apart, and perhaps most importantly, you keep the spirit of Halloween, the spirit of magic and wonder, alive in your heart throughout the year for yourself and others, too. And as a reward, of sorts, this... all of this, was created just for you; a Halloween adventure of your very own.

"All that's left is for you to finish the ritual."

"So that's real?" I ask, looking from the bag back toward my doppelgänger.

"Oh yes, it's very real," the guide says. "You didn't collect all of those things, or face the terrors, for nothing. Together those five items will strengthen the barrier between the worlds until next Halloween, when a new adventurer is chosen and will embark on a story of their own."

"I have so many questions," I start to say. The guide puts their hand, which I now see as my own, on my shoulder.

"I'm sure," the guide starts to say, "but - "

From downstairs, I hear the crash of the front door being blasted into the house, followed by the shouts of the fiends from outside.

"There isn't much time," the guide says, grabbing my hand.

The guide takes me to a small table lit by a single candle with wax dripping down its sides.

"You can do it here," the guide says. "Start with the spellbook page, and use the scroll if you need help. I'll hold them off until you're finished."

I get one last smile from the face that is my own before the guide turns and heads toward the stairs, the cloak billowing in their wake.

*Start with the spellbook page,* I repeat in my mind. *Okay... let's do this.*

I reach into my drawstring bag and pull out the spellbook page, unfolding it carefully and smoothing the edges down on the table. This is the first chance I've really had to examine the page itself up close, its timeworn edges yellowed with age, hand-sketched diagrams and what I assume to be a spell written in one of the spellbook's mysterious texts. It's strange, but I can almost feel an energy emanating from the delicate paper.

"I don't need to remind you that we *are* in a bit of a hurry, do I?" the guide yells to me from across the attic, breaking my focus.

One by one, I pull the other items from the bag.

"A ticket to the midway," I say, setting the ornate ticket I retrieved from the carnival on top of the spellbook page. With a shiver, I hear the laughs of those sinister clowns on the floors below, making their way through the house.

"... and a flower most blood-red." I pull the flower from the bag, the scent of that old perfume from the Countess Dragavei's dressing room lingering around its crimson petals. A high pitched squeak from the far window catches my attention, and

I look to see two large bats flitting back and forth.

*Hello again, ladies,* I think before turning back to the task at hand.

"A piece of crumbling headstone," I say, pulling out the broken headstone piece and thinking of the undead hand I had to wrestle it from.

*Was he one of the zombies I saw coming shuffling up the driveway outside?*

"... and a spellbook page well-tread." I tap on the page beneath the other items. A cackle at the big window breaks my focus and I glance over to see three witches hovering outside on their brooms, with the one I'd confronted in the woods in front of the others, her hand outstretched as she's chanting.

*I don't have much time left.*

"Then last a spectral talisman," I quickly finish, scooping the ghostly necklace that again floats over my hand out of the bag. I gently scoot it onto the table with the other items, and adrenaline courses through me as I see all five of them laid out in front of me.

*I did it!* I think triumphantly. *Now what?*

I grab the scroll from my bag and unroll it as quickly as I can.

"'Bind them all with once-charmed thread'," I read aloud. "What's once-charmed thread?"

I reach into the bag, trying not to panic as I hear the big window's glass cracking under the witches' spells.

*Is it possible? Did I miss something? Surely the guide would have said if there was something else I needed to grab...*

I can hear the terrors surging through the house below and getting closer to the attic. I open it wide to take a better look, but, other than the midnight stone, my bag is empty.

"Hey," I shout to the guide from across the attic as loud as I can. "I don't think I have any thread, let alone any that's 'once-charmed'!"

"You have the scroll, right?" the guide calls over the shouts and stomping of the creatures coming up the stairs.

"Yes," I yell back, flipping the paper in my hands while a zombie groans loudly from just beyond the door the guide has pinned themself against.

"Then you should have the thread!" the guide yells through gritted teeth, pushing into the door with both hands.

*That's right,* I think. *The scroll was tied up when I first found it... but what did I do with that thread? I didn't put it in my bag... and I don't think I left it at home? But where did I...*

Suddenly, I remember and reach my hand into my pocket, pulling out the shimmery string that I'd stored there while I was preoccupied with first reading the scroll.

"I've got it!" I shout. "But... are you sure it'll work? That it's 'once-charmed'?"

Before the guide has a chance to answer, ghosts begin bursting from the walls, casting their ethereal blue glow through the entire attic and filling the room with their unnerving whispers. Unlike downstairs where they paid me no attention, they're all staring directly at me as they slowly advance.

"What do you think brought the scroll and the stone to you?" the guide calls back, sounding frantic. "You've had that bit of magic all along!"

I look down at the items on the table, understanding what I need to do to finish the ritual. I roll everything together in the spellbook page, quickly folding the ends neatly into themselves until the four wares are packaged in the fifth like a simple parcel. The guide won't be able to hold the door much longer. Without warning, the big window shatters and the witches fly through, followed by the bats.

I grab the thread and loop it around three times, trying to swat the bats away in the process. The ghosts are closing in and there's a whoosh of air from the witches rushing past on their brooms again and again, their cackles ringing in my ears.

Trying to stay focused, I tie the thread into a simple knot. From across the attic, I hear the guide yell as the door splinters under the pressure from the clowns, zombies, and who knows what else clamoring on the other side.

*Keep going,* I tell myself. *You've come this far; you've almost done it. Keep going.*

I tighten the knot and release the ends; the wares remain

suspended in the air bound by the once-charmed thread. For a moment, nothing happens and I'm worried the ritual didn't work. But a hush falls over the attic as the wares start rising into the air, now glowing a bright, white light.

I look around and all of the horrors that surround me are staring wide-eyed at the parcel, which continues to glow brighter and brighter. I follow their gaze and gasp when I see the package is starting to come apart in the light, dissolving into little pieces that spread over the attic like a cloud.

The pieces suddenly converge into a small orb and there's a boom followed by shrieks from the monsters all around me as the orb explodes over the attic. The white light of its shockwave is blinding as it surges through the room and out into the world. Soon after, the attic goes silent and the brightness subsides.

"I did it!" I yell once I can see again, beaming as I watch the shimmery remains of the wares float around in the air. The witches are gone, and so are the bats; the sounds in the house below have quieted. No stomping of feet, no clowns laughing or zombies groaning, not even the whisper of a ghost.

All is still.

"Now what?" I call to the guide.

"Now this."

I turn around and again come face-to-face with myself. The guide is right behind me, smiling with a hand outstretched and their fingers, my own fingers, reaching toward my face.

And just as I feel the brush of a fingertip on my forehead, I awake with a start back at home. My fuzzy blanket with the pumpkins is still draped over my shoulders, the wax that remains at the bottom of the candle has hardened, and the book is still in hand, though I'm holding it face-down on my chest.

I breathe in deep, looking around the room. Everything is as I left it, and there's a lingering spice from the candle in the air.

"I'm home," I say, my voice scratchy from sleep. According to the clock on the wall, it's half past midnight which means its officially Halloween.

"Wait," I say aloud, straightening up in the chair. "Did... did it really happen?"

I grab the book and, realizing that I'm at the end of "The Thirteenth Story", flip back several pages to see how it began.

I skim a few lines and stop.

It begins just the way I remember it, with a story in a book then a poem and three knocks on the door... I lived that. I experienced it, I saw it... or maybe I had just read it all?

"A story for the reader, a Halloween adventure all my own," I say sleepily as I close the book. "One that I can revisit, again and again."

I finish my cold cider and sit for a moment, listening to the wind. I replay the events from the night in my mind as I recall them. The carnival, the theater, the graveyard and the woods, even the haunted house; I remember being there, how each place felt, how each place smelled, and what it was like to face all of those horrors, one after the next.

But I'd done it. I'd bested them all and collected each of the wares to complete the ritual and keep the veil between the worlds intact. And, in doing so, I'd saved Halloween.

"So in the end, 'The Thirteenth Story' was *my* story," I say with a tired smile, picturing myself standing alongside the rest of the characters from the stories in the book, another hero of Halloween. I gently close it and put the book on the coffee table next to the candle. I'll definitely read this one again.

Not long after, my eyes grow heavy and I yawn; it's definitely time for bed. I stand up and toss the blanket back on the chair, stretching with a groan as I do. I turn out the lights and head for my room. Whether it all happened or not, it was real for a time. At least it felt like it was real to me.

"Happy Halloween," I say quietly to myself, settling under the covers.

Maybe it's the plush blankets, the wind blowing outside like a midnight lullaby, or simply exhaustion from the night's outing... or *reading* about the night's outing, whatever the case may be... but my room feels extra cozy tonight, and it's not long before I feel myself drifting off to sleep.

"Happy... Happy Halloween..."

# AUTHOR'S NOTE

When I was growing up, there were few things I enjoyed more than reading or writing. I could lose myself for hours in one book and then the next or spend whole afternoons just scribbling pages of notes and ideas in one "Writing Notebook" after another. So it should come as no surprise to those who know me that despite whatever passion I'm pursuing at any given time (and there have been quite a few!), all roads eventually lead back to writing and storytelling, and that's even true of my love for Halloween.

As we were preparing for our second year of posts on *Your Best Halloween Ever*, the idea to write and share original stories on the blog came about. (If you're unfamiliar, we are a seasonal blog with daily posts in the fall leading up to Halloween, featuring recipes, costumes, playlists, and more!) My first novel, *Cityscape*, had been out for a few years, but I hadn't been writing as much since my career in the events industry was keeping me especially busy at that time. There was something that immediately excited me about returning to writing, and writing scary (-ish) short stories no less!

I set about working on my six initial stories, and even from the first few days plotting them out, I felt like I had happened upon something special. Writing those stories felt like getting reacquainted with an old friend. Before I knew it, it was time to start releasing them on our site, and as anxious as I had initially been about sharing them with the world, I was humbled beyond words at how well those first six stories were received. People weren't just reading them; they were sharing them with their kids! Their families! They were creating new Halloween traditions involving stories that had started in *my* mind. For those responses and more, I will be forever grateful.

I shared another round of stories during our third year of *Your Best Halloween Ever*, and by then I was already starting to think about releasing them in a book, too. With twelve completed stories by the end of Year Three, it was only natural to include a thirteenth, print-exclusive story not just as a way to incorporate a fittingly creepy number, but as a thank you for those who bought copies of the book.

And while those thirteen tales have now come and gone, there is one final treat to share before we part ways; a favor for that old friend, if you will.

Like a lot of kids growing up in the '90s, I was a huge fan of pretty much any serialized chapter books I could get my hands on. None were as dear to me, though, as R.L. Stine's classic *Goosebumps* books. From their iconic covers to the plot twists and turns, I raced through each book as they were released. Eventually, I even found myself trying my hand at writing my own scary stories (or what was "scary" to a nine-year-old circa 1996). I can still remember grinning from ear to ear when my fourth-grade teacher agreed to read one of my stories to the class a week before Halloween.

That story was called "It Happened on Halloween Night", and I had been working on it for weeks in my free time: writing, revising, and writing some more until I had it just right. I even typed it up on the family computer, which at that point was a suitcase-looking monstrosity with a little green and black monitor built into its base. The story was well-received by my classmates, and hearing it read out loud by the teacher was surreal in the best way imaginable. I decided then and there: I was *going* to be a published author someday.

For years afterward, I kept "It Happened on Halloween Night" tucked away in a shoebox. I continued writing, working on stories that were scary and others that weren't, evolving my style and trying new writing techniques as I'd learn about them. But I never forgot about that old Halloween story, and when I started putting this book together, I couldn't help but think, *Wouldn't it be something if I included "It Happened on Halloween Night" in* Thirteen Tales for Halloween?

So, I decided to do just that.

This was to be a collection of Halloween stories, after all, and it just felt like a moment where life could truly come full circle to close with one of the first Halloween stories I'd ever written; it just felt right. I've updated the story's formatting so that it has a better layout on the page, but as an homage to my younger self who spent so much time on it, I've left the story just as I wrote it all those years ago. It certainly reads like a nine-year-old wrote it in the mid-90s, but revisiting "It Happened on Halloween Night" as an adult, it's hard to deny there's just a sense of unabashed gusto between the lines that's unmatched.

As kids, we so often lack the self-doubt that creeps into our psyche over the years; our inner critics aren't as loud as they become later in life. We just go for it, whatever "it" may be, and seeing that on display - in a version of my own voice, no less - was moving in a way I never expected. And honestly, it made me more excited than ever to keep going, keep writing, keep telling these stories. Because if my nine-year-old self knew that someday he'd be publishing a book of Halloween stories, and that "It Happened on Halloween Night" was even included, he'd be absolutely beside himself with excitement... though truthfully, he probably wouldn't be very surprised, as I was quite the determined kid and, again, had already decided that I'd be a published author one day.

And that day is today. So after all these years, it's my pleasure to present the *final* final tale of *Thirteen Tales for Halloween*: "It Happened on Halloween Night".

# IT HAPPENED ON HALLOWEEN NIGHT

It was the week before Halloween, and Geary Blak was getting ready for his favorite holiday. He was planning tricks, practicing screaming and howling, and making costumes. He LOVED to scare people! But this year he scared the wrong kids.

"The Zomboids" are what they wanted to be called, and so they were. But the Zomboids would scare Geary, which is VERY unusual because no one could scare Geary. But the Zomboids had a strange power, a mysterious power, an evil power. And they just might scare Geary to… THE DEATH!!!

"So, Gerald, did you get the scoop on the Zomboids like you said you would?" asked Geary.

"Yeah. Zarrie, Zesta, and Zonna are the girls and Zane, Zicco, and Zage are the boys. They always wear black," said Gerald Scarlet.

"Great! Did you get what they're afraid of?" asked Geary.

"No. But from what I heard they aren't afraid of anything!" said Gerald.

"Come on, they have to be afraid of something!" said Geary.

"Nope."

"Okay, I guess I'll have to do some research of my own. Bye."

"Bye."

That night, Geary's TV in his room was flickering. Then Zesta and Zicco's faces materialized on the screen. Zesta asked, "Is he the one?" Zicco answered, "Yes, he is." Then both faces faded.

\* \* \*

The next day was Monday. After breakfast, Geary went to school.

"Geary, hey Geary, wait up!" It was Gerald.

"What?"

"I found out what the Zomboids are afraid of!"

"What?!"

"I can't tell you here. Meet me in the graveyard tonight, at midnight, by tombstone #13."

"I'll be there!"

"Great see you at midnight, then. Bye!"

Geary couldn't stop thinking about what The Zomboids might be afraid of.

LATER THAT NIGHT…

Geary had to sneak out because he never would be able to sneak out with his parents knowing. He wondered how Gerald would sneak out. Oh well. Gerald never went back on his word, he'd find a way to get out. But little did Geary know that this was his first gate to pass through to becoming… DOOMED.

\* \* \*

The wind picked up as Geary walked, and seemed to whisper. This made Geary walk a little faster. In the distance, he heard a rumble which indicated a storm was brewing. This made Geary walk a little faster. Finally, he made it to the graveyard. There was Gerald, right by grave #13. #13 read:

D.O. Omed

Nobody knows where our little D.O. Omed is, but let her be there forever.

1955 - ????

Geary looked a little more closer before going over with Gerald. A little drizzle had started to fall.

"There you are, Geary, I was starting to think you weren't coming."

"So, Gerald, what are they afraid of?"

Gerald started to tell Geary when it started to rain. The two boys ran into the crypt. Gerald was in the dark corner. Then a loud, ear piercing scream traveled through the air. Geary asked Gerald if he heard it, but Gerald didn't answer. He pulled him into the light. And shrieked!!!

It wasn't Gerald! For there stood a monster! With ebony hair, and emerald skin, with flaming sapphire eyes, and with big chestnut nails, and razor teeth, and blood red lips! It was a monster, indeed. Then it said "Oh, Geary? IT's... Geary it's me, the REAL Gerald. The Zomboids did this to me! Hurry, run! It tricked you into coming here. I can't hold him much long...er. Oh Geary want to play tag? I'm it!!!"

Outside, it was pouring down rain. Geary didn't care. He ran all the way home. When he got home, he remembered what grave #13 had said:

**D.O. Omed**

Nobody knows where our little D.O. Omed is but let her be there **forever**

1955-????

\* \* \*

The next day was Halloween. Geary was off that day. He wouldn't even think about last night. But tonight, he would have fun. Tonight was the one night he could reveal his true self. He still didn't know what the Zomboids were scared of, but he was dressed as a vampire.

Later that night, around 10:00 p.m., he was looking for the Zomboids. He just kept on going until he came to the graveyard. Shuddering, he remembered last night. He went on until he came to the edge of town. Then he turned back. But this night would be his final night before... DOOM.

As he was walking home, he passed the graveyard. Out of wonder if the Zomboids were in the graveyard, he walked in. It was 11:52 p.m. He wandered through a couple of times. Then went into the crypt. When he got in he noticed a small circle pattern in the floor, that wasn't there last night. He bent down to rub it off. When he did, he discovered it was a hole. He heard some chattering in the hole. He bent down further to get a better look. And... he fell through. He went through a hole of bright colors. Then he fell through to a medium sized room. Then, a voice that sounded like Zarrie, said "Welcome to DOOM!!!"

"That hole was a portal to our dimension. We wanted to come here, but thought of no way to get here. Finally Zeke, our faded brother, thought of the idea. Unfortunately he, what your people call it? Died? In the making of it. Now we have come here to have our fun, and terrorize," explained Zage.

"Hey, that is my job, to scare."

"Now it's ours!" snickered Zane.

"And you will be our first victim!" bursted Zarrie.

And Geary knew the end was near.

"What are you gonna do to me?" asked Geary.

"We'll torture you."

"How?"

"That's for us to know, and for you to find out," said Zonna.

Geary noticed that Zesta had been quiet through all of this. Then, Zonna's voice boomed.

"Welcome to the obstacle course! If you survive, you might get out. But that's a mighty big if."

Then a ghost rose. And boy, was he hungry! He began chasing Geary. Then Zesta said "Didn't you get the message on tombstone #13? You will be doomed forever!"

## THE END

# ABOUT THE AUTHOR

Born and raised in St. Louis, MO, Andrew Noles has been a storyteller – and Halloween fanatic! - since before he could even write, dictating stories to his parents when he was just a few years old and planning out costumes well over a year in advance.

Over the years, he followed this passion for storytelling across various media and industries before launching the Halloween blog *Your Best Halloween Ever* with his partner, Devin, in 2018. Featuring daily posts in the fall with tips, tricks, and treats for your best Halloween ever, the blog is viewable year-round at yourbesthalloweenever.com.

Andrew continues to reside in the suburbs of St. Louis where he is often to be found working on projects of the writing, baking, or crafting variety… and is likely already decorating for Halloween.

His first novel, *Cityscape*, was released in 2014.